The Locker Notes

MIKE DERRICO

Paperback ISBN: 978-1-7354767-2-8
eBook ISBN: 978-1-7354767-3-5

Cover & Interior formatting by Abbey Suchoski.

For Tom, Chris, Rob, Eric and Eric

Contents

PART ONE

Desire & Memory

1

Cool

The sixth grade school year began with a teacher's strike. During the first two weeks of September 1980, the teachers of the Cypress Elementary School blocked the corner of Oakwood Avenue and Cypress Estates. We heard rumors of a strike during the final weeks of summer break but hardly understood what it meant. Just what the hell was a teachers strike? Did it mean we wouldn't have school? Were the teachers mad at the students or something? Didn't they like their jobs? My eleven year old mind couldn't grasp what was going on. I didn't understand the concept or meaning of a strike. All we knew was that school was starting and the teachers weren't going. Did that mean we didn't have to go either?

On the first day when my mom drove Tommy Dewhirst, Marc Rinaldi and me past the picket line, it just looked like a bunch of angry teachers holding a bunch of angry signs. Much to our disappointment however, school would not be canceled nor delayed. A substitute teacher would be assigned to every classroom, and school would begin as scheduled.

I had been friends with Tommy and Marc my entire life, and not one school year from kindergarten through fifth grade were either of them in my class. Sixth grade was going to be a little different, as Marc and I would both have Mrs. Painter as our teacher during the final year at the Cypress School. Tommy however, would be unfortunately unfortunate to the point of parody...something that reveals itself a little further ahead in our story. Either way, the final year at Cypress was something to look forward to since we would no longer be the little kids climbing our way to the top. We would rule the school, being both feared and admired by the younger kids who looked up from their lower ranking, aspiring to that day when they too would rule the school. That's really what elementary school felt like. This year however, I was dreading as much as looking forward to. Everybody pretty much knew each other by the last year, and even if you didn't interact with everyone, you still knew who everyone was. Everyone had their own reputation. Some were tough, some weak, some funny, and some much friendlier than others. There were the smart kids who paid little attention to anything that wasn't school work, and were often referred to as dexters. That rather 1970s term later became known as a nerd in the Eighties. There were the populars and the unpopulars. There were two types of popular kids... the ones who were the objects of somebody's crush, and the ones who could kick the ball on the roof of the building during lunchtime kickball games. These ones usually always excelled in sports and were always picked first in gym class if they weren't already captains. Tommy was good in sports and was always involved in the kickball games. Marc, on the surface, was a tough kid who palled around with all of the actual, real tough kids. Underneath, he really wasn't, although he could kick my ass if he wanted to.

Me?

I was something else.

I was *cool*.

Or at least I was at one time.

The part of me that wasn't looking forward to the new school year was the part that knew Kevin Weir and Ashley Drake would be in my class. Weir was the toughest kid in the Cypress School since Derrick Adler had moved on to middle school. Back then, middle school was referred to as "junior high," so from here on in, that's what we'll call it. Back to Weir. Weir was famous. Everybody knew him, and everybody either loved him, feared him or both. The few kids who hung out with him were pretty scary too, but they were older and no longer went to Cypress. He knew who I was through Marc, but he had never spoken a word to me. I wanted both to be friends with him, and avoid him. We had never been in the same class, but he got along good with Marc, and since Marc and I were good friends, he didn't bother me. He didn't talk to me, but he didn't bother me either.

Ashley Drake was the most diabolical girl in the school. I had a history with her that went back to second grade. There were other evil girls in the school, but Ashley was the devil. She and Kevin Weir would both be in my class, and I wasn't looking forward to interacting with either of them. With Ashley, I knew exactly what to expect. With Kevin, I didn't know what would happen and didn't want to find out. I guess I began the sixth grade school year pretty frightened. I entered the classroom wearing a brand new Grateful Dead iron-on t-shirt. I had lots of rock and roll shirts, and I knew that Kevin Weir liked the Grateful Dead. I really didn't know many songs from them other than "Truckin" and "Casey Jones," but I told myself that I would get into them with the new school year. I was a big fan of rock music, and that was one of the things that initially made me cool.

But in the 1970s, there was this band called Kiss. They were probably the most popular band of the later part of the decade. Yet, besides Tommy and me liking them, it was nearly impossible to find anybody else who not only liked them, but didn't completely hate them, or hate us for liking them. Girls mostly hated them. Me? I was borderline obsessed with them, and they became something of definition for many, many moments of my childhood.

In the classroom, Joey Franco, one of Weir's friends, popped his head in the door from out in the hall. Franco was in Mr. Hardenberger's class in the room next to us, but needed to talk to Weir. In the process, he noticed my shirt.

"Hey Devine," he called to me. "Name five songs from The Grateful Dead." I was propelled into immediate embarrassment.

"And don't say "Truckin" or "Casey Jones.""

It wasn't always like this though...at least not when I was cool.

———

One night during the summer of 1976, I got down on my knees to pray to God. I had recently begun catechism classes, and was told that God answered all our prayers. This whole imposition of Confraternity of Christian Doctrine, aka CCD on our lives, came as me, Tommy Dewhirst and Marc Rinaldi found ourselves in a position where we had to go learn about Jesus Christ once a week. All our parents were probably locked in some dialogue where they were weighing out whether they should hand their kids over to the Lord, or continue raising us in the Godless state in which we existed. That night, I asked God to send me the first Kiss album. I didn't have it, and needed it for my collection. Since God answered our prayers, I expected to wake up in the morning to find the record at the foot of my bed, right where I asked God to leave it. I woke up the next morning and began to cry as I looked and found nothing. From that point on, a lifelong question arose over whether or not God really existed.

If you grew up in Oakwoods in the 1970s, rock music was probably the biggest thing in a kid's life. Sports were popular to a certain degree, and the town certainly had its share of jocks, but for the most part, every kid was a fan of rock music. The boys wore their hair long and the girls looked like sluts. Every day, I'd watch the older kids walk up Sycamore Drive and past the fence at the top of the block. They wore Led Zeppelin and Grateful Dead shirts, work boots, chain wallets dangling down their legs, bandanas around their heads, and denim jackets with the sleeves cut off. I was only six when I first became aware of the older kids walking up the street past my house. I marveled at how they were dressed and always wondered what they were doing and where they were going. Soon after that, I discovered Kiss. It was sometime during the Bicentennial summer of

'76, when Marc Rinaldi and I wandered into his older sister Elena's bedroom. She was around 13, maybe 14. It was the 1970s of films like *Over the Edge* and *Little Darlings,* and if you had teens back then, it was a terrifying age to be a parent. It was especially dangerous if you had Kiss on your bedroom walls. One day she was out with friends when Marc decided we should snoop around her bedroom. Immediately, I spotted them from across the room as I went in, and walked over to the poster on the wall. At first we didn't know what to make of it. We chuckled a bit over how stupid they looked. They had long hair and wore makeup...lots of makeup. I laughed out loud nervously, but realized my laughter was forced. Marc also pretended to laugh. I looked intensely at Ace Frehley, the lead guitarist and studied him. I had no idea who he was at that point, but for the sake of the story, it was Ace Frehley. There was something about him that transcended every negative idea that we thought we had about the poster. Something about the way he held his Gibson guitar. The way he crouched down...the knee bends...the puckered lips...the tight black outfit...the long hair. It seemed to represent everything outside the norm. It screamed a certain "fuck you" to everything that was considered safe and good. This was something I didn't even get from Fonzie, my television idol. I mean, I still loved Fonzie because he had shaped my coolness at such an early age. At the time, *Happy Days* was my favorite TV show and the Fonzie character played by Henry Winkler had become a sex symbol, and bigger than the show itself. Fonzie was so cool he could get any girl he wanted. All he had to do was snap his finger, and girls would come running. But as I stared up at the Kiss poster, I was instantly pointed in a direction that would inform the rest of my early childhood. Yeah, we pretended to laugh at the idea of grown men dressed in black spandex and wearing face paint. But they had guitars. Electric guitars. The thin kind that you wore low. Not the big fat kind with the hole in the middle that Elvis and the country people always wore up to their chests. Suddenly we weren't laughing anymore. Because as that kid who was obsessed with Fonzie, I had known all about cool, and considered myself to be cool. But this was next level. This was life-changing. So as I would re-enter school that following September, I went fueled by some newfound rock and roll sensibilities along with my ever-present belief that I was Fonzie, and I too snapped my fingers at the girls. And when they didn't come running, I ran after them.

When I was that young, my initial instinct was to not care what people thought of me. I was cool...far too cool to give a shit. My best friend Tommy was cool too. Although my discovery of Kiss happened in Marc's house, he wasn't as obsessed with them as Tommy and I were. At the Cypress School, the kids laughed at you for being a Kiss fan, especially the girls for some reason. Elena liked them and she was older, more mature, and obviously knew better than any of them. In second grade, the average kid was listening to Muppets and Sesame Street records. In the face of such scorn and torment, I brought a Kiss album to school for Show and Tell. As I stood in front of the class holding a copy of Kiss *Rock and Roll Over*, the class reacted in disgust.

"Do your parents know you have this?" the teacher asked.

"They bought it for me," I said with a sense of pride.

It's true...my mom bought me my first Kiss album. She was raised on Doo Wop, and my dad, Frankie Valli and the Four Seasons. I don't think they had any clue what their seven-year old was really involved with. By 1978, I was pushing nine, and Tommy and I ate, shit and slept Kiss. Our parents didn't seem all that concerned at first… at least not at that point. I suppose they thought Kiss was a cartoon or something. Whatever the case though, my parents never really deprived me of getting something they could see I really wanted. They could be overprotective at times, and usually said no to a lot of things, but if you begged and pleaded enough, they would bend. When it came to Kiss, they bent.

Sometimes.

———

Rock and roll music has been the backdrop of our lives in the small suburban town of Oakwoods. Through the second half of the twentieth century, it dominated pop culture. Being born in 1969, I missed the first fifteen or sixteen years. One thing we know, or at least has been suggested, is that it is made by the young for the young. When Mick Jagger said that he didn't want to be singing "Satisfaction" at the age of 40, he probably meant it. When Bob Dylan said never trust anyone over 30, he probably meant that too. Both men were well into their thirties at this point in time, and both were still active. Jagger still had some time to go before he could retire at 40. Rock and roll however, seems to be an on-going experiment. In the 1950s, they didn't know how long it would last. In the 1960s, it became a medium of information, and redirected youth culture. In the 1970s, it exploded into various unforeseen entities such as glam, progressive and corporate rock. The same would happen in the last decades of the century, as we would come to find out that we can't predict the outcome like we thought we could some fifty years ago. We have found out that yes, unfortunately we are going to watch our rock heroes get old and die, just as surely as we will face our own mortality. But in the face of age, we have found that rock and roll, a music born out of defiance will not simply bow out. The spirit has transcended age, and has shown us that Mick Jagger and Keith Richards will do their thing well into their sixties and seventies. Most rock artists have transcended time this way. But let's stay in 1976 for now...back when it was still fairly early in the experiment, though we didn't yet know it because there was that ever-present sense of doom in the air and some asshole here and there was always preaching about the end of the world. But, every generation lives at the end of the world. Jim Morrison probably said it best: "The future's uncertain, and the end is always near..."

This was the era of the double live album. In kindergarten through first grade, it was Kiss *Alive* against *Frampton Comes Alive*. If you liked Kiss, you were probably a boy. Girls liked Peter Frampton. Within a year, the girls would like disco. The boys would still like Kiss. A new cat from Freehold, New Jersey named Bruce Springsteen released his breakthrough album *Born to Run* late in 1975 and some critic predicted he would be the future of rock and roll. Bob Dylan, who had come out of hiding a year before, began his Rolling Thunder Revue Tour that November. But the early 1970s were a sort of hangover of the Sixties, and no one particular artist or band stood out. The Beatles had been broken up for over five years, although there were always rumors of a reunion. Paul McCartney was active and successful on the pop charts with his band Wings. George Harrison had recently wrapped up his first post-Beatles tour to disappointing reviews from those critics who had a problem with the Hare Krishna thing and that his voice sounded like shit. There was this Beatles cover band on Broadway called Beatlemania that would surface a year or two down the line, and would become one of many elements of Seventies kitsch. They meant well, but it was too much too soon. People just did not want to accept that the Beatles were no longer together. Within another year, there'd be a Hollywood version of *Sgt. Pepper's Lonely Hearts Club Band* starring The Bee Gees and Peter Frampton.

Things had changed.

The Rolling Stones had recently replaced Mick Taylor with Ron Wood, and were touring the world, but critics at that point were already calling them "old." I had their *Hot Rocks* album. It was the first record I ever got, just to let anyone wondering know that I was still aware of other music besides Kiss.

In the first months of 1976, I had become painfully aware of the coming Bicentennial. The subject dominated the media and everything all around us. As the year progressed, we began seeing increasing amounts of red, white, and blue everywhere we looked. The reason it was painful for me, was because of a particular exercise that I had to do in my first grade class. As the nation's 200th birthday approached, the entire school prepared a gigantic showbiz extravaganza to be staged in the "All Purpose Room." Every grade had a different role. It was the responsibility of the entire first grade class to learn some sort of choreographed flag waving performance. And I had no clue. I could not learn the damn thing for anything. I just couldn't deal with it. I was grilled by Miss Collins, my first grade teacher on a daily basis. Miss Collins was around 117 years old in

1976, so I would imagine that she has to be dead by now. This woman was so Old World that she spoke with a snobbish British accent. She constantly used lines like "You will do as you are told to do." Anyway, she put me on the spot in front of the class almost every day during the second half of the school year just because I couldn't learn this flag dance thing. She even called my mom in for a meeting to explain to her the severity of the situation:

Here was the end of the world. People were going to die. There was going to be a death count. I was committing crimes punishable by my own death. But first I'd be taken away and thrown into the school basement where hungry alligators awaited me in a pit of boiling water. This was serious. All because a six year-old kid couldn't commit to memory some bullshit flag dance. The teacher even went so far as to give my mom her own flag to bring home with mine so she could work on it with me. I still didn't get it. Maybe subconsciously, I knew I wasn't a flag waver. I did however, do my civic duty in the '76 presidential election by "voting" for Jimmy Carter because he had more hair than Gerald Ford. Maybe I was born a liberal before I was even politically aware.

Let's put it all in perspective. It was 1976. We'd just had our asses kicked in Vietnam. We had endured the Nixon Administration. With our 200th birthday celebration on the horizon, our country had been repeatedly embarrassed on a global scale. The nation needed healing. Maybe subconsciously at the age of six I didn't feel it necessary to wave the flag. It made my life miserable for the last few months of the school year until it was decided that I wasn't fit to participate in the Bicentennial celebration. And they broke the news to me as if it were some sort of punishment for not learning my part.

They showed me alright. And guess what...as usual, I didn't give a shit. That summer, I would discover Kiss, and Kiss would make me cooler than I already was.

But just what was so cool about cool anyway? Well, for starters, it wasn't just in the music you listened to. It was in the attitude. It was everything that rock and roll entailed. As you come to get older and branch out in your artistic tastes, you find these sentiments are also contained in jazz, blues, literature, painting, sculpture, cinema and other genres and mediums of pop culture. There also seems to be a feeling of being "one up" on everybody else. If you played it cool, you gave off the idea that you knew something that nobody else did. Even if you didn't, the idea was to create the illusion that you did. There was always a sense of pride in being the only kid in class with a rock band on his t-shirt or being the only kid in a class of twelve boys who didn't watch the game the night before, and while everybody was talking about it, you were too cool to seem that common. It was also about knowing the obscure song on side two of an album while everybody else only knew the single on the radio. In short, you were a fucking snob. Something holier than thou. You'd even have a girlfriend later in life who would refer to you as pious. Little did you know that you were laying the groundwork for all the neo-hipsters that would walk the earth at the turn of the century. I was a pioneer in that respect. But being a little kid in the mid-1970s, it was more about banging on the jukebox like Fonzie and having the music suddenly start to play. It was also about standing out in a crowd. The funny thing is a few years later when you reach junior high, you run in the opposite direction under pressure to look and be like everybody else. How and if that happens probably has a lot to do with a child's personal experiences in elementary school. Sure, I was cool in my own head, but how people perceive you is a different story. And just how cool could a seven-year old be anyway? And did a seven-year old really understand the other implications of cool such as hip? Cool and hip were two different monsters. Anybody could be cool, really. But hip...that was about really knowing something that nobody else knew.

Or was it?

Was it really just about non-conformity?

How about being tuned in to the cosmic order of things and not revealing how or why? Didn't it all go back to the attitude?

Did a six-year old really think about these things?

Did a six-year old know the difference?

Did I know the difference?

In reality, you were a little kid living in a middle class suburban town like many, many others throughout the United States. It was Anytown, U.S.A. In your case, it was Oakwoods, a miniscule area between two major shopping malls in central New Jersey. You lived on a street in a development that contained rows of houses that all looked identical. In the center of town was Luigi's Pizza...the one establishment that predated everything else. Your town was barely on the map, although millions of people from around the tri-state area all rushed in during the holiday season to shop at the malls. Central Jersey seemed to be the shopping mall capital of the world, and if you drove a car there during the holiday season, you were miserable for approximately 40 days because you could not get out of your own development and onto the major highways due to the large volume of cars with New York plates congesting the area. Yes, it was the mid-

1970s, and tons of hairspray and fake tans were not yet in vogue, so it was impossible to distinguish the Staten Islanders from the rest. Staten Island, it had been suggested, was a holding cell for Brooklynites who wanted to move to New Jersey, but couldn't take such a giant leap all at once. It was a place to get their feet wet...sort of get used to the phenomenon of trees and grass in front of their homes. On your block were white descendants of European immigrants. In your school, among a population of some 400 kids, only two were black...and it made you wonder why. You were taught to respect others, and that we were all children of God. In your neighborhood, you had friends who were your own age who your parents let you play with. There were also older kids who did different things. At night, they walked up the block and went into the woods. Your parents watched them suspiciously. You, however, watched them and saw how cool they looked. Within two more decades, your story would become a cliche, as the "portrait of suburban New Jersey" would be a worn out genre studied by at least a half a dozen major filmmakers by the turn of the century. Your only consolation is that everyone experiences absurd and somewhat scarring moments in their childhood. And as long as some segment, some sentence, some word, some *something* in your story connects with somebody out there, your story has a purpose.

Between my family and Tommy's family, things have always happened simultaneously. Our parents all grew up together in Elizabeth, New Jersey. They went to high school together, went on double dates together, got married around the same time, had me and Tommy around the same time, got their first apartments at the same time, and moved to Oakwoods at the same time. There were all kinds of creepy things too. Like one day in 1972, my grandmother died while she was in the hospital. A few days after that, Tommy's grandfather keeled over and dropped dead right there in the Dewhirst's living room during Tommy's third birthday party. At this early point in the story, I feel it necessary to acknowledge that our story jumps around from year to year and back again with the timeframe, but it's quite essential to the story and to finding out who Eugene Devine is (that's me,) and how he got that way. So, one night during the early summer of 1973 while our moms were in the hospital giving birth to our little brothers, I slept over Tommy's house with his grandmother supervising us. It was then that I discovered my fear of snakes.

There were two single beds in Tommy's room. Tommy wanted me to sleep in the bed that was next to a dresser serving as a stand for a snake tank. When I refused, it became an argumentative issue... two four-year olds in a disagreement over sleeping arrangements.

"What's the problem? Why don't you wanna sleep next to my new snake?"

"I don't wanna sleep next to the snake," I said. "You sleep next to it."

Tommy remained polite, innocent and insistent. "But you're a guest here, and the guest gets to sleep next to the snake," he said, sounding much less like a four-year old than a salesman pitching some demented idea that sleeping next to a snake was a privilege or something.

"I'll sleep on the other bed," was all I had.

He didn't want to hear that.

"You sleep next to my snake. You don't upset the host. You sleep next to snake!"

"No!" I shouted, suddenly wanting to go home...wishing his dad, Big Tom was upstairs to intervene. I backed away and stopped in the doorway. Tommy looked at me and smiled as he realized I had fear in my eyes.

"You're afraid of the snake."

"No, I'm not," I shot back, ashamed.

"Yes you are. You're afraid of the snake!"

"No!"

"Afraid of the snake!"

"Stop!"

As I stood in the doorway, I turned my back for a few seconds to face the stairs that led down to the living room. In those few seconds, Tommy proceeded to come up with an act that would scar me for the rest of my life. As I had my back turned toward him, he reached into the closet, pulled out a monster-sized rubber snake, and dropped it around my neck. At the very feel of it, I jumped out of my own skin and ran down the stairs screaming. Tommy grabbed the snake from the floor and started down the stairs after me.

"Afraid of the snake!"

Incidentally, that was one of our last nights as only children, because into the world, two mysterious beings appeared. In Tommy's house later in the week, was this screaming and crying force of nature. It was a baby. Its name was Christopher. In my own house, this kicking and cackling thing appeared on the chair in the living room.

It too, was a baby. Its name was Franklin. Franklin and Christopher would be our little brothers. They too, would grow up in Oakwoods.

————

Tommy Dewhirst and I got bored very easily. So we invented a Doing Machine. Whenever we were looking for something to do, we just climbed into the Doing Machine and decided what to do. This involved us ducking under Tommy's backyard deck and sitting under the stairs. We'd punch in a bunch of imaginary buttons, feed a blade of grass through an invisible computer, and wait for the information that would offer us options of what we could do next. And there were always plenty of things to do. And usually, we did one of them. One of those choices was always playing *Happy Days*. *Happy Days* was our favorite TV show. A half hour sitcom situated in Milwaukee, it ran on Tuesday nights at eight on ABC. Our own sitcom, situated at Tommy's house on White Birch Road in Oakwoods, was a little less attractive. I always insisted on being Fonzie. Since I was always the Fonz, Tommy was Potsie, although he wasn't always happy about it. The fact that we played this would never be revealed to anybody else, especially in school. At home and in private, I played Fonzie. In school, I became him. Not that I looked like him or anything. I didn't have the cropped up slicked back hair. My hair hung straight down. In fact, all our hair hung straight down...mine, Tommy's, Marc's... Ritchie's. It was the mophead look. In the mid Seventies, the running joke about haircuts was that the barber placed a cereal bowl on our heads and cut around it. Besides our hair, Tommy and I, dark brown, and Ritchie, dirty blonde, we were pretty normal looking little kids.

I mean average, I guess. No real distinguishing features that made us stand out from the general population of the school or neighborhood. No deformities or noticeable flaws that could draw unwanted attention in a child's life, thank God. No one was too fat or too skinny. No one wore glasses, which exempted us from being called Four Eyes. For the most part, we were all spared the typical clichés of childhood torment, at least physically. But as "normal-looking" as I was, I became the Fonz in school. Why? Because I was cool. Needless to say, I became terrified of anything made of rubber. Especially snakes. So I suppose there was nothing cool about that. Tommy knew this, and because of it, he played on my weakness and terrorized me with his collection of rubber snakes. When I wasn't looking, he'd hang them around my neck or put them on my shoulder. He'd throw them at me. He'd smack me in the face with them. Even rubber garden hoses...anything that was long that moved or appeared to move in an undulating motion was a snake to me...belts, wires, anything. At Tommy's house, before entering a room, I'd ask if there were any rubber snakes in the room. He'd say, "No, come on in," knowing that he had one hidden, just waiting for me. When I was finally convinced it was safe enough to go in the room, he'd whip one out at my face. My next door neighbor, Ritchie Burke, also caught on to my fear of snakes and how Tommy would torture me with them. Eventually, he began doing the same thing. Ritchie was two years younger than me, but we still became friends growing up. He had two older brothers who were seniors in high school and listened to lots of cool rock music. They would occasionally let us hang out in their rooms and talk to us about what bands we should listen to. Really cool guys, but even they would occasionally tease me with Ritchie's rubber snakes.

Rubber snakes seemed to be a common thing in Oakwoods during the Seventies for some reason. The same way every kid has video games today, everyone had a rubber snake back then. Eventually, Tommy would become obsessed with reptiles, especially snakes. In time, the rubber snakes would become real snakes. Plenty of real snakes. In tanks. Snakes in tanks in the basement. Snakes in tanks in the bedroom. Snakes in tanks all over the house! A typical average day that consisted of an encounter with one of Tommy's creatures and his deliberate torment would go as follows:

Tommy: What do you wanna do?
Eugene: I don't know. What do you wanna do?
Tommy: No idea.
Eugene: Well, we have to do something.
Tommy: I think this is a job for the Doing Machine.

And so, we duck into our tiny space under the stairs of the De-whirst's backyard deck and scramble our imaginary computers for something to do.

Tommy: Hmmm...let's see.
Eugene: Hmmm...something is coming up.
Tommy: What does it say?
Eugene: Play *Happy Days*.
Tommy: Nah. We always play *Happy Days*. This one over here says play sports.
Eugene: Sports is stupid.
Tommy: *Happy Days* is stupid.

Eugene: No sports, I wanna play *Happy Days*.
Tommy: Only if I get to be the Fonz.
Eugene: No. I'm the Fonz. You're Potsie. Let's go.

From there, I crawl out from under the Doing Machine and Tommy follows me.

Tommy: Why am I always Potsie?
Eugene: Because that's who you are. Potsie. I'm the Fonz.
Tommy: I wanna be the Fonz!
Eugene: I'm Fonzie! You're Potsie!
Tommy begins scowling, growling and grimacing.

Tommy: I wanna be the Fonz!
Eugene: I'm the Fonz! I'm Fonzie!

Tommy jumps up and down furiously and runs into the house. He reappears a minute later clenching rubber snakes in each hand, and begins chasing me around the corner as I run away, hysterically crying all the way home. He tails me at my heels all the way to my house, snakes dribbling out of each hand and bouncing with each footstep as he runs. As I reach home and turn onto my property, he keeps running up the block as if he were never chasing me and just out for a jog, still with the snakes raised toward the heavens.

———

There was Oakwoods, and there was the other side of Oakwoods, known as *old* Oakwoods. If you lived in old Oakwoods you went either to the Delta School, or the Fruit Tree School. Everyone else in Oakwoods who went to public school went to Cypress, unless you were one of the unlucky ones who went to Our Lady of Peace.

Nestled between Cypress Gardens and Wellington Drive, on a piece of land known as Cypress Estates, the Cypress School sat in five brick buildings in the middle of a hilly grass patch creeping up the ass of the Garden State Parkway. The five buildings that made up the Cypress School were the main unit, the first and second grade unit, the third and fourth grade unit, the fifth grade unit, and the sixth grade unit. Kindergarten, music, art, gym and lunch were all held in the main unit. The main unit however, featured a strange extension meant for all types of purposes. Accordingly, it was called the All Purpose Room. This was a large, dark and ominous room where we had gym, ate lunch, watched plays, went to chorus and listened to Officer Anderson speak about right and wrong. Even when the lights were on, the All Purpose Room was still dark and dreary. The lights always made it seem like it was raining outside. We'd spend time in this room every day of our lives from 1974 to 1981. I was happy though. I found out that I would be going to kindergarten during the AM session, which meant that I'd be home just in time for the *Batman* re-runs on TV. At this point, it would probably do some good to mention that Tommy and I were separated when school began. Well, sort of. I did AM classes, and he did PM...and over the course of our entire run at Cypress which would last the next six years, it didn't seem like we would ever be in the same class together.

The thing that frightened me most about starting school, was that everyone was telling me that I was a big boy, and that I was going to go to school, and in school, they give us milk and I'd have to drink it all because I was a big boy. The main offenders here were my mom's Aunt Rose and our neighbor Rose Giovanni. The Giovanni's lived next door to us on the opposite side of the Burke's. Aunt Rose used to watch me while my mom was out, and she would take me over to the Giovanni's house where we'd hang out in the basement. Rose Giovanni was in her 50s or 60s, chain smoked Lark cigarettes that she kept in a leather cigarette case and drank a shitload of coffee. The percolator was always going and leaving the constant aroma of fine Maxwell House brew in the air. The mid-1970s were a time when coffee's popularity was on the decline with younger adults opting for colder beverages over hot...and if it had be hot, they chose instant coffee without the caffeine. But not the two Roses. The two Roses were speed freaks who loved their caffeine, as did all our parents and most of the adults we knew. Rose and Aunt Rose would sit there for hours in the basement drinking their coffee, smoking cigarettes and talking. It was a finished basement with Astroturf on the floor and a handful of vintage salon blow driers with the chairs underneath. It was a rather memorable room, as was just about every room in the Giovanni house...everything meticulously placed, not a speck of dust anywhere or newspapers hanging off the dining room table or anything like that...nothing that ever looked lived-in. They had that old ornate European-style furniture in the living room...everything marble, glass and gold...couches and chairs upholstered with plastic protective covers that every Italian grandmother had in their homes...the kind your skin would stick to in the summertime. But it was furniture you weren't allowed to sit on in a room that you weren't allowed to go in, and it was usually referred to as the parlor. Everyone else had living rooms, but people like the Giovanni's had a parlor. They had a parlor, a basement with Astroturf, lots of coffee and cigarettes, a poodle named Sha-Sha and a house full of expensive shit that you couldn't use or touch. But all of that is beside the point. What I'm trying to say here is that they kept telling me I was a big boy even though I was only five. I was only five and they kept telling me I was a big boy and that I was going to grow big and strong. But they made it sound as if it were all dependent on drinking milk. They kept mentioning the milk. There was milk at school...that we got...and we had to drink it all. We had to finish it. All of it. Rose and Aunt Rose drilled this into my head in the days leading up to starting school. From there on, I kept envisioning the gallon of milk sitting in my refrigerator at home. I had no idea that small milk cartons existed. I had no idea of the existence of any other kind of milk other than that big fucking gallon bottle that I'd recognized as milk for the entire five fucking years of my little miniscule life. And until then, that had been my only experience with milk. How was I supposed to drink all of that milk? How much time were they going to give me to drink all of that milk? Would I get in trouble if I didn't finish all of that milk? Would they laugh at me? Yell at me? Beat me up? What was going to happen to me?

———

School wasn't what I expected when I first walked in. My teacher, Mrs. Greco greeted me as I walked up the stairs with my mother on the first day. She already knew my name. My mother stayed at the door as she watched me walk into the main unit's kindergarten section. She'd return later in the morning to pick me up. Prior to school starting, I had pictured a classroom with rows of desks with chairs attached to them. What I got instead looked more like a kindergarten class...big tables with wooden blocks on them, toys all over the place, and little empty squares called cubbies to put your things inside. I can't recall too much about my classmates except that there were those who got along, those who didn't get along, the kids who smelled and the kids who didn't. Then there was me. I was cool.

My biggest problem those first few years of school was wanting to be older...actually believing I was older. I idolized Fonzie, so at the age of five or six, I thought I could get any girl I wanted. I had a few girlfriends those first few years...Leslie Tindal in kindergarten, Haley Benson in first grade, and Lauren Davis in second grade. By the end of the year, I was fed up and ready for first grade and a real classroom. I wanted my own separate desk. The kind with the chair attached to it...not stupid tables that we had to share while we played with our blocks and tinker toys. What we got instead were desks and chairs separate from each other, and at the end of the day we had to turn our chairs upside down and place them on our desks so that the janitor could sweep after school.

Coinciding with the start of first grade was a new TV show called *Welcome Back Kotter*. It was a show about a teacher in a Brooklyn high school, and his unique and often bizarre students. Gabe Kotter's students were nicknamed "Sweathogs," and he had such a connection with them, that they were always visiting him at home, many times coming in through the ground-level window of his Brooklyn apartment. I found it both cool and amusing. Something I might try. But

I had no idea where my first grade teacher Miss Collins lived, nor could I see myself climbing into the fourth grade teacher Mrs. Aaron's basement window of her suburban home on Sycamore Drive in Oakwoods, New Jersey. So I let that idea go. At least until I reached fourth grade and she became my teacher.

———

"You're stupid," the nasty slime of a girl whispered to me in class. "You're stupid for liking Kiss, and you're stupid for thinking you're cool."

I ignored her.

Mrs. Aarons was in the middle of cutting a girl to pieces for having a messy desk, so Ashley Drake used the fact that the teacher was distracted as an excuse to abuse me like she so often did. She was mean from second grade, and that's around the time certain people started chipping away at my cool, but it was in fourth grade where I completely climbed into a shell, terrified to come out.

"You think you're cool, but you're not."

I used to love going to school in those first few years since it was a place for me to chase girls around and showcase my cool. Ashley Drake became my reason for hating school. Well, her and Mrs. Aarons of course. I used to hear stories of how unreasonably strict things used to be in the classroom. Teachers beat students with yardsticks, rulers...anything they could get their hands on, really. I think when we started school in the mid 1970s, we were on the cusp where the modern age was just on the horizon if not already somewhat in motion...but that Old World cruelty was still a reality, even if it was in its last dying days. We caught the tail end of it. Teachers like Mrs. Aarons still existed. What made matters worse, was that Mrs. Aarons lived on my block, just three houses away.

"I don't care what your mother said. When you're in school, I'm in charge and you will do as I say. And I'm telling you to get out your math book."

Poor little Dana Kaschak sat at her desk looking up at Mrs. Aarons with the trusting eyes of a child who had no idea how cruel and fucked up the world could be.

"I left it at my grandma's house. My mother said she'll write you a note if..."

"Likely story, Dana. Can everybody sympathize with Miss. Kaschak? She left it at her grandmother's house."

I had no idea what sympathize meant, but I sat there watching with a sense of both dread and relief. Dread that I knew exactly what was coming, and relief that I wasn't the one it was going to happen to. What followed was typical of any class that ever had Mrs. Aarons. Once she had any reason to focus negative attention on you, your desk was getting dumped.

"I bet you didn't even take it home," she sneered at Dana. "I bet if I search that rat's nest of a desk you got there, I bet I'd find all sorts of things you lost."

Dana pleaded.

"But I'm telling the truth."

"Oh get away," the teacher snapped, motioning for Dana to slide her chair away from the desk. "Get back."

Before she could give Dana a chance to move, she pulled the child, still in her chair, away from the desk and turned the desk over, spilling its entire contents on the floor. The little girl looking terrified began to cry. Mrs. Aarons ignored her and proceeded to turn the incident into a lesson.

"Everybody take a good look at Miss. Kaschak. This is not the way to keep the inside of your desk clean. If I need to provide further demonstration on how to keep the inside of your desk clean, I'll do it. And if you were this sloppy and irresponsible, you'd be crying too."

It was almost standard procedure by some of these older fossils of teachers in the Cypress School to randomly single out a kid on any given day, dump their desk, and then deliver a screaming sermon to the entire class on how bad that kid was. They'd carry on and on about how messy and sloppy, and how dirty, inadequate, incapable and unworthy...completely reducing the child to tears and probably scarring them for life. And it didn't matter if Dana Kaschak got it today. The next day, it could be you.

Mr. Hardenberger was another one. He taught the fifth graders, which meant that if you were Derrick Adler, you got to put up with military tactics like marching back and forth in a straight line all day, and the constant drilling and grilling and dissecting of students at random. Nobody died, and nobody was beaten at Cypress, but the psychological warfare of some of the teachers who acted like they just stepped out of the Massachusetts Bay Colony proved too much for some kids. On better days, a teacher carrying on and on in response to a simple question would be almost inevitable. A typical exchange with Mr. Hardenberger on a good day might be something like what I overheard in the hall one day when I was asked to walk across the playground to the fifth grade unit and deliver an envelope to him. As I handed him the envelope, he thanked me and I walked out. Derrick saw me, and I suppose he wanted to bug me, so he raised his hand and asked to use the bathroom. Just then I walked out of the room and stopped outside the door to listen to the teacher's response.

"No, Derrick, you cannot go to the bathroom."

Derrick wasn't having it.

"But, it's an emergency," he said, sounding desperate.

Mr. Hardenberger wasn't having it either.

"Derrick, I said no."

"But..."

"...because it takes time away from the lesson if you get up and go to the bathroom, because next there's gonna be a big parade to the bathroom and everybody is going to want to go to the bathroom, and I don't think it's necessary for 25 people to get up and go to the bathroom. Do you really have to go or do you just want to waste tiiiiiiiime?"

"I really gotta..."

"And that's why you can't go to the bathroom. You people better shape up or ship out. You think you've got it bad now? You just wait til they get you in the junior high."

———

During the first grade school year, catechism was imposed on our lives. Since Ritchie Burke attended Catholic school, he was exempt. But the rest of us...Tommy, Marc, and me, had to endure one hour a week at Our Lady of Peace learning about Jesus Christ. This would happen every week until eighth grade. In retrospect, it was probably the obvious thing for all our parents to do, by sticking us in these classes in preparation for our communions and confirmations, and to avoid their own souls from being damned into hell for not giving their children up to the Lord Jesus Christ. Church itself was a very funny thing, because although our "religion" said on paper that we went to church on Sundays, in practice, we only went on Christmas and Easter, and the occasional wedding and funeral. Later in life, I learned to question most of what I was taught. I often wondered what I would do if and when I ever had my own kids, and what I would tell them when it came to the subject of religion. Do I raise them in the traditional family manner? Or do I tell them what I really think? Guilt would probably consume me, and have me baptize the kid immediately, as my questions and beliefs should probably yield to the fear of dishonoring the family lineage. At least from there, just in case they were right, the kid will have a fighting chance in life.

On the morning of my first communion, my brother Franklin swallowed a penny. As my mom was in the kitchen doing mom/kitchen things, I was in the living room with Franklin who was playing with an empty plastic gallon bottle that once had milk in it. My mom had rinsed it out and given it to him to play with. At some point, he got hold of a penny and was shaking it around at the bottom of the bottle. It wasn't really registering with me what he was doing as he put the bottle to his three-year old mouth. A few minutes later, Franklin got up and started rubbing his stomach.

"Mommy, stomach hawts," he yelled while walking into the kitchen.

"Franklin, go play," she said in that dismissive parent voice that tells you that they're so consumed and stressed by what they are doing, that you could tell them, "Mom, I going out to do drugs," and she would say, "That's nice, dear."

Franklin stayed in the doorway.

"Stomach hawts, Mommy!"

I felt the need to cut in, fearing he might have swallowed the penny. So I asked him.

"Franklin, what did you do with the penny you had?"

"All gone," he said with a knowing look of dread. Mom still wasn't paying too much attention.

"Mom," I screeched, growing more concerned, "Franklin was drinking out of the bottle, and I think there was a penny in there."

She looked up.

"Franklin, what did you do with the penny? How did he get a penny?"

I shrugged and Franklin pointed to his stomach.

"Penny all gone."

"Oh Jesus Christ," my mother shrieked. "Did you see him put it in his mouth?"

Somehow I knew this was all going to fall on me.

"I don't know," I pleaded. "He had the bottle by his face, and the penny was in the bottle because I heard it clanking around."

She shot me a dirty look and turned back to Franklin.

"Franklin, did you swallow the penny?"

"Swallow penny! Stomach hawts!"

"Oh Jesus Christ almighty!"

This went on for a few more quizical minutes before my mom finally accepted that Franklin had swallowed a penny. After that, she sent me and my dad to church for my communion while she spent the rest of the morning in the ER with Franklin.

There was much concern around the event. My mom came home with Franklin a few hours later with news that he would live, and that the penny would eventually come out of his ass. Later in the day, a party was held in the basement with my entire family... grandparents, aunts, uncles, cousins...all seated around a table eating pasta. It was a "first communion" party held in my honor. But the big news of the day was the baby. No matter how old Franklin was, he was still referred to as the baby at certain times. Normally, he was Franklin. But whenever a bad situation arose where a finger could be pointed at someone for being irresponsible, he became "the baby." The overlapping conversation told the story:

Aunt Rose: "Where is the baby now?"
Aunt Marie: "Did the baby poop?"
Aunt Jess: "Poor baby!"
Grandma: "What happened to the baby?"

Eventually, it was time for my mom to put Franklin on the bowl. The entire family eagerly followed her upstairs so they could obtrusively stretch their necks into the bathroom, while anxiously awaiting the turd that would pop out of my little brother's ass. I stood behind my family all gathered in the doorway of the bathroom, listening to the overlapping talk of crap and coins.

Aunt Jess: "Push Franklin, push!"

Cousin Lucas: "Come on Franklin, you can do it."

Aunt Marie: "You're gonna have to get the strainer, Luanne!"

Uncle Tom: "You remember the time Joseph swallowed the quarter?"

Aunt Rose: "He's gotta push, Luanne."

Aunt Marie: "The strainer Luanne, the strainer!"

Aunt Jess: "Oh yeah, Joseph and the quarter. That was scary. Remember that mom?"

Uncle Jimmy: "The penny...it's gonna come out his ass?"

Suddenly, I realized that I was no longer in the picture. The family gathering had gone from my "first communion" party to the "we're all waiting for the baby to take a shit" party. Nobody was paying any attention to me anymore. And when the turd finally exploded out of Franklin's ass and everyone applauded, I became jealous and began to cry. Not cool.

2

Lizard With a Brooklyn Accent

As my mom drove us to school that first day of sixth grade, we drove past the picket line and the first person I saw was Miss. Tripe, the music teacher. I began flashing on thoughts of how we were expected to be in chorus once the year got underway, and how much I dreaded the idea of singing in front of the entire school. It was a sixth grade tradition, and from what we had been told all through elementary school, everyone had to participate. I was one to always dwell nervously on the future and play out the worst possible scenarios in my head, along with the potential embarrassment that could come my way. So in typical Eugene Devine fashion, I sat in my mom's car some nine months away from the sixth grade concert, worrying about chorus. I knew in my head I was a rock star, and that the Fonzie coolness of my early years at Cypress was still somewhere to be sought out and dug up. The introverted coward who suffered stage fright, barely able to speak in front of people let alone sing, was light years away from the legendary icon who would prance shamelessly around his bedroom playing guitar on a tennis racket instead of doing his homework.

I suppose there were lots of things that bothered me about starting sixth grade, but music shouldn't have been one of them. But my fears took over and had their way with me. Looking back, I can't help wondering if Miss Tripe had made us sing Kiss and Led Zeppelin songs instead of Broadway showtunes and kiddy songs, if I would have shaken off my stage fright. But it was still the idea of singing in front of people that I couldn't get over, and not the actual music. The songs were fun to laugh at all year long during music class. I didn't mind music class. It was gym that I hated. From the first day of first grade it had been a sickening experience. And although I no longer dwelled on that, it's still worthy of a flashback or two for further understanding of Eugene Devine. And mind you, reader...these flashbacks are random and only sometimes connected, if not totally linear...if you haven't noticed by now. And though some stand on their own, they all serve a purpose in the progression of our story. And so we return to the flashbacks.

I can't recall how I met Marc Rinaldi or how he comes into the picture. It seems to have been sometime before the start of kindergarten. In fact, I was somehow introduced to a whole new crowd down the street from me, or as my mom would say, "down the block." Any time I was going over to Marc's, I was going "down the block." It got to the point over the years where anything involving Marc Rinaldi or Marc himself, was referred to as "down the block." I'd tell mom I was going out to play with my friend, and she'd say, "Down the block?" It eventually got to a point where my friends were renamed for where they lived in proximity to my house. Marc became Down the Block. Tommy became Around the Block, and Richie became Next Door. For example, if Marc called on the phone, my mom would call me and say "Your friend is on the phone."

"Who?" I'd ask.

"Down the Block!"

Marc Rinaldi lived down the block. Across the street lived Derrick Adler and his little sister Stephanie. In the first few years of Cypress, I became a target for Derrick and Marc. They made fun of me because I watched *Happy Days*. They also laughed at me because I was an Elton John fan. Oh yeah, I almost forgot to mention that sometime in 1975, Ritchie Burke's older brothers threw a party when their parents weren't home. Ritchie and I were playing in the basement when we curiously wandered into his brother's room. They were in the yard hanging out with their "big kid" group of friends. They all listened to rock music too and eventually turned us on to groups like Led Zeppelin, Blue Oyster Cult, Be-Bop Deluxe, and Pink Floyd. They'd laugh at us when we eventually got into Kiss. Kiss wasn't taken seriously because they wore makeup and younger kids who probably shouldn't have liked them practically worshipped them. But Ritchie and I were seven and five years old. Any rock music in our lives should have been commendable. That day, Ritchie's brothers were blasting an Elton John record out the window. They had them all...the yellowish album where he's holding his arm up, the album where he has the beard, the album where he doesn't have the beard, the album with the big blue letters on it and the one with the blue background where he's smiling and wearing his pants up to his chest. He was the biggest rock star in the world for a few years and we discovered him just at his peak.

But anyway, Marc Down the Block and Derrick Adler made fun of me for liking Elton John. But that was alright. I was secure when it came to music. No one could shake me. I was already a veteran. At the age of five, I had been rockin' for years already. I danced with the refrigerator to "Get Back" at the age of one. I mouthed the drums to "Get off My Cloud" by the age of two, and I bought my first official album *Hot Rocks* by the Rolling Stones at the age of four. By the age of five, my rock and roll credibility was impeccable. Nobody was going to mess with me. And any motherfucker who has a problem with Elton John, I dare to listen to *Tumbleweed Connection* and not be shaken by it.

Even though Marc had the occasional mean streak in him if Derrick was around, he stayed my friend through most of our childhood. He was the same age as Tommy and me. Derrick, who was two years older than us, was an instigator who usually sparked some trouble between Marc and me, and then took Marc's side. Deep down, Derrick liked me, but he also loved as much bullshit as he could create in any given situation. He was the strongest kid in the Cypress School, so it didn't hurt knowing him. If he ever saw I was in any real trouble with someone else though, he'd jump to my defense and kick their ass if need be. So in that respect, he really was my friend.

When you went to Marc's house to play, it usually involved violence. He had a tiny obsession with weapons. In his room, he had a wide assortment of guns, knives, bows and arrows, chains, ropes, whips, handcuffs and a basement with a darkroom. His dad built it to develop photographs, but Marc liked to use it as a torture chamber. I know this makes Marc seem pretty sadistic, but this really was my first impression of him, even at that young age. In reality, he was harmless. One on one, he wasn't bad at all, and could be your best friend. In a group, he could sometimes get mean and single you out. The running myth/joke about hanging out with Marc was that if a crowd of people were involved, it usually ended in someone in the group being singled out, picked on, beat up, tied up and then thrown into the basement for hours at a time. That said, I never witnessed anything like that ever happen. Plus, I was close enough with him that he always kept me on his side or stayed on mine...so I never had to worry about him turning on me. Except for that one time he rolled me up in a carpet and left me there while he went into the bathroom to take a shit. Funny thing is... his grandfather was sitting in a recliner two feet away from me. He was looking at a crossword puzzle with a magnifying glass and had no idea I was rolled up in a carpet behind his chair while the deafening music played on the stereo, and the southern accent sang to me from out of the speaker on the floor next to my ear..."Hey, won't you play another 'somebody done somebody wrong' song." In some ways, Marc rubbed off on me, but only in extremely small amounts, and not enough to affect me in the long term. It did however influence the first bout of creativity in the somewhat artistic mind that I would later develop. We'll get into that a little further along in the story.

————

The neighborhood was young. Barely two decades old, Oakwoods had been built between 1957 and 1959. One generation had already exhausted its time there and although there were still some older families on our block, most of the houses belonged to young couples in their late 20s and early 30s. That meant lots of kids between the ages of five and ten. The older couples already had teenagers. Those were the couples like Richie's parents whose oldest kids were driving age. But the older couples often mingled with the younger couples and just about every house and family socialized with each other. Spring and summer nights were always filled with our parents all gathered talking in the street. Some nights they'd randomly put out lawn chairs in front of someone's house, and that would be their spot for the evening. Us kids would run around and play while the adults talked...every parent occasionally glancing over to check on us. Not all households seemed all that normal, however.

There were two rather dysfunctional families on Sycamore Drive...the Allen's and the Merker's. Yes, every family is a little dysfunctional, but these two were a little exceptionally exceptional. The Allen's lived across from us. It was George, an emotionally unstable alcoholic, his wife Nadine, and their two daughters Alicia and Rebecca. Alicia was the same age as Tommy and me. Rebecca was the same age as Franklin and Christopher. None of the other kids in the neighborhood seemed to like the two girls, nor were they very popular in school either. Because of circumstances that I don't remember, or perhaps have blocked out, my mom used to offer me up like a human sacrifice to the Allen's so Alicia would have someone to play with. And Franklin had to play with Rebecca.

I imagine scenarios of little children being raised in jungles by animals. I imagine uncivilized little demon creatures running wild in anarchic frenzy. I'm not really sure how the Allen girls were raised. I don't know what exactly they were taught, or how or why. I was too young to understand or even begin to contemplate it. I don't think the poor girls were given baths very often. And I know Alicia was never potty trained. I know this because she would go wherever she was, and at the moment that she had to go...kind of like a dog. On two separate occasions one summer, she raised her dress and crapped on my lawn...once on the side of the house, and once right in front. And with no shame at all...like an animal, she did it right in front of me. This was around first or second grade, so I know she was old enough to know better. I was too traumatized to even talk about it or tell on her. I think some neighborhood dog probably got blamed when my dad stumbled across it while mowing the lawn. In the Seventies, it wasn't yet politically correct to clean up after your dog. It was also common to see litter strewn about in the streets. It wasn't the norm to hold onto your garbage until you found a garbage can. If there was no can in the immediate area, you threw it in the street. Streets were always decorated with crushed soda cans and Burger King bags. And there was dog shit everywhere you looked. Every lawn had dog shit. So it was pretty easy for little Alicia Allen to get away with crapping on peoples lawns.

The other family, the Merker's, lived further down the street. Barker Merker, an acid casualty, was an absent father who would pop in and out of the lives of his family every once in a while. His wife Lula was forced to raise the three children on her own. Together, Barker and Lula produced two sons; Big John the Bouncer and Kenny Longlegs. Also living in the Merker house was Barker's mother, also known as Granny Morbid, and his nephew Malbert. Malbert Merker's parents (Barker's brother and his wife) left him on Barker's steps when he was a baby, and they never came back. Malbert read books and was rarely seen. Big John the Bouncer, the oldest, born in 1964, was the neighborhood pervert. He was always spotted in the 7-Eleven trying to buy porn magazines. Kenny Longlegs, born in 1966, was covered in burn scars since the age of one, after having been accidentally dropped in the fireplace by his drunken father. The big rumor on the block was that the kids kept Granny Morbid tied up and locked in the basement where they would perform experiments on her. Derrick Adler always talked about it, and swore that he went up to the basement window one night and saw the kids sticking a needle into Granny Morbid .

The stuff of legend in smalltown U.S.A.

But anyway...

The Giovanni's were one of the older couples on the block who took a few of the younger couples under their wings. As I mentioned, my mom and Aunt Rose always went over there during the day to hang out with Rose Giovanni. Rose's wise guy husband was Vinnie. Vinnie was in his late 50s and seemed to be connected to organized crime, as were a lot of shady people I vaguely remember who used to hang around the Giovanni house. He spoke in a thick Brooklyn accent, pronouncing words like water as "waw-da." If he liked you, he usually referred to you as cocksucker. If he didn't like you, you were also cocksucker.

During the Bicentennial summer, an overabundance of fireworks in the neighborhood spilled out far past the Fourth of July and into August as every night was gleefully seasoned with explosions in the sky. The scented sulfuric essence of gunpowder remained a constant, while a smoky fog always seemed to waft in from somewhere. Random blasts and bombs bursting in air...sky rockets in flight...the summer was a kaleidoscope of sensory overload. The Giovanni's 20-year old son, Vinnie Jr. danced down the driveway wearing cutoff shorts and no shirt, a transistor radio in his ear and the Sylvers "Boogie Fever" blasting out of it for the circle of adults to hear.

"I took my baby to the pizza paah-laahhh," he sang with a sense of bravado, winking as he strutted past me.

"Get the hell outta he-ah," his father barked. "Go in the house and get a shirt on. And put on some slacks!"

Little Vinnie ignored him, turning onto the sidewalk to head out for the night. Big Vinnie continued.

"Everybody's gonna think yaw a quee-ah! My own son...actin' like a fuckin' quee-ah!"

We kids just usually looked at each other and smiled, knowing Vinnie was saying bad things that kids shouldn't hear. But that was Oakwoods...a bunch of well-meaning responsible young adults trying to raise their kids right, sprinkled with older jaded fuck-ups who had watched their dreams die and were taking their miserable lives out on their rebellious teenagers. Vinnie Jr. wasn't one of the older kids that I would see walking up the street at night. He didn't bother with them and was off on his own non-rock and roll trip, embracing the early emergence of dance music, which was slowly seeping into the suburbs.

"Guys, cover year ears when Vinnie talks," Tommy's dad, Big Tom playfully warned us. Vinnie wasn't amused.

"Hey kids," Vinnie drunkenly said to whoever of us may have been listening. "He wants you to think I'm a bad guy."

He pointed at himself, looking directly at me.

"I may be a tough guy, but I'm not a bad guy. Do you think I'm a bad guy?"

I laughed nervously. I looked at my dad who offered me a reassuring smile, probably realizing how fucked up Vinnie really was, but knowing better than to say something. Vinnie then turned to Tommy.

"What about you, Snake Boy? Do you think I'm a bad guy?"

Big Tom cut in.

"So, Vinnie we need to get back. What's this thing about a lizard? What did you need me for?

"Ah, the lizid," Vinnie remembered, placing a bottle of Shaeffer on the surface of the driveway where the concrete meets the lawn while clumsily getting up from a folding chair. Long story short, Vinnie's rich brother, Peter had died several weeks earlier. Peter was a well-to-do music professor whose eccentricity and homosexuality remained scandalous in the Giovanni family. But that aside, there were a number of items that Vinnie was inheriting from his brother... things that he already wanted taken off his hands like Peter's library and the entire contents of his office. Vinnie was dreading the entire idea of it and couldn't even bring himself to go back to his brother's

Brooklyn brownstone. Peter's partner Walter had been staying away from their home with his sister in Sheepshead Bay, but made it clear to Vinnie that he wanted certain things out of his sight that he simply couldn't deal with. One of the biggest problems in terms of Peter's possessions was his monitor lizard, and Vinnie wanted no part of this either. That's where Big Tom came in. Big Tom had become accustomed to dealing with lizards and snakes and reptile removal in general. Some very brave and demented collector, for example, was getting rid of a Gabon viper that he had somehow managed to get into his house years earlier, and Big Tom had recently used a newly-built noose contraption to capture it from its tank in order to properly secure it in a wooden crate and somehow get it to Florida. Big Tom was not concerned with how this person got the snake to Florida, nor did he ask. His only job was to get it from one tank to another without getting killed in the process. Vinnie was in the process of trying to work out some sort of deal with Big Tom if he would take care of the lizard situation, perhaps arrange with some of his lizard people to have it moved to a lizard place.

"I got this lizid that I have to get rid of. It was my brotha's. Waltah my brotha's queeah friend don't want it, and neitha do I."

As Vinnie was telling this to Big Tom, George Allen walked over from across the street...causally strolling, face down with his arms folded behind his back as if handcuffed, looking both deep in thought and without a care in the world. He stopped on our group of parents and kids as if he had just happened upon us without expecting it and was somehow surprised to find us in his path. He just listened as Vinnie explained his lizard situation to Big Tom.

"A lizard, huh?" Big Tom said, not really interested, but politely acknowledging him.

"Yeah. A lizid. You have any people you know who might want it?"

Vinnie handed George a beer and sat back down next to Big Tom. George remained standing above them.

"Yeah, I think I can ask around," Big Tom replied. "I know some lizard people. What kind of lizard we talking about?"

"I don't know, it's a big lizid. One of those dragon lizids"

"Like the Komodo Dragon?" George asked, cutting in.

Vinnie looked at Big Tom as if to establish a mutual silent agreement of disgust at George's very presence.

"Yeah cocksucka, like the Komodo Dragon. It's a big muthafucka. That's how bored my brotha was. Rich, bored cocksucka. I think he bought these things just because he could. If I had his money, I'd burn mine."

"Yeah," George said, opening his beer. "But won't you get some of that money now?"

My dad and Big Tom looked at each other, both visibly cringing.

Vinnie looked at George with his well-known scrunched-up face and furrowed brow.

"Why, you cocksucka. I don't count his money, I count my own. I work for a living. That's what I do. I work!"

Nearly every adult either let out a chuckle or an uncomfortable smile. They knew Vinnie very well, and they knew how proud he was on the subject of money. They also knew what he did, didn't really fall under the category of work. Yet, the working class hero rap always surfaced within a few seconds.

"What are you laughing at cocksuckas?"

Feeling for her husband, Rose Giovanni attempted to take the conversation elsewhere.

"I can't believe Walter is taking the Picasso," she said, chucking a cigarette butt into the street. A cluster of flying burning embers seared my arm as the butt blew past me and landed a few feet from the curb.

Indifferent or incognizant to the fact that she had just burned me, Rose opened her little cigarette purse and reached for another Lark.

"His brother has a Picasso and one painting that's also attributed to Picasso...and of everything in that house, Walter is keeping the Picassos. Can you imagine? To have a Picasso..."

"Screw Picasso, that fuckin' degenerate," Vinnie charged. "He was a degenerate and Waltah's a degenerate, so it makes sense. It's very fitting that he has his Picasso. You call that art?"

"I think Picasso was a fine painter," George cut in. "Maybe even the most important of the twentieth century."

Vinnie scrunched his face.

"Why you cocksucka...you *would* think something like that."

Big Tom busted out laughing, unable to control himself.

"And what are *you* laughin' at?"

"They're laughing at you, jackass," Rose reminded him. "They know how this conversation goes."

"Fuck's that supposed to mean?"

"It means everyone knows your rant about art. And sports. And music. And politics. And the gov..."

"...Well, it's pornography, I tell ya. You degenerates call that art?"

Everyone began exchanging glances, bracing themselves. For what they were about to hear were the ramblings of one Vinnie Giovanni, who had to tell the same story over and over again as if he were telling it for the first time. But Vinnie's memory didn't serve him well very often, and he didn't realize that he had told the same story dozens of times to the same people. So when the subject of degenerate art came up as it often did, everyone knew that it would lead into one of Vinnie's "Years ago" stories.

"Years ago," he began.

"Oh Jesus Christ," my mom shrieked, getting up from her chair, folding it and heading back up the block to our house while Franklin walked with her, holding her hand.

"Come on Eugene," she called back. "It's getting dark."

"I'll be up in a second," I responded, sitting on the curb flipping baseball cards with Tommy.

"Years ago," Vinnie continued, "I was doin' a job knockin' down a joint in order to build Doubles in the basement of the Sherry-Netherland. I went into that place. You can't believe the money. You would eat off the bathroom floor. And we had to knock it down. I remember I went in the bathroom to start rippin' it apart. I walked in? Cocks and balls everywhere! Everywhere you looked was cocks and balls. Cocks and balls on the walls...cocks and balls on the floor. Fuckin' degenerates that designed this place I tell ya. Even the faucets on the sinks were cocks!"

Vinnie's warped and distorted memory didn't allow for him to realize that what he was referring to as "years ago" had only taken place within the past year and a half, as the private Doubles supper club had just recently opened in Manhattan.

"Watch your mouth around the kids, Vinnie," Big Tom scolded.

Vinnie continued, unphased.

"Then one day we were rippin' out the toilets. I looked at one and you know what was painted at the very bottom of the bowl?"

He stared at George. George already knew what was painted at the bottom of the bowl, but he humored Vinnie anyway.

"What was painted at the bottom of the bowl?"

"An eyeball."

"Nooo shit!" George smiled. "An eyeball?"

"A fuckin' eyeball. So it could stare up at your dirty stinky asshole and watch your balls dangle over the wawda."

Tommy and I were now cracking up on the curb.

"I remember right before we did the job," Vinnie continued relentlessly. "Some old lady walked in out of nowhere and told us to save one of the bowls because she was gonna buy it."

"What did she pay for it?" George asked

"The fuck do I know?" Vinnie shrugged.

"I got a bust of Voltaire from my father," George said, as if suddenly remembering it and just needed to add it to the conversation. "I'm not sure how much it would be worth though. Can't be much."

Vinnie scrunched his face and bared his teeth.

"You fuckin' candyass! Voltaire."

———

In February 1977, four native New Yorkers, Paul Stanley, Gene Simmons, Ace Frehley and Peter Criss were about to live out their childhood dreams and headline Madison Square Garden for the first time. Their popularity was steadily on the rise, and by the end of the year, Kiss would be the biggest rock band in the world. Across the Hudson River, I was quickly beginning to idolize them...wanting to be them...wanting anything but the gruesome reality of my second grade life.

By that year, Ritchie Burke had also become infected with Kiss. It had been a year since I'd discovered them. Around the corner, Tommy had caught it worse than any of us. He quickly surpassed me in the number of Kiss albums owned. One of our newest pastimes was to stage fake Kiss concerts. I did Kiss concerts with Tommy, Ritchie and Marc, though never collectively. One time, Ritchie and I took a pair of broom sticks that had horse heads attached to them and used them as guitars. We stood out in his driveway and proceeded to act out the entire note-for-note, word-for-word concert from the *Alive* album. We even had a small audience of some teenage girls who were walking up the street and stopped to watch us for a few songs. The horse heads on broomsticks were not the only objects that would serve as guitars. I played guitar on tennis rackets, wooden cooking spoons, and anything I could find that was conducive to jamming out. It was the tennis racket acting as guitar that became my favorite thing to play with as a child since I didn't really play with toys that much. I wasn't interested in toys. I either played Fonzie or rock star. If I did feel the need for toys, I went over to Ritchie's where he had every toy and game in the world. Our favorite was a game of army figures called Battleground. On rainy days when we couldn't go outside, Ritchie and I would set up his entire living room with hundreds of little soldiers, tanks, canons, and barbed wire fences. The set came with cardboard landscapes, fake bodies of water, booby traps, land mines and everything else that the hell of war entailed. We also played with Fisher Price Adventure People and games such as Life, Operation, Hungry Hungry Hippos, Connect Four, and Perfection. Yes...Perfection! You gotta move 'em fast. Because the pieces pop up before you put in the last!

That summer, some maniac named David Berkowitz, who called himself the Son of Sam was a year into a killing spree in New York City. You couldn't listen to the radio or watch TV without hearing the name Son of Sam. One day, I was down the block playing with Marc, when he decided to play a joke designed to scare the hell out of a five year old Stephanie Adler. He had with him a fairly large vintage countertop transistor radio and a small tape recorder. Into the recorder, he taped some music that he interrupted with a fake news flash (his own voice). The "news" said that the Son of Sam had moved from New York City to Oakwoods, New Jersey, and was preying on little five-year old girls. He was last spotted at Oakwoods Junior High. Well, Oakwoods Junior High was just up the block and a fence. That's all that came between the Son of Sam and little Stephanie. Next, Marc unscrewed the back of the radio, and planted the small recorder. We then walked over to the Adler's house where Stephanie was sitting on the front stairs. He played the tape and held the back of the radio towards his body to hide what he was doing. Now mind you, the joke did not work. The whole thing was lost on her. The news played out, and she hadn't even been paying attention. What was he supposed to do? Reach inside the radio, rewind the tape, and play it again? The plan may not have worked, but it was an example of the warped but creative brilliance of the very young Marc Rinaldi, who lived down the block.

———

Once a week in the Cypress School, the class lined up single file and walked outside across the playground to the main building where we had music class. Miss Tripe, as previously mentioned, was the music teacher. She was a middle-age heavy-set woman who always wore dark blue polyester suits and far too much rouge on her face. Facially, she looked like Mama Cass meets Liberace. She tought us songs out of the music books...singing them to us at first...and then as we learned them, we would have to sing them in unison. The books were color coded according to grade level. We sang songs like "Cotton Needs Pickin," "Good Old Electric Washing Machine," "Erie Canal," "Old Polina," "Khumbaya," "Scratch Scratch," "Don't Count Your Chickens," "Grab Your Bicycle Buddy," "Pay Me My Money Down," "Don Gato" and "There's a Hole in the Bucket." While the music played, Miss Tripe walked up and down the rows between the desks, frantically swinging her arms around in the air with her finger pointing as if she were a conductor. We sang these songs, while she swung her arms around the entire time. And when she wore short sleeves, you could see the fat jiggling from side to side. The peculiar element of some of these songs we were singing like "Cotton Needs Pickin,'" an old slave song of the racist South, was that they were part of a book of American folk songs that was in the school curriculum...and nobody really thought anything of how seriously fucked up it was for a class of suburban white kids to be singing so joyously about slaves in a cotton field.

Towards the end of the school year, Miss Tripe would let us bring in our own records to play. The girls always brought the *Saturday Night Fever* soundtrack and Andy Gibb. They'd all get up and dance in the back of the room, while the boys sat there and laughed.

One time I brought in *Rock and Roll Over* from Kiss. The girls all sneered and made nasty remarks, and Rachel Santos even went so far as to hit me just for having it. What I found amusing though, was not their reaction to Kiss...but Miss Tripe's reaction. When I gave her the record, she looked at the song list on both sides. Without so much as asking me about the songs or which song to play, she immediately skipped the first two and went straight to "Calling Dr. Love," as if she already knew it. Now granted, the song was being played on the radio for a brief period in early '77, but is it possible she was that in touch with rock radio? As the song was finishing, David Kirschner remarked at how cool Ace Frehley's guitar sounded as he bent those eerie- sounding, feedback-lined notes during the fade out. Miss Tripe then cut in.

"That's not a guitar, it's a motorcycle."

They argued back and forth for a minute. Kirschner insisted it was a guitar, but she kept insisting rather authoritatively, "It's a motorcycle!" For you reading this, please refer to Kiss *Rock and Roll Over* and go to the end of the third track, "Calling Dr. Love" if you are unfamiliar with what I am talking about.

———

One thing I always hated about the Cypress School was that we only had music and art once a week, but gym we always had twice. In the mornings, the All Purpose Room would become the gymnasium. In short, gym was a pretty scarring experience through most of my childhood. The more tolerable days were when we played kickball and you could blend in with the crowd...except of course when it was your turn to kick...times when you were literally on stage, and it could be pretty traumatizing. That was most of the time. If I wasn't able to blend in with the defense in the outfield during kickball, I usually felt onstage in some other activity, ready to make a complete ass of myself. We either had to do back flips or somersaults or cartwheels in front of everybody. I wasn't very flexible and just couldn't get the hang of flipping over. In truth, I was afraid of landing the wrong way on my head and breaking my neck. Then there were the days when Mr. Minuchie, the gym teacher, would pull the ropes down from the ceiling. We'd have to climb the ropes all the way to the top while the class watched. I usually only made it up a quarter of the way and got rope burn on the way down. Then Mr. Minuchie got creative. We'd have to grab two ropes, one with the left hand and one with the right on either side of us, and do back flips between the ropes...a game called Skin-the-Cat. I couldn't seem to get away from the back flips. The girls tormented me for sucking at everything. Scrawny little Ashley Drake with her wrinkled clothes, messy long brown hair and very dangerous pair of boots was a large source of that torment in gym class. I guess that goes without saying by now. Not even those homely sad eyes could conjure up so much as a turd's worth of empathy for this girl. I can't say it enough. She really was the anti-Christ.

At lunchtime, the All Purpose Room became a cafeteria. The crowd was especially loud. Every day during lunch, Mr. Tutundjian, the principal would walk in. Noise level didn't matter when Mr. Tutundjian spoke. His overly bass-like voice always rumbled over the crowd. You could feel it thumping in your chest when he spoke, but you could never make out actual words with the crowd noise. We'd all be talking on one end of the room, and from the other end we'd hear "Ourrum. Rrrruugarrawarf! Rrrruugaroaragrum sprarffaganarum! Aurrrgggrumm!! Arrrrgggrrrrrrgggggrggrrr!!" Yes, it sounded more like animalistic, almost Sci-fi character-like growling.

But as threatening as he sounded, he was really a nice guy. His voice shook the room, and he was always oblivious to the noise level of the crowd. He just spoke over it. He'd often come in and speak to the teacher's aides. He'd come up to Mrs. Santorini and say something like "Aurrruugarum. Mofomorarafim nuroooragerrrrrr!!" And Mrs. Santorini would respond without missing a beat...as if she actually knew what the hell he was saying.

Mr. Wagner, the janitor, unlike Mr. Tutundjian, had no tolerance for noise. He was a tall, thin, wrinkled man with a 1950s crew cut. He looked near retirement age, as many did in that school. Most times when you saw him, he'd have a seething uptight look on his face as if he were just looking to start some shit with someone. He had that "go ahead, press my buttons and see what happens" look about him, and behind that look was the face of someone who had been in that school for decades. He was in high demand in the Cypress School, and everyone seemed to want a piece of him. If one combs through the staff of any school district today, they'd find custodians and tech support playing different roles...both of which require staff members to fill out "job reports" only to wait days, sometimes weeks to be addressed. Mr. Wagner was a janitor, and he was a janitor in a time when janitor wasn't dressed up in fancy names in politically correct efforts to dignify positions that people once looked down on. Mr. Wagner was the janitor and he did his job with pride. He did it all, and he was the only one doing it. And when somebody called him, he was always right there. He didn't give teachers the runaround that contracts and job reports created. This was all during a time when parents and grandparents told kids to stay in school and go to college because you didn't want to end up sweeping floors like a janitor or working public sanitation like the garbage man...and that's exactly how they were talked about...these people weren't sanitation work-ers...they were called garbage men as if they were the lowest form of human existence and their lives were irrevocably fucked. Janitor was a job nobody seemed to want, but somebody always had, and Mr. Wagner fit the part. He wore the shoes and he had the face. It didn't lie. He meant it. It was in his eyes, buried deep. He had janitor lodged in every wrinkle on his skin, around his eyes and his mouth. He even had janitor hair. Occasionally, you'd see him talking to other staff members, but on most days, he only seemed to know one word.

The noisy lunch period could never escape the inevitable one word that always came out of Mr. Wagner's mouth. He would do his job as we ate. He'd be in the background almost unnoticed. As the volume level grew, it became evident in his face that he was growing increasingly agitated. He'd stare out into the lunch crowd for several minutes, most kids having no idea that he was about to boil over. Then in his final moments of patience, he'd look intensely at the left side of the room and then quickly spin his head to the right. His face would become grimaced and contorted. The eyes would squint, the fore-head would wrinkle, and the mouth would get all pursed. As you got to know Mr. Wagner, you'd know what was coming. You'd hold your ears and look away as he inhaled one enormous breath. Then in one raging moment, he'd let out a single roar that jolted the All Purpose Room to a complete silence:

"HHHEYY!!

The All Purpose Room also served as the auditorium. Folding chairs to accompany every student and teacher were set up for events such as concerts and assemblies. Assemblies were always a treat for us because it meant that we got out of class and didn't have to do intolerable things like math. It didn't matter what the assembly was for. Any time away from the classroom was welcome...except of course for gym. Did I mention I hated gym?

The most consistent visitor to the Cypress School was an Oakwoods policeman named Officer Anderson. He showed up at least twice a year and always spoke to us about safety, not taking candy from strangers, drugs and stuff like that. I somewhat had a fear of the police with no real reason other than instances when me and my brother would be out with our parents someplace, and if one of us was acting up, my mother would either pretend to call the manger or find a nearby police officer. We could be anywhere...a store, a restaurant...and if one of us wasn't behaving, she would say "That's it, I'm calling the manager and he's going to call the police." Then she would stand up and look desperately around the room as if it were a real emergency. It always seemed to work on the both of us. I remember one time we were at some event on my mom's side of the family, and some acquaintance of someone was a cop who showed up to the function in uniform. Franklin and I were sitting in the garage, and this guy got out of his car and began walking up the driveway. Franklin, who was probably around four years old, immediately screamed out "No! Noooo! I'll be good," and then started crying as the guy approached us and went into the house. I wasn't nearly as bad as that, but I always had a natural guilt complex even when I didn't do anything wrong. So when Officer Anderson walked into the All Purpose Room and there were a few hundred kids in there, I was always paranoid that he would see me and single me out for some reason. No matter how innocent I was, in my mind the cops were always going to get me.

The most memorable assembly happened in fifth grade when Officer Anderson, a few other police officers and a detective came in with a giant glass case filled with drugs, and displayed it in front of the entire school. They went drug by drug, pointing each one out... informing us which drug we were looking at, and then about its effects. They let us come up to the front class by class to see the drugs close up. They showed us marijuana, cocaine, heroin, angel dust and a bunch of different kinds of pills. They showed us all kinds of plastic bags, needles, burnt-up spoons, pipes, bongs, a pack of EZ-Wider and how to roll a joint. Then Officer Anderson gave a long rap on why drugs were bad and why we shouldn't use them.

———

Television in the Seventies contained 13 channels. That was it. And most in the area couldn't get channel 1, 3, 6, 8, 10, and 12...which limited us to seven measly channels. When you watched a movie that you missed in the theater, you first waited several years before you could ever see it on television. When you watched it, the profanity and nudity was cut out. To add insult to injury, the movie was interrupted by commercials. This was just a fact of life. There was no DVR or TiVo or taping of your favorite programs and movies either. You didn't spend the night doing other things while knowing your show was being recorded and that you could watch it anytime you wanted. If you wanted to watch something, you remembered the time and channel, and kept it in the back of your mind that you had to be home and in front of the TV when it started. If you missed it, too bad...you were fucked.

We had one of those wooden sets that stood on legs, which in the Seventies were about the best things you could buy. Ours was a Zenith Marseille that had a very distinguishing but unflattering feature. The channel changer was a button on the front of the TV that made a loud obnoxious noise that resembled the sound of somebody sneezing. Every time you changed the channel, you heard this ridiculous sound. These were the days before remote controls, so if you wanted to change the channel, you had to get up off your ass and walk to the TV. Sometimes my dad would call me downstairs from my bedroom just to change the channel. One time the channel button got stuck and the channels didn't stop changing. The TV just kept going around and around in a rapid-fire endless cycle, changing channels by itself. No matter how hard we tried, we just couldn't stop the channels from changing and we had no choice but to turn the TV off. When we turned it back on after a few days, the channels were still changing. So we left it off for a few weeks and forgot about it, resorting to an old black and white set in the meantime. I remember taking it upon myself to turn the TV on one day when nobody was around, thinking it would be back to normal...but the channels were still going round and round. The channels changed by themselves for several weeks until one day we turned the TV on and they had somehow stopped. Finally, we could watch color TV again. Good times!

———

In the 1970s, before cable TV, VCRs, DVDs and multiplexes, there were buildings scattered throughout New Jersey. The buildings consisted of a small lobby and two rooms. Each room had seats and a giant screen...many of those screens above an old abandoned stage. Some of the older buildings even had balconies. These buildings were called movie theaters. Back when architecture was a language, these decorative structures passed through Art Nouveau, Deco and numerous other styles of elaborate ornamentation. These movie theaters had character. And unlike the soulless multiplexes of the future, each theater showed usually no more than two films at a time. Decades later, the multiplexes were built to maximize profit...each new bland structure featuring more and more screens. As the twentieth century pushed toward the new millennium, the trend of mass-produced diarrhea in large volumes passed off as movies had become the norm in Hollywood. These features were often referred to as "feel-good hit of the summer" and "number one movie in America." The price of a movie during the last quarter of the twentieth century increased five-fold. In 1977, one could see five movies for the price of just one of today's films. Without cable and video, it was common for people to go and see certain movies two, three, four, maybe five times in a theater. That summer, one film would change the course of the silver screen forever. The highest number of theatrical viewings of this film gave kids bragging rights for the next three years leading up to its sequel three years later. In a way, it opened up Pandora's Box for the future crap that we had to endure for the rest of our own personal eternities...the predictable cliché of the summer blockbuster and its inevitable sequels. In 1977 however, it was all new, unknown and unprecedented. What had happened with the album format in rock and roll, where suddenly, artists were selling more copies of albums than ever before, also happened in Hollywood as the blockbuster film phenomenon began that summer in much the same manner, with a relatively small movie starring a bunch of unknowns called *Star Wars*. The only other film before *Star Wars* that saw lines wrapped around entire blocks was 1973's *The Exorcist*. *Star Wars*, however, happened on a much larger scale. The marketing of the film was unlike anything ever promoted before. There were action figures, clothes, bed sheets, etc... At one point, you got a free Star Wars glass with the purchase of a Whopper at Burger King. You even got a *Star Wars* glass just for filling your tank up at certain gas stations. You name the merchandise, and more likely than not, they had it in *Star Wars*.

Disco was becoming a thorn in the side of rock music as '77 pushed onward. Like most other trends of mid-century pop cultural significance, it started underground in New York City as early as the late Sixties. It broke however, in 1977...as did punk. When we say "broke," we mean it reached the mainstream suburbs and mass popularity. Both forms of music had been around a while. It would be another year however, for punk to really be bastardized by mainstream popularity and new wave. Disco on the other hand went mainstream and got bigger and bigger. Like *Star Wars*, it took one film to change everything. In the final weeks of 1977, perhaps the defining year of the Seventies, *Saturday Night Fever* was released. Disco's explosion in the suburbs is largely owed to the film. In terms of showing the Brooklyn disco scene, the film came out a few years after the fact. Based on a 1975 article in *New York* magazine, the effect on the rest of America was almost unexpected. Like *Star Wars*, it was a phenomenon. If you liked rock music, it was the culprit for years of bad music and we saw it as the enemy. For the next two years, disco pretty much informed pop culture and how people dressed and wore their hair. It even informed the drugs they took. As rock fans, we all claimed to hate it and insisted that it sucked every chance we got. But we really had no idea what the true origin of the disco hate was all about with older people...I mean we were kids for Chris'sakes. None of that racist, homophobic sentiment that was fueling the anti-disco crusade way back to the Stonewall even entered into our realm of thought and experience. Again, seven and eight year olds in late Seventies suburbia only knew that rock was cool and everyone older than us was saying disco sucked.

Not the girls though.

The girls latched onto whatever watered-down version of disco culture that was permitted into the suburbs by 1978. They all had the *Saturday Night Fever* soundtrack and all went to see the sanitized PG print when it hit the theaters. Yeah, disco was the shit in more ways than one. But I was a born rocker. Few other boys other than Tommy, Marc and me really cared about rock music at that point...at least not the ones who were our age. So it was us against the girls. And the girls liked disco. It was war. And we had to stand and fight alone... especially being Kiss fans.

———

The Drug Fair in Oakwoods was a collage of overlapping scents that could stick to your clothes, permeate your hair and etch itself into your psyche to the point where you could still smell it from memory as an adult. One could walk in and instantly catch a whiff of rubber beach balls, garden hoses and lawn fertilizer...that combination of fragrances that could only be associated with a Drug Fair.

One day during the sweltering summer of "Baker Street," I walked into Drug Fair with my mom who was using the pharmacy. As I waited, I wandered through aisles of assorted junk and came to the books and magazines. This was where I'd check for recent issues of Creem and Circus to see if I could find any new pictures of Kiss. From the entrance of the aisle though, I spotted something different though that lured me all the way in. There in a shapeless mass of random miscellaneous items, sitting all alone on a shelf glaring out at me...almost glowing...were four giant red letters on a book cover... spelling out KISS.

I hurdled through an obstacle course to get to it.

Could it be?

I got there.

I picked it up.

I couldn't believe what I was holding.

A Kiss book!

Not a music *magazine* or anything like that.

It was a *book*!

A real *book*!

About Kiss!!

The Great American Novel!!

The first ever book on Kiss!!

By Creem Magazine's Robert Duncan!!

From their early days in Queens and the Bronx right up to the 1977 *Love Gun* Tour!

I held it tightly. I had to have it. It was only two dollars, and it was the last one. Somehow, I had to convince my mom to buy it for me. She couldn't possibly deny me the only Kiss book in Oakwoods. I clutched onto that thing and raced down the aisle maneuvering through the maze that was Drug Fair and finding the pharmacy where mom was.

This wasn't going to be easy.

Kiss was responsible for everything terrible in the world. But school was out. There was nothing that could possibly get me into trouble that could be blamed on Kiss if there wasn't any school.

And guess what...

She got me the book.

In the end, I didn't really have to convince her. I kind of knew that I would get it, not because I was spoiled or anything. I really wasn't. It's just that my parents never really denied me of anything that they could see I really wanted. This of course was before Kiss became problematic.

When we left Drug Fair, mom dropped me off at Tommy's house. We spent many hours at each other's houses during the summer. It was that inseparable bond that began at childbirth and saw us literally shitting our diapers together in those early years. I got out of the car and went up the walkway. Donna, Tommy's mom, opened the front door as I ran up the stairs. She waved as mom beeped the horn and drove off...the loud rhythmic hum of the 1965 Lemans rumbling away as she got to the end of White Birch Road. I walked into the house, proudly showing Donna my new Kiss book.

"Oohhhh myyyy God," she gasped. "Tommy's gonna love that!"

We walked from the living room through the kitchen.

"He's outside in the swimming pool with Christopher," she said, directing me out into the backyard. From the kitchen to the glass sliding doors, which were only about two steps, I must have had a million things racing through my head. I hadn't been this anxious to show something to Tommy since the day I got my first Kiss record. Opening the door, I could see Tommy and Christopher splashing about in the pool. It was a circular above-ground pool, which sat on the other side of the yard, across from the giant maroon-colored deck.

"Wait 'til they see my book," I thought.

I was on top of the world.

I was the king.

I had the biggest dick of anyone in Oakwoods that day.

I had the story of Kiss in my hands.

I stepped through the doors and walked out onto the deck. Tommy was gonna be impressed.

But wait!

What if he already had his own copy? It was the last book there. There were people who had obviously bought it before.

Nah.

Donna would have said something when I showed her my copy. Since we were only eight years old, and our parents were still buying our Kiss merchandise, she would have recognized it. It was hard to impress Tommy when it came to Kiss. Although I had the first Kiss record between the two of us, he quickly surpassed me in getting the entire collection very quickly. By the summer of 1978, he had all six studio albums and both of their live albums. I remember one day Big Tom was freaking out while comparing the studio albums *Hotter than Hell* and *Dressed to Kill* with the live album *Alive*.

"Look! This song is called 'Parasite!'"

He was incredulous.

"So?" Tommy responded, confused.

Big Tom held up two of the album covers.

"This record has 'Parasite' and so does *this* record. It's on this one, and it's on *this* one! The same song on *two records*!!"

He didn't seem to realize that one was a studio recording and one was a live recording. Not through any fault of their own, but our parents were Baby Boomers. They grew up during the Fifties and early Sixties. With the Sixties, you could have gone one of two ways: the side before the Beatles and Bob Dylan...or the side *after* the Beatles and Bob Dylan. Both roads had their cultures. The former road saw albums simply as records...merely collections of songs that you heard on AM radio. The latter road saw the evolution of the pop 45-rpm single into album-format FM rock. In the 1970s, as I mentioned earlier, a new trend occurred...the double live album...which every major artist would release during that decade. These were two staples of the latter road. Our parents, who identified much more with the Fifties and early Sixties, were on the pre-Beatles side...which meant that the concept of *album as art* was completely lost on them. And live albums were just collections of songs that you already paid for on all the other records. There was no difference between studio versions and live versions. Songs were songs, they thought. Big Tom ripped into what he perceived was a scam, holding the studio album and live album in front of us.

"Look! 'Cold Gin'...'Cold Gin'! The *same songs*! 'Rock Bottom' on this one...and 'Rock Bottom' on *this* one! Doesn't anybody know that they're being ripped off?! Can't people see the same songs are on *both records*?!"

He threw the albums down on the kitchen table.

"Cold Gin?'" he asked, disgusted at the title. "*I'll* give ya cold gin!! The songs on these records are the *same*!"

Going into the backyard, I was positive that I had stumbled upon something that Tommy hadn't yet seen. Not that we were in competition or anything. It wasn't like that at all. Kiss belonged to both of us, and we shared them proudly. I was just dying to let him know this book existed. Then he would get his own copy anyway. I was psyched.

"Tommy," I yelled. "Look what I got!"

I stood on the deck looking out across the yard at him and Christopher in the pool.

"What did you say?" Tommy asked from inside the water, not hearing me.

"Look!" I screamed holding up my new book.

"What is it?" he asked.

I started to walk down the stairs but stopped dead in my tracks at what I saw. A wall of water spilled out of the side of the pool.

Just then, Satan disguised as a four-year old Christopher Dewhirst jumped out and ran towards me. He ran stiffly and robotically across the grass and toward the stairs...the weight of his wet shorts clinging to his skinny body and the water falling off of him.

"Rrrrrunndick dunndick dunndick dunndick dunndick dunndick dunndick..." his voice buzzed as he ran. The little fucker was speaking in tongues.

"Rrrrrrrrunndick dunndick dunndick dunndick dunndick...."

He looked like one of the little fireplace creatures in *Don't Be Afraid of the Dark*. He reached the stairs and without so much as slowing down, climbed up to meet me. He then grabbed the book, snatching it from my hand. Before I could realize what was happening, he turned around and ran down the stairs. Then he started for the pool.

"Rrrrrunndick dunndick dunndick dunndick dunndick..."

His voice trailed off as he then did the unthinkable...tossing my Kiss book into the water.

I froze. I was unable to move or speak. Tommy burst out in a fit of ungovernable laughter that went on and on and on...accenting a scene that seemed to play itself out in slow motion. Christopher then got back into the water as if nothing had happened, leaving me standing on the stairs...my empty hand still holding the invisible book...and my big dick shriveling down to a grain of rice.

3

The Walls are Blank

It was during the fourth grade school year when things started to get shaky with school and Kiss being an inadvertent cause of trouble in my life. One day, Tommy and I were walking through the vast stretch of lawn in front of the Cypress School, headed home. We walked past the ice cream truck which sat everyday like a mechanical child molester in the parking lot of the Cypress Gardens apartment complex alongside the school. The truck was strategically placed there around 3 o'clock every afternoon because it knew kids were getting out of school. There was a fence separating the Cypress School from Cypress Gardens, and the kids would get to the ice cream truck by crawling through a hole at the bottom. We looked over at the truck as we walked past it. We needed to catch up to Elena Rinaldi and her friends who we walked with. The only time we were allowed to walk home from school at that age was when we walked with Elena. She would often come to the school to get Marc. Marc would usually be off walking in another group with Kevin Weir and his band of outsiders. Elena still managed to keep us all in her sight.

"We have to go to the ice cream truck one day to get Kiss cards," Tommy said looking back at the truck. "They come with bubble gum. I'm getting money from my ma."

Kiss bubblegum cards? Cool.

"How much do they cost?" I asked.

"Only twenty five cents a pack."

At home, my mom didn't want to hear it.

"Kiss cards? Didn't I just buy you the record?"

"Yeah," I said, "but they have lots of records. It's not just *'the record.'* These are cards. It's different."

"You're getting a little too much lately, Eugene. Did you finish your CCD homework?"

"Yes," I said, pacifying her. "Now can I have 25 cents for Kiss cards? It's just 25 cents. I just want one pack."

"Eugene, I said no."

"But...but...please? Tommy's getting them."

"I don't care what Tommy is doing. I'm not his mother, I'm your mother."

And that's the way most disputes were ended anytime I wanted something that I wasn't going to get. I'd play the "Tommy/Marc is doing it" card, and most times lose miserably.

That year, a whole barrage of Kiss merchandise hit the market. There were Kiss dolls, Kiss alarm clocks, Kiss lunchboxes, pinball machines, Colorforms, clothes, do-it-yourself makeup kits, tampons and of course bubblegum cards...which seemed to be the hottest thing you could buy. They cost 25 cents a pack, and in the late 70s, that was a lot of money. I remember that time in life very well…when as a kid you could hold a quarter in your hand and actually feel like you had something big.

One day Tommy and I were walking across the grass outside Cypress, and came upon a crowd of kids watching a fight between Kevin Weir and another local tough guy named John Denton. Weir was kicking his ass and stomping him in the stomach while he was down. Witnessing this made me fear Kevin even more. He pretty much had the fight won in the first few seconds, but before most kids knew it was over, they ran from all corners of the front yard of Cypress. As the kids on line at the ice cream truck all cleared out to see the fight, Tommy couldn't help but notice that there was nobody at the truck.

"Look, there's nobody at the ice cream truck!" he screamed and took off. I followed behind him.

"Oh man, I'm gonna get more Kiss cards," he said with his voice shaking as he ran.

"Ma gave me a dollar for cleaning my room. I can get four packs!"

We stopped running as we approached the truck…the famous Oakwoods ice cream truck. And this was no ordinary ice cream truck. This was a patented Carvel truck that didn't just stop at the school. Frank, the legendary owner and driver of the truck would make his way through Oakwoods every night shortly after dinnertime. Every night like clockwork, he'd drive up the block with his signature rhythmic ring of the ice cream bell:

Ding ding ding

Ding ding

Three rings followed by a pause and then two more quick rings.

Ding ding ding

Ding ding

Frank was a fixture in the neighborhood and everybody loved him. He also ran a small mini-diner called FOOD down the highway on Route 1 South. Much to our disappointment as we got to the truck that day, we realized it wasn't Frank behind the window. It was the Other Guy. Nobody liked the Other Guy. It must have been Frank's day off. The Other Guy came to the counter at the side of the truck. Just then, I remembered something. I reached into my pocket and pulled out two ten dollar bills. Tommy looked at me, stunned.

"That's some hefty cash you got there!"

"I forgot I had this, it's from my birthday money," I told him.

The long lanky figure known as the Other Guy leaned out of the truck.

"What can I get ya?"

I held up one of the tens and boldly asked "How many packs of Kiss cards can you get with ten dollars?"

A few older kids walked up behind us.

"A whole box," the Other Guy replied.

A whole box?!

"Woah, a whole box," Tommy exclaimed. "You'd have the whole set!"

He was right. I'd be rich with a whole box of Kiss cards. I'd have the entire set. Probably three times over! I didn't have to think about it for very long.

"I'll take it," I said without any further thought, and gave a ten to The Other Guy. Tommy's mouth dropped open.

"Woah, you're really gonna get a whole box?"

I looked at him and extended the other ten dollar bill. "Do you want one too?"

Another look of shock.

"What?"

"Come on, take it. Then we can both have the whole set."

The older kids were looking at me as if to say *look at this idiot little kid giving away money.*

"Woah, thanks Eugene!"

Instead of handing him the ten, I gave it to the Other Guy and said proudly, "Give us two boxes of Kiss cards!"

The other kids in a growing crowd looked on in a combination of shock, disgust, amusement and probably jealousy.

"You guys just bought an entire box of Kiss cards?"

"Two!"

"You guys are gay. Kiss sucks!"

We left behind a trail of "Kiss sucks" comments as we walked onward and headed home.

What I never thought to ask the ice cream guy was exactly how much the cards really were. I mean, did those boxes really cost ten dollars each on the nose? I didn't even think to wonder if maybe he owed me change, or if he had in fact ripped me off. But change wasn't a concept I understood at that point in time. I suppose money wasn't either. It didn't even occur to me that whoever had given me that ten dollar bill probably busted their ass for half a day to earn it. And I gave it away, just like that. It was no longer in my pocket. But what I got in return was invaluable. As I handed the Other Guy my ten, he may as well have handed me gold.

A whole unopened box of Kiss cards!

But again, it never occurred to me...the hard excruciating labor that someone had to go through to make that ten. The way I saw it was, I received money for my birthday. And I suppose it was mine.

To keep.

Or spend.

Perhaps save.

But save is not a word a kid that age understands.

So spend sounds better.

So we spent it on something we liked.

No guilt.

I often think back and wonder what my mom would have preferred I spent my money on.

Clothes?

Probably clothes.

A kid that young doesn't like clothes. If a wrapped present doesn't clank around and make noise when you shake it, the kid doesn't want it. I wanted Kiss cards, and so I got them!

We walked back to the curb holding our boxes of cards, smiles from ear to ear. The Other Guy drove off, the Carvel truck disappearing up the block as the bell called out to the other young victims of Oakwoods:

Ding ding ding

Ding ding

Ding ding ding

Ding ding

The question of my mom became a rapid reality as the bells faded off and Tommy opened his mouth with "Wow, I can't believe we have the entire set. I can't wait to show this to my ma!"

I stopped in my tracks with my eyes bulging out of my head. Suddenly I was worried.

———

At home, I snuck through the front door with the box of cards under my sweatshirt. I ran past the kitchen and up the stairs without my mom seeing me. As I got to my room, I heard the phone ring. It was exactly what I was afraid of.

Mom: Hello?

Donna: Hiiiiiiiii.

Mom: Gypsy!

Donna: I just called to thank you.

Mom: For what?

Donna: For Tommy's cards.

Mom: What are you talking about?

Donna: The Kiss cards that Eugene got Tommy. Oh my God, Lu-anne, he's so happy.

Mom: No idea what you're talking about.

Donna: Eugene bought Tommy the whole set of Kiss cards. Come on Luanne, you weren't behind that?

Mom: Are you on drugs? I don't even allow Eugene his own Kiss cards.

Shortly afterward, my mom ripped into me about spending twenty dollars on Kiss cards, and about how it took someone a long time to work for that money, and she made sure she said everything possible to make me feel guilty about having committed such a crime. Needless to say, I was grounded...or as she would say, "punished."

"You're being punished! Go up to your room and don't come out. Do not touch the record player or the TV. When it's time for dinner, I will call you. You just wait til your father comes home!"

It was the first in a series of punishments that would be caused by Kiss.

There was many a night where I would watch out the window for whatever was happening with the older kids. There were Ritchie's older brothers and their friends and girlfriends who were always sitting on their cars talking, smoking, and drinking. They cracked jokes and laughed long into the night. Sometimes I would fall asleep and wake up hours later and they would still be there...seemingly right under my window since Ritchie lived right next door. Then there was the other group of kids who would silently walk up Sycamore until they disappeared from sight. It's impossible to overstate how badly I wanted to be ten years older between the ages of five and twelve. I knew there were adventurous things out there just past my window and none of it involved school or parents telling you it's past your bedtime.

One day, my sense of adventure felt a little bigger than usual, so I decided to do something a little on the risky side. Watching the Sweathogs on *Welcome Back Kotter* had given me the urge to crawl through a teacher's window...and up until then, I passed. As much as I dreaded Mrs. Aarons, I figured I could climb through her basement window and say hi...just like the Sweathogs did with Mr. Kotter. I didn't think she would mind either, if I invited the other guys. So I took Tommy, Franklin and Christopher. It was broad daylight, yet we acted as if we were criminals creeping invisibly among the shadows of night. We ducked behind and into some bushes alongside of Mr. Manzo's house, which was two doors up from my house. The Aarons home was next to the Manzo home. As we were huddled together, Christopher jumped out looking like a deranged four-year old commando firing an invisible machine gun.

"Rrrrrrrrrrrrrrundick dundick dundick dundick dundick dundick dundick dundick..."

"Shut up assboy," Tommy whispered while pulling him back into the bushes. "This is a secret mission."

I thought to myself for a few seconds after Tommy's words. Was it really a secret mission? The Sweathogs didn't sneak around before entering Mr. Kotter's place. They just unapologetically showed up and announced themselves. So without further hesitation, I walked ahead toward the Aarons house and crouched down at the basement window. It was half opened with a screen underneath. I peeked in and tried to lift the screen with the tips of my fingers, but there was no way to open it from the outside.

"You can't open it from the outside dorkmaster," Tommy called out, still walking toward the window. Christopher stayed in the bushes while Franklin walked around the lawn aimlessly.

"It needs to be broken," Tommy informed me.

Broken?

Did I really want to do this?

"Come on, Eugene, you gotta break it."

"Break it?"

"How do you think burglars get in?"

"They break in." Duh, I thought.

"Of course they break in," Tommy snapped back. "That's what burglars do. They burgle."

Franklin sat down on the lawn and looked up curiously. His eyebrows raised as his mouth dropped open.

"Are we gonna bawgle da house?"

None of us were aware of the man crouched down on the other side of the window. He was listening to us plan the burglaring of the house. The reason he was on the other side of the window was because he was Mr. Aarons. As owner of the residence, and someone who lived there, he had every right to be concerned about some kids outside the window who were about to burgle his home. And so, out of nowhere, his head popped up in the window like a Jack-in-the-Box, scaring the shit out of me, sending me clear across the lawn and into the street.

I looked back.

"Nobody is burglaring anything!" Mr. Aarons choked out in a gravelly voice.

Tommy took off and bolted down the block. Franklin was still sitting on the grass. I motioned to him *let's go*. He just looked at me and laughed.

"Go on, get outta here!" Mr. Aarons shouted from the ground-level window, looking like some disgruntled guest star on the bottom row of *Hollywood Squares*. It made him the perfect and vulnerable candidate to absorb one of Christopher's deadly assault attacks. Little did Mr. Aarons know that one of us had remained in the bushes, which were not visible from the window. As the irritable man stared at us, he didn't see or hear Christopher running down the side of the house. It was only as he got close and approached that he heard the footsteps and then the dreadful sound.

"Rrunndick dunndick dunndick dunndick dunndick dunndick…"

The four-year old leapt through the air and landed with his ass pressed against the window, on which he released a rapid fire round of flatulence in Mr. Aarons's face. He then spun around, grabbed Franklin by the hand and ran with him down the block to catch up with me and Tommy.

"Wow, I thought we were gonna see Mrs. Aarons in there," I said catching my breath. "Ya know…the same way the Sweathogs always see Mr. Kotter and he's always glad to see them. I didn't know we'd see Mr. Aarons."

"Yeah," Tommy shot back. "I didn't even know there was a Mr. Aarons. Who'd wanna marry that skank?"

Mr. Aarons watched us in disgust from his Hollywood Squares window.

"I know who you are, and I know where you live, you little shits!"

Suddenly, I was nervous.

"What if he tells my mother?"

Franklin caught up and apparently wasn't as concerned as I was. Granted, he was only four years old and didn't fully understand.

"I not hearing of it," he charged, grimacing. "We went visit him at his house, and he yell at us! I not worry about nothing! Asshole!"

The Locker Notes

In case I haven't illustrated the absolute disdain I had for Mrs. Aarons, let me be clear. She was a bitter, old and decrepit fecal specimen of a woman, who played a significant part in scaring an outgoing kid who thought he was cool into an introverted shell of what he once was. She worked hand in hand with some of the most malevolent girls I ever crossed paths with as a child, and when Ashley Drake called her attention to how messy the inside of my desk was, she didn't waste any time in making an example of me.

"Oh, really," was her only response to Ashley's tattling, as she walked over, pulled the desk away from me and turned it upside down. The next step was usually Mrs. Aarons screaming at the student to clean it up, but to avoid further humiliation I immediately dropped to my knees and began sorting out the mess while the entire class watched me. Ashley looked at me with a satisfied smile. I didn't cry though, unlike most students who had their desks dumped. That's one thing I never did in school was cry. But no matter how bad things got, I somehow managed to never fully come out of my own world.

"You're in your own world!" Mrs. Aarons would often bark at me.

My own world consisted of plunging to the bottom of my imagination and staying one or two levels below the surface of total consciousness. It was my way of shrugging off the reality of it all, and perhaps blocking out incidents that I didn't want to acknowledge were really happening.

One of the common complaints all of my teachers had for my parents was that I didn't pay attention in class...that I daydreamed. In today's world of inventing disorders that never existed in name before, simply to sell some drugs, doctors call it Attention Deficit

Disorder, and in retrospect, that's probably what I would have been diagnosed with. Back then, there was no Attention Deficit Disorder…kids were just considered stupid. We didn't take medication for it. We just stayed stupid.

One time, I was so lost in thought during a lesson that I couldn't even hear Mrs. Aarons talking. The entire physical plain of the classroom got filtered out by whatever was going on in my head. Suddenly, as I snapped out of it, Mrs. Aarons was looking at me. The class was silent. They looked at me too. Everything stopped.

"Yes or no, Eugene?" she asked.

I stared at her for what seemed an eternity.

She waited.

The class waited.

Yes or no.

It was a simple question.

I had to say something, and since I had no idea what she was talking about or what the question pertained to, it could have gone either way. I figured I had a 50/50 chance, so I just answered "no." When Mrs. Aarons shut her eyes and shook her head, and Ashley Drake burst out with an imposingly loud "Duh!" it quickly became clear to me that the "yes or no" did not pertain to anything she was teaching. In fact, there wasn't any "yes or no." Mrs. Aarons looked over at Ashley in response to her outburst, smiled and said to the class, "I give you all permission to laugh at Eugene."

And laugh they did.

She wasn't done though. She walked over to me and took the pencil out of my hand.

"And just what are we doing over here Mr. Devine?"

"He was writing Kiss on his math book," Ashley informed without hesitation.

"Oh, is that so?"

I couldn't tell who I hated more, Ashley or Mrs. Aarons. Why would I ever have ever wanted to go near her house that one time? She grabbed my hand and pulled it off of my book, where I was hiding the letters KIS...

I was particularly proud of my artwork when it came to band logos, but on this occasion, I was drawing the logo inside the actual book rather than on my paper bag book cover. Ashley wasn't done either.

"Mrs. Aarons, look at the inside of Eugene's desk. He hasn't been keeping it neat."

Mrs. Aarons shot her a disapproving glance.

"Miss. Drake," she said, removing her glasses. "If I wanted your input, I would ask for it."

Whenever the glasses came off, it was a sign that she was getting ready to erupt and had reached the point of no return. She dug her thumb and index finger into the tear duct corners of her eyes, clasping the top of her nose and then pulling away as if picking out sand or some gook. She looked at her fingers and rubbed them together, disintegrating whatever she had just scraped away. For a brief moment, I was shocked that she would actually reprimand Ashley considering both of them were partners in bitch. Ashley paid no attention to her, opting instead to stare at me with the same satisfied wicked grin on her face.

That nasty grin.

And her obnoxious big brown hair that hung over and into her face, draped over her skinny shoulders, and sitting like a dead animal on her head. If I were any stronger, I could have turned her upside down and used her as a mop. And those piercing malicious brown eyes, that in combination with the smile, almost gave off the impression that she was only joking, and was somehow just seeking my attention. The thought did occur to me. But she was as persistent as a fluorescent-green-phlegm pneumonia cough when it came to making my life miserable in the classroom. Therefore, I didn't let any other curiosities get the better of me, as to what her intentions were behind all the misery. Mrs. Aarons picked up my book and looked at the Kiss logo, only three quarters completed, and not by any means meant to be seen or judged by anyone at that point in time.

"Kiss, huh? I think your mother and me are going to have a talk."

I stared down at my desk. She still wasn't finished.

"Hmmm...what do you have in this desk?"

She reached inside and pulled out a crumbled sheet of paper. Then she pulled out an old brown paper lunch bag. Then more crumbled paper. She lifted the bag in front of my face.

"What do we have here? What do we have the garbage can for?"

I just looked at her blankly.

"Here. Let me help you. I have a solution to this problem. And we'll just keep doing it until we get it right."

And right on cue, she pulled me away from my desk as I was still seated, dragging me and the chair together. She then picked up the desk and turned it upside down, once again spilling my Cypress belongings onto the floor. The class gasped, fidgeting around nervously and uncomfortably. Ashley laughed. Mrs. Aarons then leaned in and got in my face.

"Now clean it up!"

And so I dropped to my knees emotionless, and began sorting through the mess as the class watched.

———

"Did you know Kiss is gonna be in concert on TV?"

Tommy ran across the Cypress School lawn to catch up with me. I stopped in my tracks.

Did he just say Kiss in concert?

On TV?

"No way," I screamed. I was no longer thinking about the desk-dumping I had just received an hour before.

"They are! But it's not regular TV. It's some special type of TV thing called Home Box or something. My grandparents have it. I'm gonna sleep over to watch it in a few weeks."

"Home box? That's a type of TV?"

"I'm not sure what it is. I asked my ma, and she said we don't have it in Oakwoods." His grandparents lived in Elizabeth, New Jersey, two blocks away from my grandparents.

"You're grandparents live in Elizabeth near mine, right?"

"Yep," he said. "You should come and sleep over too, so we can both watch it."

I was baffled at what a home box could possibly be.

"Why can't we get home boxes in Oakwoods? Don't they sell them at the mall?"

"No. I asked my ma and she said that it's part of cable...something called cable. It's this rare form of television that you can only get in Elizabeth."

"A cable? Like a special kind of cable that connects to the home box?"

"I don't know. Something like that."

Then I thought of my dad. He would probably know.

"My dad is always playing with wires and cables and tools and electrical and 'build it' and 'fix it' type of things. Maybe he has a home box with a cable in the garage."

"You should ask him."

At the dinner table:

Dad: A what?
Me: A home box
Dad: A home box?
Me: Yeah, a home box. Do you have one?

Dad looks over at mom.

Dad: Do you know what he's talking about?
Mom: I have no idea.

Dad looks over at me.

Dad: What the hell are you talking about?

Franklin looks up from his food.

> Franklin: Yeah, what the hell are you talkin' 'bout?
> Dad: Hey! Watch your mouth!
> Me: Can we just get a home box for the TV?
> Dad: But what the hell is a home box?
> Franklin: Yeah, what the hell is a haw bock?
> Dad: Hey!

Just then, my mom had a stunning realization.

> Mom: Oh, he means that Home Box Office channel. They call it HBO. That's that cable television that Donna's mother and father have in Elizabeth.
> Me: Yeah, that! Can we get that?
> Mom: You're not even supposed to be watching TV. You don't go spending twenty dollars on Kiss cards and then expect to watch TV.
> Dad: Eugene, I don't think that's available in Oakwoods anyway.

Dad was right. This thing called cable television was in its infantile stages during the 1970s, and half of America still had no access to it. The concept of it appealed to everyone...movies uncut and commercial free. But in the immediate future, it was the Kiss concert that lured me to it. It was either sleep over Tommy's grandparents' house or miss the Kiss concert. So I asked to sleep over. Mom wasn't too keen on the idea.

"Why do you need to sleep over his grandparents' house? What is so important that you need to see?"

"The Kiss concert."

"Oh, Jesus Christ almighty!"

Enough said. After dinner, I was sitting outside on the front stairs as I did so often with Franklin, Tommy, or just by myself. Even though there was an entire world outside, my own narrow experience didn't consist of much outside the confines of my own house and front lawn. Other than Tommy, Marc or Ritchie's house, I wasn't allowed to go anywhere. Sometimes it was a wonder my mom even let me walk home from school. I stared down toward the bottom of the block where Marc lived. It was difficult to see certain houses and lawns while looking from my stairs because of the enormous trees in front of every other residence. The sky over each street in Oakwoods was lined with endless chains of telephone wires connecting houses to poles, and poles to more wires. The wires were occasionally obscured by the trees, which sometimes caused problems after a storm or something. Every once in a while if a tree grew too high or a branch crept along a wire in such a way that would compromise safety or power, the electric company would come and cut away branches, leaving some trees ridiculously shaped. But in the modern world, it wasn't the hideous wires that threw a monkey wrench into an otherwise picturesque landscape of trees against sky. It was the trees that rudely interrupted the stretch of power line highways imposed on the landscape some time during the middle of the twentieth century. Our section of Oakwoods had been built during the late 1950s, and the power lines connected it all. Trees freshly planted back then had accumulated some twenty years worth of growth in an all out race for the heavens…only to be rudely cockblocked by these manmade formations of cables connected to wooden phalluses sticking out of the ground like middle fingers. Yes, they were necessary to live in modern suburbia or anywhere else for that matter, but they sure were a fucking drag to look at.

I heard my mom creep up behind me from behind the front door. I turned around to look at her.

"What are you doing?" she asked. I turned back around toward the street.

"Nothing. Just sitting here."

Behind the door, my mom gazed down the street to see a group of older kids turning the corner and walking toward us. I knew what was coming next like I so often did.

"Eugene, come in the house. Those hoodlums are coming up the block."

And there it was. The kids that I was sweating every time they walked by were viewed suspiciously by my parents as something dangerous.

"I don't want to," I told her. "I'm just sitting here."

Maybe they were dangerous. Who knows? I myself always wondered what they did once they disappeared at the top of Sycamore Drive. Yet, there was still that element of mystery that intrigued me enough to watch them from afar and then pretend I didn't see them as they approached closer. Inside the house, the phone rang, taking her attention off me. She walked away from the door as I watched her go back to the kitchen through the screen. Then I turned back to see the kids coming toward my house. As they passed me, I crouched down to pretend I was tying my sneakers, so it wouldn't look as though I were watching them. I peeked up though, and one of them saw me. He was wearing a Grateful Dead concert jersey, had shoulder-length dirty blonde hair and surprisingly didn't seem much older than me. He looked as though he could have been a younger brother of one of the older kids. He was smoking a cigarette, and when I caught his eye, he smiled at me malevolently. Even as they were well past my house, the one kid kept looking back at me with the same creepy smile. And then suddenly they were gone. They went beyond the point that my eyes would allow me to see from my front stairs. The rest was one big question mark.

"Eugene!"

My mother sounded furious.

I was afraid to turn around, but I did.

"Get your ass in this house, now. Right now!"

I got up and opened the door. She wasted no time, pulling me by my arm into the house. *What the hell*, I thought.

"That was Mrs. Aarons on the phone. Apparently, you're failing math?"

I forced a surprised look onto my face.

"Is that what she said?"

"Oh, she had a lot to say mister."

She picked up a piece of Mead notebook paper where she had scribbled down notes as the teacher was talking to her.

"Failing math...daydreaming in class...drawing pictures of Kiss faces on your desk!"

I stood there, somewhat scared but still dumbfounded at where the real crime was. That's what my parents never understood. There were kids my age doing all sorts of ungodly things that were so unspeakable, that my dad would label them "riff raff." You had no chance of redemption in my dad's book if you were considered riff raff. So, there was riff raff outside doing their riff raffy things, and all I did was like Kiss.

"You're punished for the rest of your life," my mother said satisfactorily. "Don't even think to leave your room."

I wondered if Mrs. Aarons had told her anything about writing Kiss in my math book.

"Oh, and she said she caught you writing Kiss in your math book? Is that what you do? You can't do the math work, but you'll write Kiss in the book?"

As I walked up the stairs and into my room, I realized she was right on my heels. I entered the room and she followed close behind, pointing at my walls where about half a dozen Kiss posters resided.

"This is what's corrupting your mind! This is the shit that your mind is infested with. Well, I got news for you mister. There's going to be no more of this shit while you're in school!"

She then did the unthinkable by mindlessly tearing all of my posters off the wall. Every single one of them. It wasn't even like she took the thumbtacks out and took the posters down. She just ripped them off the walls and then proceeded to tear them into pieces, thus making them unusable and adding insult to injury.

"You're sick with this Kiss! No more Kiss! Enough with the Kiss!"

Even if it was Kiss's fault, she ended up tearing everything else off the walls too... not just the Kiss posters. Bucky Dent and Shaun Cassidy also had to suffer for what Kiss made me do in school. The Bucky Dent poster was just given to me by Marc for my birthday a few weeks before. Now it lay at my feet in shreds. She slammed the door after walking out of the room, but immediately slammed it back open. It bounced off the wall, the doorknob cracking a circular indentation into the paint.

"Clean up this mess and throw everything into the garbage. Now. *Right* now!"

As she slammed the door closed again, I flinched and dropped to my knees. And for the second time that day, I found myself on the floor surrounded by a mess that I didn't make, and forced to clean it up.

Hours later, I watched out the window as the older kids made their way back down the street. They emerged from the monstrous wall of foliage beyond the fence. Some kids would climb the fence while others crawled through the hole that was torn into the bottom. As they passed my house, I thought about my life and what their lives must be like. I thought about how I had just been handed down another in a series of punishments over Kiss, and how none of those kids didn't have to worry about grades, being grounded or being home at a certain time. As they walked passed my house and off into the next part of their night, I got into bed and stared at the ceiling. Or so I tried to stare at the ceiling, which is usually what I did...but something caught my eye. The blank emptiness of my walls distracted my focus. Until that moment, the rock stars and sports figures on my posters were my friends throughout so much of my childhood. They protected me at night. They watched over me as I slept. How much could a kid that young really elaborate on translating these ideas to an adult? But there was an unspoken sense of community on my walls...a comforting familiarity of all that made me happy in life.

All of that was now gone.

And now there was a sudden disquietude about the walls as I quickly scanned over them, not really wanting to look at them for too long. I reached over to my lamp on the night table next to my bed. I very often fell asleep with the light on, but unable to look at my newly naked walls I turned out the light and tried to fall asleep. As I fell asleep slowly but surely, I did so while thinking about how unfair some things were.

When you're young, the world is black and white. Before the world becomes black and white, you exist as a baby, a toddler. You learn to crawl. You learn to walk. You exist in an unsuspecting innocence that may cause you to put your hand on a burning stove without knowing the danger. Eventually, you learn right from wrong. You pick up the learned behavior of your parents, and ultimately, it is precisely right and wrong which defines the universe. This is where curiosity comes in. Curiosity leads to questions. When those questions remain unanswered, they somehow lurk beneath the surface of your conscience, in a constant dialogue with itself. They long to probe the surface and penetrate the line of black and white. It's like when you're told not to go past a certain point, like the end of the block. You are only given so much physical space to play with as a child. The end of your block is the end of the world you know. What you find after it

may be something horrible.

Or maybe not.

Yet, you wonder. When you're young, you play it safe. If your parents' eyes are windows into an unsafe world, you learn to see through those eyes. Maybe your parents don't realize that they are in fact injecting a fear into you because they themselves are afraid. But that's another issue altogether.

The end of Sycamore Drive was the edge of the world for all I knew. The bottom of the block was an outlet to the back roads of Oakwoods, the main highways and ultimately toward the rest of civilization. The top of the block was met by a fence which stood behind the last houses in a field of overgrown grasses. From my front stairs, one could only wonder what lay on the other side of those houses. As you walked up the block and got closer to the point where you were no longer allowed to go, the fence became visible. Beyond it were only trees and sky. The junior high was off to one corner surpassing Sycamore, but the rest was the Forbidden Zone. That's at least what I called it, maybe from having watched *Planet of the Apes* on the ABC 4:30 Movie at some point as a kid. The Forbidden Zone was the point in which you fell off, had you continued past the fence. I literally envisioned it as falling off the earth. Big kids walking up the street always continued past the fence. They were always going back there...somewhere.

Eventually, I'd walk further and further toward the fence if I went up there, going a little past my limits each time. At night I'd lie in bed thinking about going past the fence. I'd plot and plan how I might get up the nerve to go all the way in. Some nights, the fence haunted me as I lay there in the dark thinking to the beat of the suburban silence. But what I always noticed no matter how quiet it got at night, was how there was never really any complete silence in the suburbs. Even what we thought we knew as silence was marked by the eerie ever-present hum of humanity in some unseen background. In the daytime, there were layers of sound that you could peel...lawnmowers, dogs barking, cars driving by, kids playing, birds chirping, music blasting. Take it all away, and there remained the quiet still of night. But it wasn't like the quiet of a wheat field in some hick town somewhere, cut off for miles from the rest of the civilized world. There were always audible reminders of the roads on the outskirts of town...the happenings and goings-on outside of Oakwoods...mostly the sound of the highways and infrastructure... the trucks, buses, cars and trains...always farther than Oakwoods, but still too close to ignore or forget about. Every single non-descript outside sound too far for definition seemed to merge into a single moan. Strip away the layers of summer, and it was still there. Even without the crickets and the air conditioners...even on the most desolate nights, the monster in the distance always roared.

I sat up on a bed of tar and asphalt. The warmth of my room and the slight breeze coming through the window had given way to forceful gusts of wind. I hadn't noticed the shift in light, or that familiar objects in my room were missing. I looked up at the ceiling but only noticed the sky and the piercing refulgence of a street light shining down directly over me. Everywhere else was darkness and complete still. Aside from the trees, nothing moved. I looked around and saw Marc's house to my right, and immediately, it hit me. I was outside...in the middle of the night. Realization of something like that would normally freak me out since I was always afraid of getting in trouble, but the sudden shock and surreal element of where I found myself upon waking up, was instead luring and intriguing at first. It had to be two or three in the morning...and instead of being in my bed I was somehow sitting in the middle of the street all the way down at the bottom of Sycamore Drive.

This wasn't happening, I thought.

How did I end up outside and all the way down the street? A hollowing chill speared through me and sliced directly up my spine to the point where I wanted to curl up in a fetal position and huddle myself for warmth right there in the street. Instead, I got up.

From the bottom of Sycamore, I stood directly in the middle of the street, my vision perfectly centered with houses on my left and houses on my right. Between the houses and the street were sidewalks on either side, with trees lining the entire length of both sides of the block. The symmetry of my view could have come right out of a Kubrick film. I could have been standing inside a photograph, I thought to myself. Nothing moved except for the leaves on the trees all shaking and waving in an unsettling manner...unsettling enough for me to know I wasn't in any photograph...but standing outside.

In the middle of the street.

Down the street.

In the middle of the night.

Another cold chill traveled up my spine. I needed to get home. I needed to get home quick, and I needed to get home unnoticed. What were my parents going to say when I knocked on the door? What was I going to tell them? Where had I been? How the hell did I get there?

But that wasn't my main concern.

As I started up the street, I could see the fence at the top of the block. I could see the wooded area behind it. It was by no means an inviting scene as the branches and leaves waved eerily ahead of me and on top of me. Yes, on top of me. Those trees lining the block on both sides extended out enough to provide a leafy canopy-like cover over the street. I was frightened as I saw the movement of the trees at the top of the block, and I knew I had to walk toward them in order to get home. But it was the sound and the feeling of the branches and leaves above me, at my side, and now behind me, that bothered me much more than the sight of the woods.

I started to run.

The devil snapped at my heels.

I kept my head down as I tore up the street, refusing to look back at whatever horror might be behind me. I could actually hear my heart racing to the beat of my bare feet against the coarse pavement. Sycamore became a treadmill as I ran and got nowhere. What was really about twenty seconds seemed an immeasurable amount of time as I went from running in place to being about ten yards from my house. I gathered the guts to look behind me, and when I saw there was nothing following me, I slowed down to a hopping walk.

...because you have to get up and see.
As I approached my house, I slowed down to a comfortable pace. I walked along the grass looking at the walkway a few steps ahead.

You have to see for yourself.

I stopped, frozen again in fear, afraid of what I thought I had just heard.

Because you know it's there.

The whispering voice I thought I had imagined...was real. Somebody was out there.

———

I couldn't move as I stood at the beginning of the walkway in front of my house. I listened.

You have to see for yourself.

"What?" I exclaimed in panic, yet somehow comforted by the sound of my own voice. I started for the stairs, but when I got to the bottom, I was distracted by the bushes next to them.

You have to see for yourself. Because you know it's there. Because you know it's there.

"Who are you?" I whispered into the bushes.

Now you can see it because you know it's there. You know it's there, and now you can see it.

The voice wasn't coming from the bushes. It sounded at first like it was right there, but then it sounded more distant. I looked around, surveying the front of the house and everything surrounding it. I began to walk up the stairs. And then the inevitable hit me. I was going to have to knock or ring the bell for my parents to let me in. Man, I was in some deep shit, and I had no idea what I was going to say.

Because you know it's there
Because you know it's there
Because you know it's there

Suddenly, I was almost knocked over on the stairs, as an overpowering gust of wind blew through me and across the front yard. Around the side of the house, the gate began to clank. The wind hit it violently in a sustained surge, bouncing the latch off the aluminum support pole to the chain link fence in a rhythmic pattern that blended in with the intense hissing of the shaking trees. It was the worst possible combination of sounds a kid could hear while stranded outside in the middle of the night.

The walls are blank.

Blank?

"What?" I said again, to whoever or whatever was listening.

Just some whispering trees talking shit, I suppose.

The next sound I heard was directly in front of me...an unsettling distraction...a chain and then a click. I tightened up as I reached the top step realizing that it was coming from inside my house. I watched helpless as the doorknob turned and the front door began to open. Behind me the voice continued to whisper.

The walls are blank.

I woke up.
Again.
But this time I was in my bed.
And this time it was for real.
The clock read 10:37 PM. I hadn't been sleeping for very long. My parents were downstairs watching television two floors below. I could hear the muffled voices of people talking on TV. I was glad it wasn't one of those nights when I would wake up and it would be sometime in the five o'clock hour where there wasn't much time left before the alarm went off. I never liked waking up in the middle of the night, but it was always easier when it was early enough to have a whole bunch of hours left to sleep before I had to get up. So 10:37 was rather refreshing as I lay there trying to gather my thoughts and push my way out of the thickness of the dream I'd just had.

The walls are blank.

I sat up.
My eyes were blurry as the room slowly came into focus. The bright light of the hall was beaming into my room, revealing the empty walls. I must have forgotten about the poster incident, because when I saw the empty walls where I expected to see something, there was nothing. My reaction was one of hair-raising terror. Something

about the sight of the hall light shining on my empty walls has been indelible. My friends on the wall were gone. My protection was gone. The door was wide open. The light outside the door was painful as I sat up in my bed in the middle of the suddenly desolate room. I was a little boy all alone. I felt myself shrink to the nucleus of an atom, as I was now under a microscope.

"The walls are blank," I whispered to myself in horror.

Looking back at that night throughout my entire life, I've always found it peculiar that my subconscious mind chose the word *blank* to describe the walls in what was probably the first real nightmare I ever had. Bare walls, empty walls...blank walls. The message was all the same to a little child. You get used to seeing those images that you approve of that serve as markers of consistency and security, and then in the flash of a wakeup, those reference points are gone. There was something about seeing the walls bare like that that had scared the hell out of me, and when I could no longer contain myself, I wailed out the most blood-curdling scream that's ever been heard in my house...one that sent my parents racing frantically up the stairs as their child screamed bloody murder.

———

While thumbing through a children's encyclopedia in class the day after the walls went blank, I turned a page and jumped out of my seat, flinging the book off my desk. It landed on the floor right beside Mrs. Aaron's desk, startling her. I ran to the back of the room shaking.

"Eugene Devine!" the nasty bitch exclaimed. I stood there em-barrassed, as the class looked at me wondering what the hell just happened. Ashley Drake let out a loud cackle of a laugh and then uttered a short and simple, "Duh." Mrs. Aarons stood up.

"Why did you do that?"

I just looked at her, growing more nervous. She then proceeded to walk down the aisle.

"Eugene, I'm talking to you! Why did you do that?"

Then she got in my face.

"ANSWER ME!"

4

The Forbidden Zone

One night I looked out my window and saw Kevin Weir and Joey Franco coming up the street with a bunch of older kids. I was glad I was inside and wouldn't have wanted to encounter them if I were out there. It was still somewhat light out, so I was able to make them out. They all looked up to no good and I could only imagine where they were coming from and what they were going to do. Rob houses maybe. Do some drugs. Get in a fight with another group of kids somewhere. I watched them pass my house, thinking about how completely different my school nights were from someone like Kevin Weir. There I was, safe in my room with my parents right downstairs. Soon my mom would tell me it was time to go to bed. Weir, on the other hand, was wandering the streets with some scary looking people. I wondered about his parents, or if he even had parents. I know he had an older brother which probably accounted for his association with the older crowd. I watched them until they vanished from my line of sight, but even though I could no longer see them I knew where they were going.

I stepped away from the window being reminded of seeing Ritchie's brothers always hanging out in the street outside our houses. I reflected on wanting to be a part of them...wanting to be older so I could do what they were doing...whatever it was that they were doing. Yet, it always remained a mystery once they disappeared off the end of Sycamore Drive. But things felt a little different that night because I knew some of the kids doing that stuff, whatever it was... were much closer to my age...and I wasn't quite sure how to feel about that. Were they meeting more kids there? Did I know any of them? Was there some secret existence of kids that everyone was in on except for me? Was I really missing something? Or was I staying out of trouble? That night I went to sleep and dreamed about the Forbidden Zone.

———

I think it was Alan Watts who said that every single thought we have is either a desire or a memory. When you're a kid, you have your entire life in front of you with very little behind you, and therefore can't spend much time living in the past. The older you get, the longer your memory gets. You spend your adult life trying to account for and maybe come to terms with unresolved stuff. You could spend years in therapy just trying to get to the bottom of why you are the way you are, and why you do the things you do, and all the little details that amount to you paying tens of thousands of dollars just to remember things you probably wanted to forget in the first place.

Some people have naturally bad memories, while others burnt their memories out on too many drugs. I was both blessed and cursed with a good memory, and have therefore been my own therapist. But if Alan Watts was right about all our thoughts being either a desire or a memory, then my childhood prior to any length of memory was just filled with desire. Desire for an electric guitar.

Desire for a new stereo.

Desire for more records.

Desire for the new Kiss record.

Desire to be cool.

Desire to be tough.

Desire to not be picked on.

Desire to get good grades.

Desire to not be invisible.

Desire to be liked.

Desire for Riley Stevens.

Everyone liked Riley Stevens. Yet nobody could get near Riley Stevens. She was a celebrity at Cypress. And if you weren't part of her circle, she didn't know you existed. When I was five or six, I always acted on my desires. No matter what it was that I wanted, I went for it. When it came to girls, I really did believe I was Fonzie, and acted like it. Those days were long over though...the days when Tommy and I were playing *Happy Days* on the side of his house, and I was chasing Haley Benson all over the playground trying to kiss her. But the late Seventies were not the same as the mid Seventies.

During the last few years of the Seventies, Tommy began hanging out more with Jay Sacco who lived a few blocks from us over on Oakwood Avenue. I spent these years dividing my time between

Tommy, Marc and Ritchie. As Tommy and Jay became buddies, they entered a new stage in their lives. They had discovered girls. Well, by this time, we'd all discovered girls. But they had discovered Riley Stevens. Riley Stevens had been in my first grade class and I really thought nothing of her at first, except that she was missing most of her baby teeth. By fourth grade however, she was slowly establishing her center-of-attention status. It was hard not to find a boy who didn't have a mad crush on Riley...and by fourth grade I too had developed an eye for her. It was a nervous, sweaty palms kind of pathetic little schoolboy crush that I had...and it was torture. As I previously stated, my attitude towards girls had undergone a few changes since my Fonzie days of kindergarten and first grade. In the years following, I experienced a scarring backlash of constant abuse from girls like Rachel Santos, Dina Bell, and Ashley Drake. So even though Ashley was my main reason for hating girls, she wasn't the only one who made my school days miserable. These girls made sure that they were as mean to me as possible...making fun of me, telling me how ugly I was, ridiculing me every time I got the wrong answer in class, every time I messed up in gym, laughing at me for liking Kiss, laughing at my Tough Skins flood pants...you name it. They also had this kicking thing. It was common knowledge. Girls kicked. In disco-era suburbia, every girl went to the mall to either buy a pair of Clogs, or these deadly brown leather boots that could shatter your shin on impact. Old class pictures reveal that many girls wore them. Ashley Drake wore lethal boots and she liked to kick people. I was her target in second through fifth grade.

Who knows?

Psychological studies attribute the reaction formation to children who display the opposite emotion than what they truly feel. Maybe they all liked me, and that was how they showed it. Either way, the self esteem took a drastic plunge during those years. I haven't gotten all psychological on myself, but if I really dissected my childhood, I'd most likely find that these girls probably effected me a lot more than I would like to admit. As much as I daydreamed about Riley Stevens in class, I could never work up the nerve to talk to her, out of fear that she too would be an Ashley Drake.

Riley wasn't in my class during those peak years of Ashley's bitchiness, so at least I didn't have to suffer potentially embarrassing situations in front of her whenever Ashley drew unwanted attention toward me. Then again, nobody put me in the spot more savagely than Mrs. Aarons. Did I mention I didn't like her? It's true. Mrs. Aarons, one of the most vicious teachers a roomful of ten year olds should ever have the misfortune of spending a year of their lives with. Out of a fourth grade school year that profoundly shaped how I saw the world for a long time after, the most embarrassing moments came not when I was ambushed by an Ashley/Mrs. Aarons setup, or not paying attention, or badly in need of a desk dumping... but after I simply disposed of a booger in my nose.

One of the more disgusting habits of school children was to stick gum to the bottom of the desk. Perhaps they were finished chewing the gum, or needed to get rid of it because they didn't want to get caught with it or were just too lazy to spit it in the garbage can. Whatever the reason, they stuck it underneath the desk. I'd run my hands along underneath and feel the gum as if it was nothing, not even considering that it had been in somebody's gross nasty mouth.

So one day, I was sitting there picking my nose as I often did when I was bored or daydreaming and I had no place to put my booger. So naturally, I wiped it under my desk. It became a habit for a while until the day Mrs. Aarons saw me wiping a booger on the bottom of the desk and stopped the entire class from even so much as breathing.

"Just what are you doing under that desk, Eugene Devine?"

If she went for embarrassment, that's exactly what she achieved.

I slouched down in my seat and muttered, "Nothing."

The bitch was relentless.

"Nothing? I saw your finger go three inches up your nose and then you proceeded to wipe it under the desk...that's what you did."

Several kids in class laughed while others screamed *eww*.

"Shut up, all of you! I want it quiet in here!"

Okay, enough, I thought to myself. I wasn't about to let this escalate into another desk dumping. I had to intervene.

"I was wiping my nose," I said, gathering the courage to look her in the face, but not the eyes.

The bitch looked at me, dismayed, as if to suggest she couldn't believe what she had just heard.

"Wiping your nose? You wipe your nose with a tissue. You were picking your nose and wiping the boogers under the desk."

A tidal wave of collective laughter from the class swept over me as the bitch stared straight at me.

"The class thinks it's funny, Eugene Devine. Do you think it's funny?"

Oh Jesus Christ on the cross, I thought. If you're going to dump my desk, just fucking do it already.

"Do you think it's funny, Eugene Devine?"

I detested with absolute fucking disdain the way she always had to call me by my full name.

I was done talking to her. Whatever she was going to do, she was going to do.

"You're so disgusting Eugene," came from my right side as I turned to see Ashley looking at me with pure hatred.

"Shut up Miss. Drake!" cried the vile woman.

Then she turned around and began walking toward me.

It was coming. I could feel it.

"Alright, stand up and back away. I want to see just how many boogers you've been wiping under here. Why, I have a mind to look under all your desks and see just who else has been wiping boogers this whole time."

She turned my desk over and observed, but was interrupted by more class laughter. She looked up at one boy who was cackling away.

"Have you been wiping boogers too?"

The kid immediately shifted his laughter into a straight face.

"No."

"Oh no?"

"No. I haven't."

The bitch then looked at a random girl.

"And you? Have you been wiping boogers?"

"No?" the girl replied, unsure of herself.

The horrid teacher looked around the room and began picking random people.

"Did you wipe boogers?"

"No."

"And you? Have you been wiping boogers?"

Just what the hell did that mean anyway? Wiping boogers.

This went on for a few minutes before she finally turned her attention back to me. She resumed her inspection of my desk.

"Mmm hmm...mmm hmm," she muttered and quickly placed the desk back down.

She crouched until she was eye level with me.

"Well, it looks like you've been putting mostly gum under here, but I can't prove that it's *your* gum, and it's very hard which means it's old, so I'm not going to ask you to scrape it off."

I guess boogers carried a more severe penalty than gum did. A quick wave of relief came over me.

Saved by the gum.

Someone else's nasty chewed-up gum.

But as usual, the bitch wasn't finished.

"Considering that I'm giving you a break Eugene Devine, you need to do the world a favor in the meantime."

"What's that?" I asked curiously, somehow convinced for a second or two, that maybe she wasn't so bad after all.

But right on cue, she lifted my desk in the air, turned it upside down, and practically body-slammed it.

"CLEAN THIS MESS OFF MY FLOOR!"

The incident warranted a phone call home and my mom wasn't happy. She asked me why I wiped boogers under my desk, and then she gave me a handkerchief to take to school.

"Keep this hankie in your pocket," she said while stuffing it into my inside coat pocket.

"When you have to blow your nose, take it out and use it. Then fold it up and put it back in your pocket."

At this stage I have to ask…

Why would anyone do such a thing?

I mean, I practically get my testicles torn off for wiping a snot or two under the desk where it's not bothering anyone, and that's considered wrong and gross. But I was supposed to carry my snot around in my pocket? It wasn't a very sanitary practice, using a hankie. I associated it with decrepit old men sitting in rocking chairs outside gas stations with shotguns in their laps. In fact, it was an old man thing that went back a few generations before we were born… old men carrying around snot rags in their pockets. They blow their snot into the rag, cough into it, spit into it, fold it up and put it back in their pocket. Then they take it out an hour later and do it all over again. Then they go home and put it in the laundry with everything else. Brilliant concept. Hankies just weren't cool.

———

One night, like many nights, Tommy and I were sitting on the front stairs outside my house…those early evening hours when there's still enough daylight to keep my mom from coming out to get me inside. From across the street we could hear what had become a very predictable thing…the Allen girls screaming or crying, objects crashing and breaking, and a screaming dialogue that went something like this:

Nadine: I don't care! I don't care! I don't care! Just shut up!
George: Nadine, just listen.

Nadine: No, I'm not gonna listen. I don't listen to you, you listen to me!

George: But Nadine...

Nadine: Lazy piece of shit. You stink like a fuckin' gin mill. You can't even get it up anymore. What have you got goin' for ya? You're just like your old man! If it wasn't for me, you'd still be livin' with your mother!

Tommy laughed.

"That's funny," he chuckled.

"She's always screaming at him," I told him.

"That's the skanky Allen girls' ma and dad freakin' out like that?"

"Yup."

It didn't happen every night, but when it did, the entire block got an earful. Nadine Allen wore the pants in their house. That was for sure.

My mom came to the door.

"It's getting dark out. Why don't you guys come in now."

Tommy turned toward her from the top step.

"Hey Luanne...you hearing this ruckus across the street?"

"That's not funny. Those poor little girls in that house. And you think you got problems?"

My mom was always doing that. Changing the conversation around to make us feel guilty of something.

"I never said I have problems," I retorted.

"I have problems," Tommy cut in. "I still don't have Kiss *Double Platinum*, and Ma promised it to me. And there's a new snake I want."

Then my mom said what she always said in response to such things.

"You guys don't know how good you have it."

As she began to walk back into the house, she turned back toward us.

"Don't be too long, it's getting dark. And stay on the stairs."

Stay on the stairs, stay here, stay there, stay in your room, stay in the house, don't go near the street, don't leave your property, don't answer the door, don't look out the window, don't...don't...don't... don't...don't.

Anyway, I guess we didn't think too much about what some people were going through in their lives, or the problems they faced. We didn't think about the magnitude of the effect certain parents had on their kids...all the screaming and fighting, and very often worse. We were just stupid kids laughing at stupid things.

———

Kenny Longlegs was six foot, three. His legs were six feet. He climbed a flight of eight stairs in just two steps. As he squantered across his front lawn and hopped the stairs, I could hear him begging his mother for ice cream money. I was walking up the block past the Merker house when I heard Frank's ring of the Carvel truck. As I walked, I stumbled across Stephanie Adler riding her bike up the sidewalk across from me. We both looked at each other in mutual amusement of Kenny Longlegs pleading for ice cream. He began to scream. The sound traveled well past Sycamore, as Stephanie and I began to laugh. She stopped her bike to listen. I walked out into the street and over to her side, to share in what had become a spectator event for two. From across the street, we heard the sound of Kenny

Longlegs getting slapped, followed by a quick silence. Then, the inevitable crying fit. As he started to cry, the Carvel truck rounded the corner and turned onto Sycamore.

> Ding ding ding
> Ding ding

> Ding ding ding
> Ding ding

The Merker door suddenly sprang open. Kenny Longlegs leaped through the air, and down the stairs all in one shot, as if jumping out a window. He landed on the grass, got up and bolted for the truck as it drove past. All the while, he never stopped crying. Stephanie and I watched as the truck went by and saw that Frank wasn't driving. Once again, it was the nasty Other Guy. Kenny Longlegs had no money, but was determined to go after the truck. He bawled stridently as he ran after The Other Guy. In a stroke of sheer malevolence, the Other Guy kept ringing the bell as he continued driving, completely ignoring Kenny Longlegs, taunting him.

> Ding ding ding
> Ding ding

> Ding ding ding
> Ding ding

Each ding shot down Sycamore like a poison arrow aimed straight at the heart of a small boy's dreams of getting ice cream.

> Ding ding ding
> Ding ding
>
> Ding ding ding
> Ding ding

His arms flailed about wildly in the air as he ran, his head bobbing up and down as if he was saying "YES!"

But really, it was no.

No ice cream for Kenny Longlegs.

> Ding ding ding
> Ding ding
>
> Ding ding ding
> Ding ding

The Other Guy made his way to the top of Sycamore and around the corner. Kenny Longlegs reached the end of the line. His knowledge of Oakwoods did not surpass Sycamore Drive. He too had reached the Forbidden Zone, and didn't dare go near it.

He stopped running.

The sound of the bell trailed off.

Kenny Longlegs, still wailing at the top of his lungs jumped up and down in place, stomping his feet angrily on the ground.

A few seconds passed.

Stephanie and I were still at the bottom of the block as we watched him. He then turned around and dashed back. Still crying, his voice shook each time his feet hit the pavement. He was obviously oblivious to the fact that we were watching him, because he shamelessly continued crying as he ran past us and onto his front lawn. He was practically growling as he approached the stairs...a variation on his anger that far surpassed what normal crying could ever measure, and so was channeled through animalistic grunts.

As he leaped for the stairs, he missed and came down on his left knee.

For a split second, there was silence.

It was that same uncomfortable silence that happens when a child falls down, gets hurt and is about to start sobbing. But Kenny Longlegs, already crying...had stopped. In an instant, he just stopped. The faint sound of the ice cream truck could be heard from around the block. Still across the street from the Merker house, we watched Kenny Longlegs sit down on the ground. He rolled up his pant leg and looked at his knee. It seemed to be a reversed effect on him somehow. Usually a kid falls down and starts crying. He went down, got hurt and *stopped* crying. At the bedroom window at the top of the house, Big John the Bouncer poked his head out and looked at his brother, Kenny Longlegs. Then he looked at Stephanie and me, smiled and disappeared from sight. Stephanie and I looked at each other but said nothing. We were now embarrassed to be there. There was an unspoken mutual agreement that we really shouldn't be there in the middle of someone else's business like that. We began to disperse...Stephanie going her way, and me going mine. We were stopped however, by a familiar sound that grew louder by the second. It quickly approached, closer and closer. Close enough for us to turn toward the bottom of Sycamore Drive and see for ourselves what had once again turned the corner:

> Ding ding ding
> Ding ding

> Ding ding ding
> Ding ding

It was then that I realized the destructive nature that the human mind and spirit could possess. To our disbelief, we watched the ice cream truck turn back onto Sycamore and speed deliberately up the street...the Other Guy returning to completely fuck with Kenny Longlegs with no intention whatsoever of stopping for him.

> Ding ding ding
> Ding ding

> Ding ding ding
> Ding ding

Kenny Longlegs sprouted up, screamed something wordless, and ran into the street past us...again, seemingly unaware that we were even there. We watched helplessly...this time in total alarm, as the friendly Carvel truck had become a vehicle of Satan with poor little Kenny Longlegs chasing after it.

"Oh my God," Stephanie shrieked in disgust.

This was firsthand cruelty.

Frank would never approve of the Other Guy's behavior, tormenting an innocent child with a truck that is supposed to bring joy and happiness. Just then, something else caught our ears, and then our eyes.

From the bedroom window at the top of the Merker house, there was movement. As Kenny Longlegs ran up the block, the curtain in the window opened all the way. A hand appeared, rolling the shade all the way up to reveal the entire window. Stephanie and I both looked at each other in a what-the-hell glance.

Then a voice from the window.

"Psssst. Hey you!"

We looked up.

Framed perfectly symmetrical from the top of the window to the bottom, was Big John the Bouncer's neck to his knees...his shirt off, his pants dropped and his penis in his hand.

"Oh my God," Stephanie gasped, covering her eyes.

She turned her bike around and rode away in terror toward the bottom of the block where she lived.

"Oh my Gaaahhhhhhhd!"

At the top of the block, Kenny Longlegs was incoherently yelling something that bore no resemblance to words. And in the middle of the block was me, nestled quite uncomfortably between two kids demonstrating two drastically different forms of screaming, one adult hijacking an ice cream truck, and a pervert in the window showing me his cock.

Tommy and I always shared a unique ability to find humor in other people's misfortunate events. The sight of someone falling down the stairs always made me laugh. In fact, I think it was more so the sound of it rather than the sight that I always found funny. One time, there was a small brush fire in the woods out behind Sycamore. By no means is this funny. But as all of the neighbors poured out of their houses that day to watch the drama unfold, Tommy still managed to find something to laugh at. While the firefighters worked on putting out the blaze, one of them had some trouble pulling the hose into the woods from the residential area where the trucks were parked. As the man struggled while lumbering slowly across the street, he lost his balance and fell on his ass. Tommy chuckled to himself and took mental notes. When we returned to my house later that afternoon, he broke out a box of crayons, some paper and made a cartoon drawing of the man dragging the fire hose. Similar drawing sprees would take place throughout our childhood every time something crazy or funny happened.

One day during the summer of 1979, Tommy and I were sitting on my front stairs watching George Allen across the street. He had just leaned a very tall metal extension ladder against his house and was getting ready to paint. We could hear in the distance the sound of Alicia and Rebecca screaming at each other in the garage. As George climbed the ladder, the girl's voices grew louder. George reached the top of the ladder, which was even with the window just in time for Nadine's head to poke out of it.

"WHAT THE HELL ARE THEY SCREAMING AT GEORGE?!!"

It was the same familiar, threatening voice that the entire block would come to know. As I mentioned, Nadine wore the pants in the house, and George was terrified of her. We've all heard of spousal abuse, or husband-beating cases. They're supposedly rare, but do happen. Personally, I think there are more than most would like to admit. It wasn't that George wasn't big enough to stand up to her. He just wasn't man enough.

"GET DOWN OFF THE FUCKING LADDER GEORGE, AND SEE WHAT THEY'RE DOING DOWN THERE!!"

"But Nadine..."

"DON'T 'BUT' ME YOU FUCKING SON OF A BITCH!!"

The two girls had darted out of the garage and around the side of the house. George could feel them creeping up. He heard them but couldn't see them. As Nadine disappeared from the window, he dipped his brush into the can of white Dutch Boy paint and began doing the trim. He struggled to keep his hand from shaking as his nerves, beyond repair, jolted about throughout his body.

He hated the bitch. First an overbearing mother, and then a hag wife who turned into his overbearing mother. What did he do in some past life, he wondered. What kind of sick perverted joke was being played on him for his life to stray in such a direction? What kind of poor schmuck gets dealt such a hand? To live hopelessly in turmoil and abuse...awash in painkillers and alcohol, and surrounded by dead ends, only to succumb to the bottomless depths of some miserable white trash existence. His whole life had been a series of mistakes, and his current existence amounted to one big clusterfuck of unfuckable proportions.

"Daddy! Daddy," one of the girls cried from below the ladder. One had begun chasing the other. Miraculously, they kept missing the ladder as they circled around it repeatedly. George was getting nervous. Afraid of heights, he didn't want to be up there in the first place. It was his nagging wife who bitched and bitched about the house being painted that finally got him up on the ladder.

"Girls," he yelled shakily to no avail.

He didn't want to look down.

From the corner of his eye, he could see the shadows of their movement beneath him. And through his fear, he could feel the fragility and threat of their presence.

The girls passed him, finally, as they ran into the backyard, their voices trailing off. Just to assure himself that everything was safe, he gathered the strength to look down. They were gone. It was just him, the ladder and the trampled grass in the morning sun. He began to hum a Neil Diamond song as it played on a transistor radio in the garage. It calmed him down.

"Play it now! Plaaaaay it now! Plaaaay it now, my baybeh! Ba-ba-ba-ba-baaah!"

He had finally begun to relax. "Cracklin' Rosie" soothed his nerves.

"AND WHEN YOU'RE DONE, CUT THE GRASS!!!" the dreadful voice squawked, as his twat of a wife's horrifying head poked back out of the window. Stunned nearly into cardiac arrest, George jerked the brush forward and lost his balance while the two girls rounded the corner to see their daddy freefalling down the side of the house.

What was another family's personal tragedy became yet another neighborhood event. As people began scurrying out of their houses to see what had happened, Tommy and I went inside to draw a comic of George falling off the ladder.

The cartoon drawings would accompany our chronology as we grew up in Oakwoods. Eventually, as we got older, we'd share lockers in middle school and high school. We'd then hang our drawings in the locker for the other to see when the door was opened. I could be sitting in class and remember some funny thing that happened when we were younger, and then I'd randomly draw a picture of it. Then I'd get a pass to the bathroom or something, and go hang the picture up in the locker. Tommy would see it and start cracking up. My reaction was always the same as his, whenever he surprised me with his own drawings. If something funny happened on the way to school or on the bus or something, one of us would draw a picture of it and the picture would be hanging in the locker by lunch time. As we'd grow older and become adults, the drawings would survive the test and decay of time, being passed around through the hands of our inner circle of friends every ten or so years to remember and laugh at these things. The older we have gotten, the funnier they have become. These drawings have become known in the mythology of Oakwoods, as the Locker Notes.

In the warmth of a midsummer afternoon, I ventured close to the Forbidden Zone. Not really sure how far was too far, I'd already gone past where I was allowed to go. Since nothing had happened as I moved swiftly through the uncut grass toward the fence, I was com-pelled onward. My heart pounded into my throat as I approached it, never having been so close before. I walked along the fence to where it ended. I stopped when I saw the opening where kids would go through. The long grass swayed in the gentle breeze. I watched it move in front and all around me. This was okay, I thought to myself. What could be so bad here, I wondered. It was actually kind of nice. It was a rather serene calm amidst the swaying carpet of grasses. Other than the warm breeze, every trace of humanity and my whereabouts seemed to vanish.

Was I still in Oakwoods?

Was my house really just down the street?

I had wandered farther than I'd ever gone past Sycamore Drive. Yet, I hadn't even so much as entered The Forbidden Zone.

Maybe it was all the Forbidden Zone.

Without warning or any indication that the scene was about to take a disquieting turn, my peaceful surroundings were no longer welcome in my mind. The serenity took on an eerie form, as something else began to unfold itself in front of me. Suddenly, the trees began to change. We'd learned about trees in school. They were supposed to be friendly. A good chunk of Oakwoods was named after trees. These trees though, had arms. Faces took shape within the cracks of the bark and began to watch me. In an instant, every terrifying image and thought I ever had in my life rushed into my mind's eye all at once. The grass, several feet tall, waved ominously in the wind, but the earth was stationary. It was solid.

Unafraid.

What could be so bad that the earth would allow happen to me? Would it watch its own creatures devour another? That was nature, and that was always a possibility. The natural world often had the potential to work more evil than the supernatural. My brain was leading me places I didn't want to go, and it was becoming quickly and painfully obvious that I possessed little to no control over the situation.

I wondered.

What was it that moved underneath me that was going to dart out, wrap itself around my feet and pull me under?

Was it possible for the earth to swallow me?

I thought of snakes.

I thought of other things too.

A girl had been missing. Maybe kidnapped. It had been in the local papers. Our parents were all talking about it. What if she was back here? What if I found her body? What if she died with her eyes open and when I found her, she was looking at me? Suddenly, too scared to breathe, I froze. Alone again under that unseen microscope, I was surrounded by an unwanted silence that even drowned out the distant hum of humanity. Sometimes the broadest daylight is creepier than the darkest night. When the imagination paints in those elements that make every hair on the body stand on end... that make the blood run cold...even the sun is no longer your friend. Shadows, after all, come from the sun. Everything has its polar opposite. When the human mind strays from reality, these opposites often intertwine and the lines get blurred. With that, I gathered the strength to break out of my frozen body cast. Letting go, I let out a scream, if only to convince myself that I still had some control...and ran as fast as I could back through the uncut yard and past the final houses, which now served as a welcome mat back into the monotony of Sycamore Drive. It was a reassuring monotony...a reminder that I would at least be safe there.

5

Sports

Ritchie Burke stood in the middle of the street swinging an aluminum baseball bat. He was having an imaginary game with himself. This was not unusual on our block. I did it too. So did Derrick Adler. Adler was a diehard Yankees fan who at the time, you'd think would kill for them. He hated Ritchie Burke, simply because he was a Mets fan. There was a brief period when Derrick and I hung out, playing our imaginary baseball games with ourselves. Then Derrick kind of disappeared for a while. He'd re-surface occasionally, but after a while, I started hanging out with Ritchie for the rest of the summer of 1979.

Let me explain the games. We'd each have our own team and our own imaginary league in our heads. You have to remember...this was all in our heads...and I mean all of it.

We'd swing a bat...at nothing.

Midair.

Whatever happened spontaneously in our mind's eye was what happened to the imaginary batter. If you saw a strike, it was a strike. If you saw a hit...well, you get the picture.

I originally started the imaginary games with Derrick. He'd be off in one corner of his yard while I was in another corner. We each had our teams and schedules. We were both the Yankees. This was possible because our imaginary leagues had absolutely nothing to do with each other. And yes, playing ball with yourself in this manner made it very easy to cheat. If you didn't go with your first impulse on vision, every swing of the bat could result in a homerun if you really wanted it to. That's why Derrick Adler's New York Yankees won the World Series every season, and sometimes even had seasons where they went 162 wins and zero losses. I had attempted playing in the little leagues, but one of the more scarring episodes of childhood happened on Opening Day before the game even started. I was six, and barely understood the game yet. As we took the field, I was told by my manager to play right field. When I asked him where right field was and everybody on my team and in the stands started laughing at me, it assured my quick choice in quitting after that game. I never went back to little league baseball, and it would take about five years before kids stopped reminding me of the right field incident.

We also had other ways of doing our imaginary games.

If it was raining and we couldn't go out, we'd shuffle baseball cards around by a certain number. If we came to a second basemen's card, it was a double. A first baseman's card was a single. Get the picture yet? More details needed? An outfielder was a flyout...a pitcher, a strikeout...a catcher, a walk...a team photo card was a homerun. I think that spells it out. We even kept our team and player statistics on paper and after each game we'd sit down to change the numbers. From an outsider's point of view, it looked like two kids sitting there doing math homework. We had our thing. It worked, and it was entertaining while it lasted.

Ritchie was just as partial to his Mets as Derrick was to his Yankees. As he swung his bat in the street, it was always Lee Mazzilli at the plate. And he was the homerun champion, smacking an average of some 100 homeruns a year. This was a little funny, since Mazz usually hit around 15 during a good year in real life. What was sad was that Mazz and a guy named Joel Youngblood who would also average 15 or 16, were the Mets' real life homerun leaders. That's pretty much how bad the Mets were in the late 1970s, and from the mid-Seventies to the mid-Eighties, they were probably the most losing franchise in New York sports. They'd been the "miracle" Mets in 1969 when they won the World Series, but even that was insulting to them since the common belief was that it took a "miracle" for a team like the Mets to win. In the Seventies, it was different. They had a manager named Joe Torre during this period, an ex-player who couldn't seem to manage them out of the cellar. After he'd go, it didn't seem he'd ever be welcome again in New York. But it wasn't really his fault. It was an inept owner that refused to put any real money into the team, leaving it at the mercy of a bunch of washed up near retirees and inexperienced mediocre farm club players. In 1980, they declared that the "magic was back." It was a slogan that wasn't really warranted by anything substantial, other than the fact that they began renovating Shea Stadium by adding new seats. It was a beautiful assortment of colors...orange, blue, green and red....each deck of seats with its own color. It was an eye-catching improvement over the mold-green and diarrhea-brown seats of the original stadium, but it wasn't enough to help the Mets win. A year later, they got a guy named King Kong to hit homeruns out into the left field parking lot of Shea. There was even a sign warning fans to park at their own risk because they were in King Kong's home run zone. But even King Kong couldn't help them out of last place. On a good year, they took fifth place while the Cubs took last. Every few years, they'd alternate between last and fifth. It didn't matter to us though. We were fans. And I was one of the rare few who could transcend the idea of "teams" and "sides," and all of the symbolism and hatred that sports entails.

I was partial to no one.

I liked both the Yankees and the Mets and I rooted for both of them.

There, I said it.

I was much more of a New York fan, and the idea of New York is much bigger than any one team.

Derrick was central in introducing me to the Yankees in 1977. They had just lost the World Series to the Reds the year before, and there was a vengeance with which he rooted throughout the 1977 season. He insisted that I was a Yankees fan, and had the strength and size over me to inform my fear of getting beat up if I didn't become a fan. My dad was a Mets fan, and between him and Ritchie, I had been much more exposed to the Mets, although I never admitted to liking the Mets in front of Derrick. Derrick's family was batshit crazy with the Yankees though. I remember one time Ritchie, Marc and I were hanging out waiting for Derrick to come outside, and Derrick's dad told us to come into the house and wait, but told Ritchie there were no Mets fans allowed in his house, and that he'd have to stay outside. And the reason I didn't see Derrick for an extended period of time, was because he threw a shit fit in my house one day when my mom called downstairs to us in the basement that Ritchie was coming over. He started going off about how I was a traitor and that I shouldn't be friends with a Mets fan. Then he started punching walls and throwing chairs around until my mom kicked him out of the house and told him to go home. At first he refused, but after throwing around more chairs and punching more walls, he finally left. My mom told me never to hang around with him again, but if I listened to her every single time she warned me about someone, Tommy would've been the only friend I had. I personally wouldn't harbor any ill feelings toward Derrick after that day, but my mom made him out to be a lunatic and carried on for weeks about how he disrespected her and destroyed her house, which is understandable regarding the former, but a little exaggerated regarding the latter. Point is, she developed this idea that he was dangerous and that I was never to see him ever again. About a year later, I saw him riding his bike up the street and coming right toward me. After I asked him if he was going to beat me up, he laughed and said no, and then said what he did was stupid. Still, I never had the nerve to tell him that I was equal parts Yankees and Mets fan, and that it was more about rooting for New York City with me. Of course if the two would by any slim remote chance, ever meet in the World Series, I wasn't sure how I would root or if I would root at all. But the way I see it, Yankees fans should hate the Red Sox and Orioles, not the Mets. And Mets fans should hate the Braves and the Phillies, not the Yankees. I didn't grow up witnessing the loss of the Dodgers and Giants to cities in California. I didn't know the experience of going to Ebetts Field and the Polo Grounds. I didn't carry that World War 2 generation's conservative contempt for change. I could understand it though. Back then, there was still an idea of sacredness to sports. The act of moving a team in the interest of money was considered more a betrayal than a business move. Within a few more decades, nothing would remain sacred...and even Yankee Stadium and Shea Stadium would both be knocked down. But to my generation, it was the Mets and the Yankees who had always been there. In my eyes, New York was family...and within that family, the Mets were the Yankees stupid little brothers, but you had to love them.

Unfortunately, rooting for New York teams also meant rooting for the Jets football team.

———

Before the magic came back to Shea Stadium, I visited the cavern of losers during the mid fall of 1979 with my dad. We went to see the Jets play the Buffalo Bills. The Jets held the same status as the Mets, and their legacy-in-the-making was a lifetime worth of miserable Sundays. In the crisp, cold November chill, it started to rain. Luckily, we were covered by the roof of the mezzanine section. The dank gray, dreary, and bone-chilling cold still made for a very unpleasant experience. As the Jets star quarterback of the day, Richard Todd couldn't complete any meaningful passes due to his go-to guy, Wesley Walker being injured, the team still managed two touchdowns. Yet, they missed both extra points...and so Todd and his fellow New York stars, Scott Dierking, Clark Gaines, Bruce Harper, Jerome Barcum and Marty Lyons fell to pieces for what was just another Sunday loss by the score of 14-12.

Although I wasn't all that concerned with the game, I began growing more and more miserable by the minute somewhere during the second quarter as I became increasingly and painfully aware of the fact that I needed to move my bowels. The combination of cold trying to penetrate me, and crap trying to exit me resulted in a contorted sculpture of a kid in a seat, squirming around in shaking convulsions. What was I going to do?

I'd never taken a shit anywhere but at home. Maybe at my grandparent's house when I slept over. Of course, when I was a baby, I shit wherever I wanted. But I was wearing a diaper then, so that's different. There were 60,000 people at Shea Stadium, and soon it would be halftime.

And they'd *all* have to get up take a shit!

What if there was a line?

I'd better get up now, I thought. There were two minutes to halftime. I began to walk down the stairs to exit my section, totally cognizant of my surroundings...screaming men...big *angry* men...all drinking beer...some smoking cigarettes and cigars...all growling at the top of their lungs. Big hairy ape-like men who were going to go home and beat their wives if the Jets lost. Big morbid and morose Neanderthal-looking creatures that drive trucks and store shotguns in the back.

And all of them were about to go take a shit.

I sped up my pace on the verge of panicking.

I got to the bottom of the stairs and turned, going through the underpass, which led to the hallways of Shea. I needed to get to the restroom before the mad rush of halftime. My intestines were cramping and poking about as I booked toward the opening that read "Men."

Before the magic came back to Shea, the stadium remained in its original condition, with very little restorative work done since it opened in 1964. The restoration I mentioned a few pages back hadn't been done yet and wouldn't begin until after the last Jets home game that year, so the decrepit seats were the same as when The Beatles played there. The place badly needed an overhaul and a facelift. The concrete stairs between each section were broken, making it dangerous to walk up and down. The paint was chipped and faded. Each seat, which saw 89 asses a year between Mets and Jets home games, needed to be replaced. And even if it was the same ass of a season ticket holder all year, it didn't change the fact that the seats were still fucked up. The restrooms were hideous. The floors were buckled and broken. Water, sewage and piss ran through the cracks in the floor and flooded other parts of the restrooms. It wasn't pleasant.

When I got inside, I had to watch where I stepped. There were three stalls...one with a door, and two without doors. I went straight for the one with the door. To my horror, I found not a toilet, but a simple hole in the ground where the toilet had been ripped out... probably by angry Neanderthal men. Given the losing history of both teams, Shea Stadium had become accustomed to lots and lots of anger over the years. Adrenaline rushed through me in panic. I looked at the next stall. There was a bowl, but no door. There was nobody there yet. If I hurried, I could sit down really fast and force it out before the rush of mad truckers came in. I quickly unbuttoned my Tough Skins and pulled them down. Just then, I remembered mom always warning me about public restrooms...that if I ever had to go, to put paper down on the seat. I reached for the paper dispenser to find that there was no paper. Quickly, I peered around into the other stalls to see if there was paper. I took a roll from the stall next to me, and tore off enough to cover the seat. All the while I could hear mom warning me about picking up something ghastly if I happen to sit on a bowl that was uncovered. People have ass diseases that I would catch, I thought to myself. I attempted to sit down, but the back of my leg knocked the paper off the bowl.

Fuck!

I reached down to pick it up.

Oh no, I thought.

It's on the floor.

The floor is wet and dirty.

I needed a new piece.

Even without mom being in the room...even with her some 40 miles away back in Jersey, she was still stressing me out. Then, in the heat and pressure of the moment, I thought "Fuck the paper, I need to shit right *now*."

I sat my ass down on the bowl, but there was no way I could relax enough to let a turd slide out peacefully. This was pressure unlike anything I'd ever experienced. A whole gang of grown furious men were about to charge in and interrupt me.

I could feel it slowly begin to emerge. But just as it began to make its way out, the sound of hairy monkey men grew louder and louder, as the very presence of the restrooms beckoned them closer. I could hear the trampling sound of halftime...the stampede to get hot dogs and more beer...the lines that would form at the food stand and in the restroom. In an instantaneous magnetic reaction, one furious Jets fan after another flocked to the urinals across from the doorless stall, and in a flash they were all taken. Everyone had their backs to me as they began to pee. A second later, in the stall next to me... the one without the toilet...someone began to pee into the hole in the floor, leaving it to splash up under the dividing wall and wet my Zips sneakers with miniscule little speckles of pee stains from some stranger whose face I never got to see. Now his pee would be on my feet in a Pointillist presentation, and I would carry it all the way back to Oakwoods.

Then, the unimaginable happened.

I heard loud hard footsteps approaching, as a giant beast rounded the corner and stopped short when he saw me sitting there.

And then suddenly, it was all over.

My ass froze up.

The turd crept back inside, afraid to come out.

I couldn't shit.

Before I knew it, two or three other people came in expecting to use my stall.

"What's going on?" one of them asked.

"There's a kid in there," the one in front said.

They formed a line, each of them looking at me in the face as if they expected me to perform a fucking magic trick. I had to shit but couldn't. How could one stand up under such pressure, expected to force a turd out of his ass with an audience of monosyllabic grunting men? Needless to say, I didn't get to go that afternoon until after I got home. The turd somehow found its way back in and kind of hung out, converting its anger into a seemingly endless series of farts throughout the third and fourth quarters. This experience marked the beginning of a life-long fear of shitting in public restrooms, among other neurotic nervous conditions that have often resulted in panic and anxiety.

———————

At the end of every school year, when we were given our last report cards, we'd turn them over to read who our teacher would be the following year. Then we'd all run around trying to find out who would be in our class. That year, something new was in the works...a first.

Tommy, Marc and me would all have Mrs. Jacobson for fifth grade. We'd all finally be in the same class. This actually gave us something to look forward to in the upcoming year. Going to school wouldn't be so bad anymore. When we walked into Mrs. Jacobson's class on the first day and Tommy and I were placed right next to each other, it was even better. This was going to be the best school year ever.

Then we went to lunch.

Then we came back from lunch.

When we came back from lunch, we all sat down at our desks.

Then the door opened, and two women from the main office walked in like storm troopers.

"Thomas Dewhirst!" one woman called out.

Tommy looked up at her.

"Would you come with me please?"

The second woman then called out the unimaginable.

"Marc Rinaldi!"

Marc looked up at her.

"Would you come with me please?"

And just like that, my two friends were taken from me in an apparent scheduling mix up. They were actually supposed to be in Mr. Hardenberger's class. I couldn't comprehend the thought. It's just too sick to even dream up.

Three classes in the fifth grade.

Some 70 students.

Two get moved.

What are the chances of them being Tommy and Marc? But you see, it's not merely coincidental, but also convenient, appropriate and essential to the continuing story of what my shitty luck had become.

Out of nowhere, I found myself pining for the past summer. Even though I'd spent it doing childish things like playing Fisher Price Adventure People with Ritchie Burke, it was more fun than the school year was going to be, given the new circumstances. Tommy and Marc were still together and I was alone in Mrs. Jacobson's class. Even though I'd spent the summer trying to make sense of Kiss's latest album *Dynasty* and the commercial disco route they'd chosen, it was much more palatable than going to school. And even though I'd spent much of the summer in the back seat of my parents 1974 Catalina, while they waited on line for hours to get gas during the shortage, it was still more appealing than enduring another year of Mr. Minuchie and skin-the-cat, and kickball, and Ashley Drake. Friends make all the difference in our lives...especially if you had a few in your class.

Surprisingly though, fifth grade made for a pretty smooth school year. Mrs. Jacobson took a special liking to me and it was nice to have a teacher on my side for once. She never screamed at me or put me on the spot in front of the class like I'd grown accustomed to. This was good because Ashley didn't have any real opportunities to laugh at me. Besides, she sat all the way on the other side of the room, so I didn't really care. As for Tommy and Marc, they ended up getting the full treatment of Mr. Hardenberger, who was not very popular in the school. He liked to teach with notes spread out on a podium or a music stand...a rather pompous practice in an elementary school. For someone of his personality, he almost didn't belong in an elementary school...the professor who never was...exercising his big dick authority on a bunch of unsuspecting innocent little kids. Tommy, Marc and Jason Sacco all hated him. They were all occasionally targets for verbal dissection. But if there was any consolation, at least they had Riley Stevens in their class.

The first four months of fifth grade were the last four months of the 1970s. As the end of 1979 approached, talk was in the air about the turn of the decade. Granted, some argue that decades actually begin on the one and not the zero, and that 1980 really marks the last year of the Seventies, but I'm anal. Therefore, we'll mark the end of the decade with 1979.

How intense a thought it was...the 1980s! We'd be flying in cars! We'd be able to press a button for anything and everything! We were going to be able to communicate through television screens! Maybe we'd be living in outer space like on *The Jetsons*! Music was going to sound a whole lot different! It was plain and simple. It was the future... and the future was almost here.

On November 4, 1979, fifty Americans were taken hostage at the U.S. Embassy in Iran. It became big news very quickly. Politically, I wasn't sure what was happening. Apparently, the Ayatollah Khomeini wanted the Shah of Iran returned for trial. He had been in New York City for medical treatment and most likely would have been killed had he return to Iran where Khomeini led a revolution. When you're ten years old, it's hard to grasp the political implications of anything. Mrs. Jacobson tried as best she could to explain it to us. But at that age, you're simply told that Iran has fifty of us as hostages, and that we're good and they're bad. That was the extent of how we understood it. As days turned to weeks, we would watch the scene on television as it unfolded night after night. We'd see footage from Iran...Americans tied up and blindfolded. We'd see furious people in Iran burning the American flag. In America, of course, people had to profit from it. T-shirts, bumper stickers and posters condemning Iran began to appear everywhere. Everywhere you went you saw BOMB IRAN, IRAN SUCKS, KILL KHOMEINI, KHOMEINI SUCKS and AYATOLLA ASSAHOLA. One month into it, Mrs. Jacobson gave us colored construction paper and had us make Christmas cards to send to the hostages. During the upcoming year, more things would happen. This guy Ronald Reagan would run for president against Jimmy Carter and he would win. He would much later start talking about Russia as an "evil empire," but at the outset of his candidacy, all this sudden talk about nuclear war would begin to permeate the air in America.

Why?

Why all of a sudden were all these bad things happening and being talked about?

President Carter seemed like a nice guy to us, and suddenly this scary man was going to be our president. It's ironic how during the hostage crisis, when Iran went to war with Iraq, we were on Iraq's side.

Future consequences of the Reagan years and our alliance with Iraqi president, Saddam Hussein, would create problems for the U.S. later on.

But we didn't care.

The American people didn't care.

All we knew was that Iraq was fighting Iran.

One thing that struck me though, even at that early age, was how our anger toward Iran was almost sports-like. We rooted for Iraq as if they were the New York Yankees. It was great to be an American and all, but our patriotism was like being on a sports team…a sort of "my team is better than yours" attitude. This is exactly why artists like Bob Dylan and John Lennon were so important. They saw through the veil of shit and hypocrisy, and painted it as they saw it. Lennon challenged us to imagine that there were "no countries" and proposed the idea of having "nothing to kill or die for." Yes, all of that naïve idealism got washed away, as the apocalypse at Altamont Speedway in 1969 flushed the Sixties down with the shit, and then Lennon put it most eloquently: "the dream is over."

The Who's Pete Townshend echoed him when he declared that the new boss was the "same as the old boss."

When I looked on the streets and saw anger toward Iran reflected in T-shirts, and then turned on the news to see these people burning our flag and screaming with absolute hatred in their voices and eyes, I saw a big concerning difference...even at that young age.

Our patriotism was blind.

Their's was real.

And it was scary.

These people *really* hated us.

It wasn't anger...it was pure raging hatred.

Why?

Why did they *hate* us so much?

Nobody ever told us.

———

Later that winter, the Olympics were held in Lake Placid, New York. I can remember almost every Winter Olympics of my lifetime, but Lake Placid stands out particularly because it was the first winter games that I was really aware of. The U.S. hockey team beating the Soviets was in the news a lot, and the teachers talked about it as if it were a big deal. I guess it was, given the new nationalist sentiment being expressed around the country. This was around the time Ronald Reagan really started getting into the public eye in his presidential campaign. He was a scary man who hid behind a friendly, deceptive smile. People seemed to like him, but word on the street was that if this guy got elected, we were going to war. There was a strong sense of "us vs. them" during this period, whether it was the Soviet Union, Iran or whoever. Whatever side Ronald Reagan was playing for in America, it always seemed to be based around having another country as our opponent.

During the time that the Olympics were going on, we had a physical fitness week in gym class. Mr. Minuchie made us do a whole bunch of exercise consisting of pushups, pull ups, chin ups, sit ups, and every other type of *up* you could think of. One day, he pulled out the giant blue gymnastics mats, and whenever I walked in the All Purpose Room to see those mats, I knew that it was going to be a class consisting of cartwheels and the much-dreaded rope climbing.

Halfway through the period, I found myself a quarter of the way up the rope while Jake Kennedy was at the very top and already coming back down. I was struggling and couldn't climb any further. As I let go of the ropes to jump back down to the mat, I noticed that Jake had already made it back down and was sitting on the floor.

"Damn, Devine. You're slow as a piece of dog shit," one boy called out. I didn't even look to see who it was. I walked back from the mats without even looking up.

"You suck, Devine!" someone else called out.

I sat down next to Jake and sneezed three times. Ashley who was sitting right there, shot me her usual dirty look.

"Eww, you're disgusting!" she barked.

Immediately, I realized that I had a line of syrupy snot streaming down my face between my nostrils and my lips, so I reached into the pocket of my sweatshirt and pulled out my trusty hankie. I pulled it to my face and wiped away the grossness.

"That's so disgusting!" she said again.

Jake smiled in amusement.

"Hey," he called out. "Look, Devine has a hankie!"

A few kids chuckled in broken assorted laughter.

"You look like my grandfather!"

Everyone was alarmed when the doors flew open in a thunderous thud. Two boys fell through them and landed on the floor, close to where we were all sitting. One boy was Rodney Sharp, a sixth grade bully. The other was Kevin Weir. Both were joined in a headlock embrace, and Weir was kicking the shit out of him...punching him with one arm while choking him with the other. The class moved back a few feet on the floor to give them space.

"Hey!" Mr. Minuchie screamed from the other side of the gym.

Meanwhile, two women ran into the room after the two boys. Weir managed to stand up while Sharp was still on the floor. He began kicking Sharp in the head. Just as Mr. Minuchie approached, Weir was grinding Sharp's face into the floor with the bottom of his work boot.

Holy crap, I thought. Not only was Kevin Weir demolishing a sixth grader, but he was probably about to kill him.

"Get him...somebody stop him!" cried one of the women in a deep raspy voice, reminiscent of a mob figure.

Mr. Minuchie grabbed Weir with one hand and pulled him off the helpless boy, walking him by the hood of his sweatshirt out of the room.

"Let's go, Weir!"

"I'm gonna kill you!" Weir screamed, looking back at Sharp who was laying on the floor moaning in pain.

"I'll kill you, man!" he said again.

"You're not killing anyone today, Little Weir."

Mr Minuchie opened the doors and pushed him through into the main lobby of the school. He then poked his head back into the room.

"Mrs. Santorini, would you please watch the class while I take him to the office?"

"Of course, Mr. Minuchie," the raspy-voiced woman replied.

She was Mrs. Santorini, a little old Italian lady with a mustache who worked as an aid around the school. She was always talking about her son, Carmen. No matter what the situation...if she got in your ear, she told you about her son, Carmen. The other woman was Mrs. Toth, the librarian. She was a gaunt stick-figured woman with broken teeth and wiry hair, who resembled a Woodstock-era Wavy Gravy.

Weir somehow must have broken out of the gym teacher's clutches when he opened the doors and charged back in. Mrs. Toth jumped in front of him as Mr. Minuchie opened the door, taking hold of him by the arm.

"Kevin Weir, you oughta be ashamed of yourself, picking on somebody younger than you!" Mrs. Toth wailed, spitting into his face.

"He's *older* than Kevin!" half the class said at the same time.

"Yeah," Mrs. Santorini said, looking down at the student who was writhing around on the floor in pain. "He's sixth grade. Why are you beating up kids older than you, Kevin Weir?"

"Because he *looked* at me!" Weir shot back as he was dragged through the door and back into the lobby once again.

Mrs. Santorini turned to Mrs. Toth in disbelief.

"He *looked* at him?"

"These kids today..." started Mrs. Toth as she began walking out of the room.

"I know," Mrs. Santorini cut in. "They'll beat someone up just for *looking* at them."

Suddenly Ashley had to put in her two cents.

"He's a bully. He deserved it."

I chuckled to myself. On that note, I thought, maybe Weir should kick the crap out of Ashley too...ya know...kind of on account of her being the biggest bully in school and all.

Rodney Sharp lay on the floor, twisting around in spastic motion. Nobody paid attention to him.

"Hey Mrs. Santorini, I made it to the top of the ropes and climbed back down before Eugene even made it halfway up," Jake boasted, grabbing the woman's attention. Ashley wasn't happy about it and she elbowed him in the ribs.

"Why do you gotta get her attention?" she whispered. "Now she's gonna come over here and never stop talking."

Sure enough.

"You should see my son-a-Carmen climb the ropes," she said in a slight Italian accent. She also had Greek in her family, so we were never sure where the hell her accent actually came from. It usually wasn't traceable, but it always managed to come out when she was talking about Carmen.

"My son-a-Carmen is like a monkey. He'll climb straight to the top and then he'll climb the ceiling. My son-a-Carmen is the best at the ropes. Oh, I tell ya...I love my son-a-Carmen. He's a little crazy, but he's a good-a boy."

Ashley looked over at me and leaned in toward my ear.

"There she goes again with her son-a-Carmen."

"Does your son-a-Carmen go to this school?" Jake asked, humoring her.

I thought for a second that she was going to yell at him for making fun of her accent, but she either didn't notice or didn't care. Usually, the Italian accent has that extra "a" added to a lot of English words, but she only said it when referring to her son.

"No, we don't live in this neighborhood. We took him out of where he was, and had to put him in a special school. He's not a bad kid, my son-a-Carmen. He's just a little crazy."

I turned around and noticed Rodney was still slithering around in place. Some of the kids just looked at him as if he were a piece of furniture or some unknown alien life form whose existence they remained indifferent to.

"Hey," Jake called out. "I think he's dead over there."

"Nah, he's still moving," Mrs. Santorini replied, taking a few steps toward the injured boy.

"He's not bleeding, is he?" a concerned Johnny Felix wondered.

"No," Jake said, "but he's slobbering all over the place. Hey Devine, give him your hankie."

Ashley was still grossed out by my hankie.

"Eww that's disgusting, Jake!"

Mrs. Santorini glanced over at Rodney from a distance, but returned her attention toward us.

"I don't think he's bleeding. Kevin just knocked the wind out of him, that's all. My son-a-Carmen, he's a bleeder. He had to go to the hospital for a bloody nose."

She began walking over toward Rodney. Mrs. Toth walked back in and also headed for Rodney, who lay on the floor groaning. As I glanced over at him, Jake reached into my pocket, pulled out the hankie and tossed it in the direction of Rodney. It landed a few feet from him. Ashley wasn't amused.

"Oh my God, that's so disgusting!"

"Seriously," Jake gasped at his own action. "That *was* disgusting. Can I go wash my hands?"

Mrs. Toth stopped walking when she reached Rodney. She stood over him and leaned into his face.

"Stop looking at Kevin Weir!" she exclaimed, warning him like a thug. As she did this, Mrs. Santorini reached onto the floor and picked up my yellow and brown striped, snot-caked piece of fine linen, and threw it onto Rodney Sharp's chest.

"Here, have a hankie!"

6

The Summer Before Sixth Grade

"We don't need no eh-juh-kayshun!" we mockingly sang as we marched defiantly across the playground.

"Hey! Teachaaah! Leave them kids alone!!"

Some teachers found it amusing. Some did not. In the early months of the new decade, teachers and authority figures had taken aim at a controversial new song that was quickly taking the radio stations by storm. Many wanted it removed from the airwaves. Yet, Pink Floyd's new album *The Wall* had become something of a phenomenon. Floyd had been successful to a degree throughout the Seventies, with the dark trippy psychedelia of albums like *Dark Side of the Moon* and *Wish You Were Here*. They sold out arenas and stadiums, yet retained a somewhat cult status. With the release of *The Wall* and its first single, "Another Brick in the Wall Part II," they kicked the door of mainstream open and entered to the shock of a disgusted adult population who saw the song as a societal threat. Many Floyd fans accepted *The Wall*, but many saw it as both a sell out, and a point of departure for the band. The new single didn't resemble anything the band had done in the past and embraced the common dance beat of the day along with the choppy minor guitar chords that many rock bands attempting to do disco were playing at the time (think "Hot Stuff" and "Miss You" by the Rolling Stones, "Straight On" by Heart, or "Shakedown Street" by the Grateful Dead). For better or worse, it turned mainstream audiences on to Pink Floyd, and it preserved their place among the greatest classic rock bands of all time. And as fifth graders, we became obsessed with it.

The early Eighties also brought new wave. The Cars and Blondie were in. Kiss was out.

That's right.

Kiss was out.

I'm not sure if it was a conscious decision to stop listening to them as much as our interests going in different directions. I think subconsciously we had begun to outgrow them and felt somewhat embarrassed of our association with them. Two years before, it had been a matter of pride. In the early eighties, it became an issue of having to jump into the closet to hide. Besides, Peter Criss had left the band and there was a new member playing drums. As a fan, I found it a bit strange and unsettling how quickly they replaced him, almost seamlessly. Anyway, it wasn't the same. Between the pop-friendly direction in which they had gone and the loss of Peter, lots of fans dropped out. I liken our disassociation with Kiss to a child who loses interest in a toy that once gave him everything he needed but put it aside when he wasn't getting that rush anymore. We were growing up, and our toys began to vary.

By 1980, Marc had mellowed a bit. I no longer went to his house afraid that I would be tied up with a rope and left in the darkroom for the day. Derrick Adler had branched out and found other friends once he started junior high. He'd pop up every once in a while, but for the most part, we didn't see him too much. Ritchie Burke had been hanging around with some other friends from Catholic school, so I only saw him occasionally. He had also spent some time off his feet after having an accident of some sort. Apparently, he fell out of the car as his mom was driving him home from school, and the car ran his foot over. I mean, how bad can your luck be for that to happen? First you fall out of a moving car. Then, to add insult to injury your own car runs you over as you hit the ground. He was okay, but had to spend some time on crutches. The next few years would be the tightest of my friendship with Marc Rinaldi. The absence of Derrick I think made that possible. Any third person in the equation often made Marc take sides against you for some reason. I was always more of a one-to-one person, never caring too much for crowds. We bonded pretty tightly for a few years in what became a unique friendship.

Three things happened. First, the dead zone that was suburbia had begun to take effect on our attention spans. We were bored. That formed the first common bond. Second, the eventual addition of cable TV into our lives would change everything. By the age of ten, I was a rock and roll encyclopedia. When cable TV came to Oakwoods the following year, I discovered the medium of film. And not just movies, but film....and to be a snob, *cinema*. Marc also experienced a rebirth in artistic spirit. I say artistic, because we were both hit with a spark of creative energy. With cable still some six months away from Oakwoods, we were still able to see cable movies on something called WHT (Wometco Home Theater) at Marc's house, and when I occasionally slept over, we'd sneak downstairs after his parents went off to bed, and watch whatever was on. When I first saw *The Godfather* and *Apocalypse Now*, I discovered not only two great movies, but it marked the beginning of my life as a cinephile. I'd dissect movies the same way I'd come to dissect music. I'd analyze everything I saw, looking for some deeper meaning in every camera angle. Friends in school were talking about the new *Star Wars* sequel and about the big *holy shit* moment at the end between Luke Skywalker and Darth Vader... and I'd be there trying to talk about the TV trailer for a new film called *The Shining* to anyone who would listen. Sure, I couldn't wait to see the new *Star Wars* movie just like everyone else, but my interest in film had also begun to take on a slightly more sophisticated criteria. I remember talking to some kid about the marriage of sound and vision being used to great effect in the TV spot, and whoever this Stanley Kubrick guy was, he was a genius. The kid told me I was weird. Marc and I also had another interest.

We drew.

This was the third thing that happened.

We started making these little comic books. Marc started doing it first. He'd draw comics of movies he'd seen. And I don't mean comic "strips," but entire movies. Then he started creating his own original story lines. I watched him. Every other day, he'd show me another new one. Most of them were violent. That violent little five-year old of years before was not at all lost on the eleven-year old. He still collected weapons...especially gun replicas that looked like the real thing. Most of his books were "shoot 'em up, cops and robbers, divorced detective, lives alone with beer cans all over the apartment, hungover in the opening scene ala *Smokey and the Bandit 2*...bloody bandaged and beat to hell but still gets his man in the end" type stories. Marc's main characters were pretty much modeled after Dirty Harry, Steve McQueen's Ralph "Papa" Thorson, and early Chuck Norris movies. They were always having cold pizza and warm beer for breakfast. I ate these books up, and soon began making my own. We both wanted to be filmmakers and directors and actors and writers and everything else. We were moving so fast that very often the hours of the day couldn't contain the time needed that our combined energies required. Days would be begin and end with us sitting at a table in Marc's TV room...The Cars and Blondie cranked from an 8-track player and the both of us turning out the most mind-blowing work.

To clarify, in order to avoid any confusion, these comics were not the same comics that Tommy and I would later refer to as the Locker Notes. These were different. These were a creative outlet shared between Marc and me. While other kids in the neighborhood were playing football, we were making comic books of our own original movies that we envisioned in our heads. We had no video cameras, crews or film budgets, so realistically we couldn't actually make movies...the comic books became our movies. I suppose if you work in Hollywood, what we were doing would probably amount to what are called storyboards.

The early comic books averaged around twenty pages. I think we began attempting to outdo each other with the length of each book, as every new project we took on grew fatter and fatter in your hands. Personally, I was into the epics. I loved long, slow unfolding movies. One of my own personal absurd creations was an imagined sequel to *Apocalypse Now* called *The Continuation*. It envisioned what happens to Martin Sheen's character after he kills Colonel Kurtz. Imagine Francis Ford Coppola finding out that some eleven-year old kid in Possum Dick, Suburbia committed such sacrilege to one of his masterpieces. For a couple of little kids, I must say that we were brilliant. It was a short-lived period in which two forces collided and stars burned so fucking brightly to the point where only memory leaves me scratching my head over how quickly it all burnt out. That kind of energy and perfect connection doesn't last, whatever it is in the arts...it's here and gone in a flash. That was the summer of 1980.

One of the things that I liked about Marc was that he wasn't into sports. I didn't mind *watching* sports, but I didn't like *playing* them. Even when Ritchie and I were doing our imaginary games, I could tolerate it. But once a real game happened, I wanted to go home. A lot of that could be blamed on school. I was never into the physical competition thing. And being yelled at by other students in gym all the time just made me hate it all the more. Which is why I was surprised when Marc asked me to join the Clara Barton Soccer League with him. How or why this came about still escapes me. We signed up during the summer, and the season would start coinciding with the new school year.

Sixth grade would start that September, and our comic book work quickly became popular among our classmates. My biggest fan was Alan Horowitz. He would read them and then wait impatiently for the next one. He was always asking for more. Alan was one of the brainier kids in the school, always reading Tolkien and all kinds of books that I still to this day have not read. Riley Stevens would even compliment me on my work. I would take even more of a liking to her that year, but I was just one of many. While Riley had become pretty, shapely and attractive, she was still cute and adorable. Most girls are one or the other. Riley could pull off both, and I had a thing for cute and adorable. When that sixth grade school year would begin, I'd have Riley in class with me. And for once, Marc would be in my class. And then... I thought that maybe...just maybe... Tommy and I would be in the same class. On the last day of fifth grade, it seemed that everybody I talked to about who their sixth grade teacher was going to be, they all said Mrs. Painter.

Tommy was just happy to be getting out of the tyrant Mr. Hardenberger's class, and he didn't care who he got for sixth grade. He had survived the worst. Yet, somehow, again, the stars were not aligned. Or maybe he had done something horrible in a past life that he was paying for. I thought of *Apocalypse Now* when Tommy showed me his new teacher's name handwritten in the sixth grade slot on his final report card. Like Captain Willard, it seemed, he must have wanted a mission.

And for his sins, they gave him one.

At Cypress, teachers were being shifted around. And just as Tommy thankfully exited Mr. Hardenberger's class, he'd find out that his sixth grade teacher would be none other than...Mr. Hardenberger.

———

Cheap Trick's *At Budokan* album had been out for a year by the time I was given a copy for my eleventh birthday, and it was during that year that I grew to love them just by what the local New York City rock station WPLJ had been playing. So when I unwrapped *At Budokan* and put it down on my turntable, it stayed there until Christmas Day when I got The Cars *Panorama*. 1980 for me was all about Cheap Trick, The Cars and Blondie. There would be lots of other music I would hear as well, such as Bruce Springsteen's *The River*, but that was downstairs in the living room where my dad was playing it.

My dad had just purchased a brand new Kenwood KX-1030 cassette deck, and we were both amazed at how we could record music off the radio. Much of the music I absorbed following my initial years of musical interest with Kiss, Led Zeppelin and the Stones, was through what my dad was taping off the radio. He had dozens and dozens of cassettes filled with Sixties and Seventies rock staples taped off WPLJ and WNEW. Through my dad's radio taping, I was introduced to bands and artists like Pink Floyd, Fleetwood Mac, Tom Petty, Joe Jackson, the Clash, the Kinks, Queen, Boston, Foreigner, Elvis Costello, Talking Heads, Patti Smith, the J. Geils Band, ELO and plenty of others. As for my interest in the Cars and Blondie, both were introduced to me by my older cousins a year earlier.

One of the more noticeable and annoying things that summer was the question, "Who Shot J.R.?" There was a TV show called *Dallas* that had been around for two or three seasons, and actor Larry Hagman played the star role...an oil baron named J.R. Ewing who was gunned down outside his office at the end of the recent season finale. The show went from a rather semi-popular weekly soap opera to an overnight pop culture phenomenon even as new episodes were no longer running. The show had gone into repeats of the previous season and new viewers were watching just to catch up on the storyline which would pick up in the coming fall. Everyone wanted to know who shot J.R. If you went to the beach or walked on the boardwalk anywhere along the Jersey shore, it was very common to see shirts that read "I Shot J.R." I didn't pay too much attention to all the J.R. fuss until later that summer, but admittedly, I too would become mildly interested in finding out who the hell did it.

Regardless of all the *Dallas* hysteria, it's the music I remember most about that summer. But that's usually the case with every summer. Summers are often measured and marked by the music in relation to our memories. That summer began with Blondie's "Call Me" playing on the radio every five minutes with "Funkytown" by Lipps Inc. taking its place. Elton John had "Little Jeanie" climbing the charts along with Billy Joel's "It's Still Rock and Roll to Me, Bette Midler's "The Rose," and a one-hit wonder named Rocky Burnette who was tired of toein' the line. The song that was probably the most unavoidable was Olivia Newton John's "Magic" from a movie called *Xanadu*, and even though I was a rock fan and wasn't supposed to like anything wimpishly un-rock, I was secretly in love with "Magic." Paul McCartney also had a huge song called "Coming Up," which kind of took advantage of the dance trend that was still somewhat going strong, even though disco had already been declared dead. Still, even with McCartney's latest solo album on the charts, there were always the ever-present rumors of a Beatles reunion, which none of them would ever confirm. The other rumor going around much later in the summer was that John Lennon had entered the recording studio for the first time in over five years to record a new album. This news we'd hear from time to time over the radio. The Fab Four may not have been working together any longer, but it was still good to have them around.

———

On a rather warm and muggy night, we were all going to go see the long awaited *Star Wars* sequel, *The Empire Strikes Back*, which was breaking all kinds of box office records. There were always lines outside the theater, and the idea was to go as early as possible or at least get your tickets ahead of time. Franklin and I sat on my front stairs waiting for Tommy's dad to drive around the block in his big brown van to pick us up. My brother and Christopher at seven years of age were happy to be going out with us eleven-year olds. Unlike Tommy and me, Christopher and Franklin always shared the same class in the Cypress school. It was a rare night for everyone. Friends and brothers alike were all going out together...and man, were we psyched. Across the street, Nadine Allen was verbally assaulting her husband.

"Hurry up, George, I aint got all fucking night!"

"I'm going, Nadine!"

"And make sure you get the Sweet 'n Low!"

"Nadine, I can't have Sweet..."

"Just GET IT George!"

We all looked at each other and knew we were about to be entertained before the movie. George Allen got into his Ford Pinto and turned the ignition into its booming explosive starting. Nadine Allen, with her hand on her hips, stood on her front stairs watching him…shaking her head.

"Fuckin' son of a bitch!" she exclaimed, turning around and walking back into her house as George began to drive up the street.

———

The big brown van turned around the corner of Sycamore and headed down the street. As we watched it coming toward us, I saw the group of older kids walking toward the Forbidden Zone. For once, I enjoyed the thought of being young. I don't think I would have preferred anything else that night aside from going to see *The Empire Strikes Back*. The three of us jumped up from the stairs and began walking to meet the van as it began to slow down. Then without warning, it happened.

BAM!!

KA-KRACKECK!!

KA-KRUNK!!

Big Tom and George Allen drove right into each other head-on.

"Holy shit! What the hell do you think you're doing you asshole?" my little brother screamed at George.

We stopped in our tracks. There was an extended moment of silence and stillness.

"Ohhhhh Shhiiiiiittt!!" Big Tom cried.

Almost immediately on impact, George threw his door open and ran back towards his house.

"Nadine!" he screamed. "Naaadeeeeeen!!"

We all watched him as if he were some ridiculous character in a TV sitcom.

"Naaadeeeeeen! I just had an accident!"

My cackling brother fell to the ground as the hysterics began on our side of the street.

"Franklin, come inside the house!" my mom ordered from the front door. He sat down on the bottom step, ignoring her.

"Franklin, I'm talking to you. I said...get inside the house!"

"But I don't wanna go in the house," he pleaded.

"Now!" she charged.

"But I wanna watch the accident!"

From across the street we could hear Nadine yelling something from inside the Allen house as George very quickly made his way back to the accident. Big Tom was standing on the side of the two vehicles looking for damage when George approached him.

"It doesn't look like anything," he told George.

"Mmmmm...what about the bumpers?" George inquired, pointing at the fact that the two vehicle's bumpers were literally locked into each other. The top of George's bumper was stuck under the bottom of Big Tom's bumper.

"Oh crap," Big Tom chuckled nervously. He peeked into his van.

"Alright, everybody out! Let's go!"

He slid open the side door, and Tommy, Christopher and Jay Sacco all fell out laughing.

"Go over by your friends!" he yelled pointing to Franklin and me, who were now sitting on the front steps watching. My mother came out and stood at the top of the stairs.

"Franklin...I'm not going to say it again. Come in the house."

"But I didn't do anything!"

"He's okay," I cut in.

"Eugene, watch him!" she said and went back inside.

Mom could be overprotective at times. Sometimes it was to the point that it could be embarrassing if friends were around, not to mention suffocating. The situation couldn't have improved or gotten any worse if Franklin had gone in the house, nor would he have been in any danger or scarred and corrupted for life if he had stayed outside. Sometimes a parent's overprotective nature is just excess karmic fear boiling over from some traumatic experience that came earlier in their own life. Granted, he was only seven. But I was still only eleven. That right there is one of the disadvantages of being the older brother. No matter how young you are, you're still older and have to take the responsibility for whatever happens.

Out in the street, Big Tom pushed down on George Allen's bumper, trying to rock the Pinto and pry the two vehicles apart. George Allen stood by, nervously. A gathering of neighbors emerged from all surrounding front doors, converging on front lawns and sidewalks to watch the latest Sycamore spectacle. We all sat amused, quietly joking amongst each other. It wasn't so much the fact that the bumpers were locked, as much as the fact that it was George Allen who Big Tom had hit that made the whole thing funny. George Allen had enough problems. He had been innocently driving up the street. Either one of them could have been at fault, I guess. Neither one moved to the side to let the other pass. It was a head-on chicken collision. But George Allen was rather gullible and unstable enough to believe that he had caused the end of the world. His self-induced unworthiness and lack of self-respect was the result of years and years of abusive conditioning and narcissistic gaslighting by his wife.

And now here was the end of the world.

There was desperation in his face.

"Oooooooooooooooooooh, how are we gonna get the bumpers apart?" he wailed, panicking like a child.

Tommy and I quietly got up and went into the house. A minute later, we reappeared with a drawing pad and colored pencils. By that time, George Allen was standing on the hood of his car and jumping up and down on it. The high-pitched laughter of Franklin and Christopher reverberated throughout the block as George bounced up and down trying to shake his car loose.

"Nadeeeeeen!" he yelled as he stomped. "Nadeeeeeen! The car's stuck!"

Our little brothers were in the grass rolling around in stitches while Tommy and I exerted a little more restrain in containing our laughter. We were about to get down to our own business.

"Nadeeeeeen!"

George continued screeching as he pounced on his Ford Pinto.

"The car's stuck!"

For a second, he stopped jumping long enough to unbutton his shirt and take it off, revealing an overly hairy chest and breasts larger than his wife's. He clearly could have used a bra. He threw the shirt into the street and began to bounce on the car again. This time his big tits bounced with him.

"Nadeeeeeen!"

He bounced and bounced and bounced to no avail. By this time, Big Tom just stepped to the side and looked over at us, smiled and shook his head.

"Nadeeeeeen!" George wailed, his voice shaking with his body. "The car's stuck!"

Then she came out.

"WHAT THE HELL ARE YOU DOIN' GEORGE?!!!!"

The horrendous shriek of a voice came from the Allen's front lawn, as Nadine finally came out of the house to see her idiotic husband embarrassing himself in front of the entire block. Standing on her front lawn she turned to see Vinnie Giovanni pulling up in his baby blue Lincoln Continental Mark V. She made eye contact with Vinnie and shook her head. Chomping on a cigar he winked and gave her a knowing smile without even having surveyed the scene. He parked, got out and sauntered slowly...moving two houses up to the cars. George didn't notice Vinnie watching him pounce away. When he saw the two cars locked together and then looked at George on top of the hood, the famous Vinnie Giovanni smile came out...which resembled that of a Maltese baring its teeth. Big Tom walked over to him.

"Can you believe this?"

"This is your van?" Vinnie said, stating it more so than asking it.

"Yeah, I drove into him," Big Tom said, almost starting to grin.

"You hit George's Pinto?" Vinnie asked, his smile growing wider.

"Yeah."

"And it didn't explode?"

"Not yet."

"Does he think he's gonna help this situation by jumping like that?"

"I don't know what he thinks. He thinks it's the end of the world, I know *that*."

"Jezzu-Chreest!" Vinnie exclaimed.

"I don't know how much longer he's gonna do this."

"Fuck this. Ya want a beer?"

"Sure."

"Come on. Hey, Rose...put the chairs out! Who wants a beer?"

And so everyone headed over with Vinnie to grab a beer and watch the drama from the Giovanni's front yard for what had become yet another neighborhood event. Tommy and I stayed on the front stairs, where each of us had torn out a piece of paper from the drawing pad. Big Tom glanced over at us inquisitively.

"What are you guys doing?" he inquired.

"Drawing the accident," Tommy said without looking up, a smile plastered on his face.

As the adults walked two houses down, Vinnie, in his gravelly Brooklyn accent, lovingly called over to George who was still on top of his Pinto.

"Hey cocksucker...when you're done jumping on the car, come and have a beer!"

Needless to say, we missed the movie. The beer and communal gathering were more important to the adults and our drawing was more important to us, and we were all much too invested in the moment to care. We ended up seeing the movie the next night anyway.

"Hey, I'll draw the guy with the big tits bouncing, and you draw the ugly bitch yelling." Tommy said to me.

"Okay," I said.

Jay just sat laughing as he watched us drawing this crazy event that had just happened.

"You guys are messed up."

He shook his head in half amusement and half disbelief. I suppose the idea of drawing pictures of crazy things that happened during our childhoods was indeed a little deranged. But it was precisely our deranged sense of humor that set Tommy and me apart from everyone else. It was as if we both functioned on the same warped mind and reacted to things with the same singular sick sense of humor...as if one demented brain controlled both of us at the same time. These are the pictures we drew of this and previous other sidesplitting neighborhood occurrences that accented and adorned our memories of growing up in Oakwoods. These would be the Locker Notes. These would be the works of art that graced the inside of the locker that we would share when we got older. And all of those years of being apart in separate classes would be compensated for. Even the thought of having a schedule...one where we switched classes every 45 minutes, where there were eight classes a day...they were eight more chances to be in the same class. And it was something to look forward to. These uproarious experiences throughout our childhood would be preserved through the Locker Notes. As we'd get even older and into high school, the Locker Notes would take on evolving levels of maturity, but nonetheless remain hilarious inside jokes. That night however, was still a long way from all of that. The reality was that we still had one more year at Cypress, and Tommy had to endure Mr. Hardenberger all over again. I didn't see him too much that summer after the movie because he was hanging out with Jay and I was hanging out with Marc. But whenever I did see him, he made it a point to whine about the upcoming school year.

That night was also the last of countless summer nights that our block would gather in the same way, as Vinnie Giovanni would be tragically killed by a falling air conditioner while walking on the Upper East Side of Manhattan the very next day. Besides being an unspeakable shock to Rose and her family, the incident would wreak havoc on Sycamore for weeks to come, as nobody could figure out the answers to questions that arose like how such a thing could happen. Was the air conditioner dropped? Was it not secured properly? Was it thrown? What was Vinnie doing on the Upper East Side? All we knew was that an air conditioner fell from a 15-story window and clunked him on the head. Our parents all gathered for nights discussing it... trying to imagine it and even recreate it in their bickering over just how the heck it happened. They argued and fought over it. And while the adults completely lost their shit, Tommy and I refrained from making a Locker Note out of the tragedy. Neither of us had the heart to draw a picture of the falling air conditioner, nor of Vinnie getting smashed in the head with it...so instead, we drew pictures of all the angry adults screaming at each other over it. Still, all of these troubles were in the near and distant future. On this night however, it was one of those treasured occasions when everyone was together...those moments that were so easy to take for granted. George was pouncing on his car, Vinnie was still alive with his head still intact, the adults were festive and Tommy and I were in the zone. And so our initial plan of seeing a movie was thwarted when some other unforeseen event took place...one that was nonetheless entertaining. In those days, we lived in the moment. So we made the best of it. We always did.

7

The Feast

The St. Rocco's Feast was a yearly staple to the summertime. Every year in mid-August my family and Tommy's family gathered in the streets of the Peterstown section of Elizabeth to attend the annual event. Sometimes we did it together and other years we didn't. It was a major happening though, that beautifully decorated the sentimental stretches of childhood…those memories that are never too painful to recall and only bring a warm fondness, and perhaps at worst, a sad longing for the past. Peterstown was also known as the Burg and was predominately Italian during the 1970s and early 1980s. Our parents grew up there, and as I mentioned earlier, our grandparents and much of our extended families lived there. It is a town that irradiates the vast reaches of personal recollection just as much as our hometown of Oakwoods. Many weekends were spent there, as Franklin and I would often fight over who got to sleep over our grandparents' house. Many a Friday night was spent with them

visiting us. We'd sit out in the backyard during the summertime...
sometimes barbecuing and sometimes just ordering a pizza. We'd
sit there until it got dark out, and then we'd sit there even longer...
the adults talking nonstop while we played, teased each other and
horsed around until we'd inevitably get yelled at. My dad's stereo was
always going at night, and whenever our grandparents were over, the
default music was always ABBA or Engelbert Humperdinck. We had
woods behind our house, and bats would often fly out and straight
up to the house before turning back. For years we thought they were
birds and then one day we found out they were bats. Between the
bats, the pulsing flicker of the lightning bugs and everything else flying around, there was far more movement in the air than there was
on the ground. The static whiz of the bug zapper always provided
background noise in addition to the music or whenever the music
wasn't playing. The bug zapper stuck out of the ground like a lamp
post but was far more deceiving...luring all the pesky little flying in-
sects into its harsh, antiseptic light and electrocuting the shit out of
them. Bug zappers were pretty popular for a short time before anyone realized what sadistic inventions they really were. Nevertheless,
it was the sound of summer on Sycamore. All of that aside, Friday
night's visit would end with Franklin or me going home with our
grandparents for a weekend sleepover.

Peterstown was full of old people. It was a grandparents' town.
We figured because our grandparents lived there, everybody's
grandparents must live there. It was full of streets made up of houses
standing closely together, most of which were without front lawns
or backyards and separated only by narrow alleys. Some houses
had driveways with no garage and some had a garage with no drive-

way. Unlike the suburb of Oakwoods, no two houses were the same. The neighborhood was much older than Oakwoods and contained a built-in sense of history about it, even if I didn't know what that history was. Every street was filled with the Italian language and there seemed to be a deli or small food store on every corner. Staple landmarks of Peterstown included DiCosmo's Italian Ice, Saraceno's Bakery, Spirito's Restaurant and St. Anthony's Church. In between were countless little stores that seemed to be frozen in a 1950s time warp, but still felt warm and welcoming. My grandfather would take me on walks and stop in to any one of the stores to pick up his daily *Il Progresso*. He'd buy me Tic Tacs and always had a piece of Juicy Fruit gum for me. If we went to the store on the corner of Second and Amity, the one with the big Coca Cola sign hanging over the sidewalk, I knew I'd be in for a treat because it was the only store where I could get Dynamints. Sometimes on days when he didn't feel like walking, he'd send me out to get him his newspaper and a pack of L&Ms, which I used to love opening for him because I couldn't get enough of the smell of unlit cigarettes. Then he'd scold me for holding the pack up to my nose.

Speaking of smells, there was a distinctive odor that pervaded throughout Peterstown...a chemical scent that wasn't good but wasn't necessarily foul either. It just became the air you breathed, and you didn't think too much about it. I imagined it as a combination of paint and coffee. In reality, it was the characteristic symptoms of existing in the shadow of the Bayway refinery, which itself sat in the middle of a large industrial wasteland that haunted Exit 13 of the New Jersey Turnpike. There was also the overpowering presence of the Tenco plant in nearby Linden on the opposite side of Route

1. The smell of Peterstown couldn't be traced to any one direct culprit, but the conglomeration of scents was unique. Days were also highlighted by trips to the open-air outdoor market which took up entire blocks on the outskirts of Peterstown...vendors selling fresh fruits and vegetables amidst an unmistakably pleasant sense of Old World community, fellowship, kinship and an unspoken feeling of age-old wisdom that accompanied the entire experience. These are the little things that you couldn't bottle or contain. Some can be preserved I suppose through photographs, but most tend to slip away if we're not careful with how we treat and process these moments. And if we're lucky, we can still access them through memories... even if most have faded to mere still images. They exist as tiny snapshots...little mysteries with enough familiarity to be a source of comfort to those who may *find* such comfort in the past. Not everyone is blessed with a direct conduit that allows such access to time and space...and not everyone is cursed with it. Some memories are just too painful and unsettling for people to want to remember. Not everybody's story has unfolded the same. Some stories unfurl through a generous grace and some through a fierce grace. Smell is a funny thing though. Smell in itself can locate lost time and space. It can transport you back. Music is another way back. But believe it or not, there's not much music that connects me to Peterstown. I remember my uncle driving a blue Duster for a short period. I remember him standing outside my grandparents' house and Thin Lizzy's "The Boys Are Back in Town" was playing. I wasn't outside with him...I was watching him through an upstairs window. I was maybe six or seven at the most. But I associate that song with the still image of him with his blue Duster through the window. For me, it's the sense

of smell that connects me back to Peterstown…smells such as those of the St. Rocco's Feast.

The veneration of saints is one of the staple customs that many branches of the major world religions share in common and carry over from centuries past. St. Rocco was a French Franciscan monk who lived during the fourteenth century who was roaming around the Basilicata region of Southern Italy during the Black Death in 1348. He was said to have cured many Italians on their death beds by making the sign of the cross over their bodies. The Feast of St. Rocco was an annual tradition in Peterstown that took place over a ten-day period during the second and third weeks of August and it was just as much a part of summer as anything that went on in Oakwoods or in any of the beach towns we'd visit like Wildwood. The feast celebrating St. Rocco was known to us simply as "the feast." As kids, we didn't really think about St. Rocco or who he was, or what the religious or spiritual connections were. All we knew was that we were going to "the feast." Most other people referred to events like this as a carnival or a fair, and I remember Derrick Adler laughing at me because he overheard my mom saying that we were going to the feast.

The feast was a glorious occasion that to a little kid, transformed the gritty but homey landscape of the Peterstown streets into a magical wonderland of carnival music, streaming lights, rides, endless food stands, games, contests, raffle drawings, cotton candy and festive voices over loud speakers informing the rhythm of the night. The dominant majestic presence that permeated the square block between Second and Third Avenues and beyond was the fine aroma of sausage and peppers and zeppoles. This was holy food, and at least for a few hours a night for that week and a half, the Peterstown section of Elizabeth, New Jersey was home to the best cuisine in the world. This was the magnitude of which our imaginations were captured by this yearly event, which may not have seemed as monumental to an adult...but to a child, it was everything.

As the summer before sixth grade was waning in its last few weeks, the Feast of St. Rocco raged on. I spent most of the week staying in town and returned each night with different company. The first night with my parents, brother and grandparents...the next night with my uncle and soon-to-be aunt...the night after that, with Tommy and his grandparents, and on the final night when mom and dad came to pick me up, everyone went together. That night, I won a goldfish after shooting water into the clown mouth and popping the balloon. I gave it to Franklin who was much happier about it than I was. As we walked along South Seventh Street, Tommy who was almost a quarter of a block down, called over to me.

"Hey, check it out!"

He was standing at one of the number wheels that also have people's names between the numbers. The prize was a record of your choice. Tommy was pointing at one of the albums on the wall as the arrow spun round to land on a lucky winner. He wasn't playing, but he was waiting for me to catch up to him so he could show me something. When I got there, I immediately spotted it myself before he could even open his mouth. On the wall, next to a bunch of newly-released records...*Glasses Houses* by Billy Joel, *Saved* by Bob Dylan, *McCartney II* by Paul McCartney, *Different Kinda Different* by Johnny Mathis, the soundtrack to *Caddyshack*, *Full Moon* by the Charlie Daniels Band...was an album cover made up of a colorful comic strip and the eye-popping title...KISS *Unmasked*. It was an album that had already been out for two months, but with Kiss pretty much off our radars, news of a brand new album had escaped both of us. It had been a period of coincidences though because I saw them on ABC Eyewitness News about a week or two earlier when they played at a small club in New York City to introduce their new drummer.

"Whoah, what the heck is that?" Tommy roared.

"Is that a new album?" I asked, almost a little interested.

Our parents caught up to us.

"Kiss Unmasked!" Big Tom exclaimed. "Are they unmasking?"

"They don't *look* unmasked!" my dad said, smiling obnoxiously as he and Big Tom shared a mutual moment of both knowing they'd once gone through hell at a time when their kids had gone crazy with Kiss.

"Ya wanna play?" my mom asked, handing us quarters to put down on the next game.

We played, but didn't win the new Kiss album.

Somewhere on the outskirts of the park area where the feast took place, was a burst of fireworks, coming from some kids on Second Avenue. Our parents and grandparents all agreed that it was getting late and that we should probably head home. We all walked along Third Avenue in little clusters...the adults all together, Franklin and Christopher together, and me and Tommy way ahead because we walked much faster than everyone else. As we moved along, I drifted off deep into thought. I thought about how it didn't bother me in the least bit that there was a new Kiss record out that I didn't have. It didn't seem to bother Tommy either. I thought about how two years earlier, we both would have acted as if it were the end of the world until we both had that record in our hands. We probably would have insisted everyone play that game until somebody won. I thought to myself...quietly amazed at just how much I didn't care...not quite knowing anything about the concept of indifference or how time changes you...but just thinking how strange it was to not be so knee-jerk when it came to some of the things we once thought to be so important.

A block buster went off in the distance, rattling my attention back to the surface of total consciousness where everyone else was startled by the blast as well.

"Idiots," Big Tom called out.

"Hoodlums!" my mom screamed. "Where are their parents?"

"Riff raff!" my dad added. "They're all on drugs!"

As we crossed the street and came upon a corner store, Tommy stopped at the window.

"Woah, check this out!"

A round of fireworks blasted off, the source of the detonations now a few blocks behind us...the feast still raging.

I strolled up to the window and peered into the darkened store that was lit by the residual glowing of a street light shining in on a magazine rack in the front where the first thing I saw was a new issue of *People*. Pictured on the cover, was Kiss. A wind wafted in from the nearby port. In combination with the river, the port contributed greatly to the aromatic character of Peterstown which was now illuminated overhead while the sky exploded in the magic August night.

8

Dreams and Dread

On the much-dreaded last afternoon of summer break, I was hanging out with Richie on his front stairs. We both attended different schools but we both began on the same day and the dread was equal. The final day before school started was usually miserable and none of us really left our houses. Richie and I hadn't seen each other much that summer, but we were next door neighbors which probably accounts for us finding each other that day and trying to make the best of the situation. He had a baseball bat in his hand with a Mets batting helmet on his head but didn't feel like playing. I didn't feel like doing much of anything either, so we just sat there looking and feeling glum. It was Labor Day and I had just come from watching the Jerry Lewis Telethon that always ran for a little over 21 hours. I'd watch it in spurts here and there and always associated it with the beginning of a new school year. Bored, I looked out the window and saw Richie, so I went out to sit with him. As I got there, his older brother Carl came around the side of the house from the backyard with two of his friends having some sort of music argument about Black Sabbath and Blue Oyster Cult. These guys were diehard Blue Oyster Cult fans and began telling us how they had just gotten tickets for the Black Sabbath/Blue Oyster Cult concert at the Garden. One of them was suggesting that Sabbath should have been opening for Blue Oyster Cult because they weren't as commercially successful and that they had lost their popularity since they now had a new lead singer. The other friend countered it with the fact that Sabbath was around first and more legendary than Blue Oyster Cult. Then the first guy started going after Sabbath's new singer, a guy named Ronnie James Dio.

"He's ancient. Did you see him? He's nothing like Ozzy!"

"He's better than Ozzy!"

"No he's not...he doesn't even look rock and roll!"

"Yes he does. Are you crazy? He was in Rainbow! Have you even *heard* him?"

"The guy is four feet tall! He has a five-head instead of a forehead! He looks like Luigi the pizza guy! He's old!"

"Ozzy's a drunk...he's finished!"

"No, I heard he has a solo record coming out soon!"

"Ozzy is finished. Nobody is gonna care about Ozzy Osbourne going solo."

Then one of them stuck a magazine in my face.

"Kid, take a look at this guy. Who do you think is cooler...this guy or Ozzy Osbourne as the singer of Black Sabbath?

I didn't know what to say. I didn't know Black Sabbath's music other than "Iron Man," and I didn't have a visual in my mind of Ozzy

Osbourne. I also didn't know the names of the guys in Sabbath, so I really had no idea who Ozzy was. Carl's friend then showed me a picture of Ronnie James Dio, who to me, looked like the guy who served the sausage and pepper sandwiches at the St. Rocco's Feast. There was no way I could be objective about it.

On the much-dreaded last night of summer break, Franklin and I were in the back seat of the car as our parents drove home from the mall. They had just gotten us brand new haircuts, which for me meant humiliation and embarrassment upon entering school the next day. We always went to an old French guy named Pierre who had snow white hair, leathery skin from too much sun and wore flowery blue and periwinkle button-down shirts with huge collars and blue polyester pants...always blue or some offshoot of blue. He was usually standing outside the Unisex on the first floor of the mall smoking a cigarette, and as soon as he was done with our haircuts, he'd run back outside to light another cigarette before we even left. This was back when smoking was permitted in places like shopping malls, stores, restaurants and movie theaters. It's difficult to imagine when it was common to see cigarette butts all over the floor inside public establishments such as these, but it was actually the norm at one time.

Upon turning onto our street while returning home from the mall, my dad drove slowly toward our house. As we got closer, I noticed something sticking out of the garbage can. Even from halfway down the block amidst the darkness of night, I saw it.

Is that what I think it is?

I was stricken with a sudden case of nerves as I leaned forward trying to peer around the back of my mom's head.

No, it can't be.

Oh my God.

It is!

It was kind of hard to mistake the leaves of the pot plant sticking out of our garbage can as we pulled up in front of the house. I immediately thought of the older kids who walked the neighborhood all hours of the night and of the kids my own age who hung around with some of them.

Well, I had no way of knowing if those same kids had dropped a pot plant into our garbage can, but given the natural guilt complex that I always seemed to have, I instantly felt like my dad was going to recognize the plant for what it was, blame those kids and somehow connect me to them. In other words, as innocent as I was sitting in the backseat of a car while seeing some marijuana from a mile away before anybody else did, I still felt as if I was about to get in trouble. Before anybody could say anything as we pulled up and backed in alongside the garbage can, I called out, "What's that in the garbage can?"

"I know what that is," my dad said calmly, while parking along the curb. "Some riff raff must have been running from the cops or something and threw their drugs in my garbage can."

This is the kind of paranoia and fear under which I would begin to live with, as sixth grade would initiate a new era that somehow through no fault of my own, always felt dangerous.

———

On the much-dreaded last night of summer break, I got into bed and surprisingly fell asleep quickly and peacefully. While asleep, I had a dream that Ronnie James Dio worked at Luigi's Pizza. In the dream, I went into Luigi's with Franklin to pick up a large Sicilian pie that we ordered over the phone. Mom stayed in the car while Franklin and I went inside. While we waited for Luigi to take our pizza out of the oven, Dio was next to him kneading flour into dough. He was wearing all white and didn't have long hair like I had seen in the magazine. He just looked like a friendly little Italian guy with a receding hairline, pressing his hands into the dough and smiling at us. The sound of the door being pulled open violently stunned everyone inside, and the look on Dio's face was one of great concern. I then turned around to see two scary-looking men dressed in suits and trench coats. It was one of those dreams where you know it's about to take a bad turn, and you try waking yourself up before the horror unfolds. I shielded by brother as if the two men had already revealed any sort of threat, and we began to run out of the pizza parlor. As I reached for the door, we heard gunshots and screaming. We made it outside, but mom's car wasn't there. Grabbing Franklin by the hand, I began running while he picked up his pace and ran with me. For some reason, we ended up behind the strip mall where there were nothing but dumpsters and loading docks. That's when we saw mom pull around the corner frantically, as if she knew something was going on. We approached the car with the sound of sprinting footsteps coming hard and fast around the corner. I pushed Franklin into the car and turned to see Dio coming toward us. The strange and totally warped part about it is that he was no longer Dio...but had somehow morphed into Mr. Hardenberger. What was even more terrifying was that when I heard more footsteps,

I expected to see the two men rounding the corner as well, but instead I felt a presence creeping in on me close up...almost breathing down my neck when I turned to see one of the men standing right behind me...pointing the gun at this non-descript pizza guy who had been both a rock star and a teacher within seconds of each other. As the man aimed his gun to shoot this person, he looked at me and smiled with nothing but the white of his eyes piercing through me.

———

On the much-dreaded last night of summer break, Tommy Dewhirst was in a dreadful mood. A little before bedtime, he went down into the basement to feed his animals. First he fed the fish. Tank by tank, he dumped their late dinner into the water. Then he went across the room to feed some goldfish to his Oscar. He did this methodically and without thinking. His mind was elsewhere. He couldn't bear the thought of another year with Mr. Hardenberger. Why was this happening to him, he wondered. It's not fair, he thought. He took a goldfish in his hand and he tossed it into the Oscar tank. The goldfish tank served no other purpose than to hold food for the Oscar. They may as well have worn a uniform with a number. I often referred to the goldfish tank as Death Row. He then went over to his king snake. He peered at it through the glass. He stared and stared and stared and stared until he could no longer see it. All he could see was Mr. Hardenberger. His face was virtually pressed up against the glass as the snake lifted its head and glanced at him.

"Line up to go to music," the snake said, looking Tommy directly in the eye. "I don't wanna hear one peep from any of you while we walk down there," it continued. "If you make me mad, I'll see that you guys stay in lunchtime!"

The snake was pissed off, and it continued with its derision as Tommy, now demoralized, looked down at the floor.

"What are you laughing at? You think it's funny? You'll see how funny it is when you get into the junior high! You'll think I was a party! I'll fix you, you little piece of..."

"I wasn't laughing!" Tommy squealed defensively. He got up and walked away, ignoring the snake as it continued.

"You had better buckle down. You better shape up or ship out Mr. Dewhirst! Your feet are going to be on the ground, you little shit!"

His oldest turtle Shit Box was next. When he went over to the tank, he was nauseated by what he found. He looked for Shit Box, but he couldn't find him. All he found was a pile of gloppy goo sitting right where Shit Box usually sat.

Through the glass of its tank, the snake chimed in.

"Yep! That's him. He couldn't take it no more, so he split." It then dawned on Tommy that the gloppy goo he was looking at was Shit Box's insides. The turtle had walked right out of its own shell in an apparent suicide and literally ripped itself apart. This wasn't good. It was a bad omen or something.

"Life in a shell," the snake taunted. "What a miserable existence! At least I can shed my skin!"

Tommy sat down on the floor. The snake wasn't finished.

"And you...you little shit! You better watch yourself in myyyyy class! You'd better show respect for what you don't know about. You'd better fear me! IIIII'lllll make you very afraid of me. IIIIII'lllll give you reeeeezon to be afraid!"

School couldn't start tomorrow...it just couldn't! But it must have been in the stars. It just wasn't good. He'd have to ride the year out and hope for better the next year. He went to bed thinking about what the next ten months were going to be like, already mourning the loss of summer break. All he wanted was to go out and play baseball. Go fishing. Listen to music...anything. It had been a good summer, but school always hung over his head. He lay in bed staring up at the ceiling. This Hardenberger thing two years in a row was unacceptable. What else could he do though? This wasn't like the twenty-first century where a kid could just request a transfer to a different class. You got what they fucking gave you...period. There was often anxiety on the night before school started, but this was nothing less than absolute dread.

Okay.

Try to look on the bright side, he thought to himself. That's part of the lesson often taught on shows like The Brady Bunch and the Flintstones. Look on the bright side.

At least it was the last year at Cypress.

It couldn't be that bad he thought, trying to convince himself.

Could it?

As he lay in the darkness, Tommy closed his eyes. The ever-present hum of humanity buzzed on, just outside his window. Some teenagers in the distance could be heard with their voices trailing away as they headed toward the Forbidden Zone. Tommy was too entranced by his own thoughts to be concerned. There on the farthest edges of summer, he began to drift off.

———

The Locker Notes

"Hey look," cried the sixth grade student. "Here comes Mr. Hardenberger. Get in line."

Another student cuts in, "It's not Hardenberger, it's Cheeseburger!"

A roar of laughter encompasses the playground.

In the classroom, the teacher is fuming already.

"Take your chairs off your desks," he barks.

The students noisily remove their chairs from the top of their desks.

"Shut up!!" the teacher cries. He goes to the podium.

"Stand up and salute the flag! Ready? Begin!" he wails as the class begins in unison:

> I pledge allegiance to the flaggeg
> of the United States of Amewawa
> And to the rePUBlic
> for which it stands
> one nation
> under God
> indivisiBELL
> with liberty and justice...for present!

"Shut up!!" the teacher cries again. Then the singing begins.

> My country 'tis of thee
> sweet land of poverty
> of thee I sing
> land where our fathers went
> and all the money they spent

on beer and whiskey

in every bar they went

Silence.

"Just for that I'll see that you guys stay in lunchtime and don't go out on the playground! You guys had better shape up or ship out! You think you got it bad now? Just wait 'til they get you in the Junior High!"

A girl in the back of the rooom raises her hand.

"Whatta you want, goddamn it?!" the teacher belches.

"Can I get a drink?"

The teacher walks over to her.

"No Jenny, you cannot get a drrriinnnnk. Because then there's gonna be a big parade to the fountain and I don't think it's necessary for 25 people to get a drink at the same time!"

Ten minutes later: "If I let you get a drink, I have to let everybody get a drrriinnnk!"

Half hour later: "Are you thirsty? Or do you just wanna waste tiiiime?!!"

One hour later: "...AND THAT'S WHY YOU SHOULDN'T DRINK!!!!"

"Now! Line up and go to music!" the angry teacher instructs the class. Little Louis calls over to Bobby, "Bobby, front seats back seats!"

"Shut uhhhp!!" they hear from the nasty man's vile mouth.

As the class tries unsuccessfully to line up single file, there is mutiny.

"I get in front," Louis yells.

Johnny is having none of it.

"No, ME!!" he cries and pushes his way to the front.

"The both of you guys get in the back! And if I hear another word, we'll march right baaaaack!!" The teacher is not happy.

"Boys, hand out books!" Miss Tripe exclaims to the boys in music class. Little Jimbo jumps to his feet to secure the books that he will pass out to the class. Some other boys go to the cubby holes at the front of the room to help with the books. Those books...those big smelly music books...a series called *Making Music Your Own*. Each grade was a different color. Every year, you'd see those colored books at the front of the room and know that you'd eventually use all of them...just like the unit buildings. When you're a little miniscule turd on his first day of kindergarten, and you see all those unit buildings spread out across the vast blacktop of Cypress Estates, each for a different grade, you know that someday you'd make it into each one. This was the Cypress stepladder of achievement...the totem pole of seniority. It was all accompanied by the knowledge that you were getting older with every building and every grade. There was that feeling of superiority over the kids who were now beneath you in grade level and age. You were now using the sixth grade music books, and this year you would be king.

Miss Tripe puts the 33 1/3 piece of vinyl onto the Univox. The kids sit waiting. The record crackles and pops and farts away. The music begins.

Lift off!

Ground Control to Major Tom!

The teacher begins to walk down the first aisle. She smiles pleasantly and swings her arms like a conductor. Her cheeks are smeared obnoxiously with rouge. She wears hideous bright red lipstick...lips puckered. She resembles a walking blowup doll in a polyester suit. The girls sing while the boys laugh. They parody the music.

"Oh, I wish I was Mr. Steven's son," Louis sings.

"Getting paid everyday!" Johnny Jabubowitz cuts in.

"He knocked me down with the end of a spar! Pay me my money down!" Louis croons mockingly. "Pay me! Pay me! Oh yeah! Pay me my bingy down..."

Tommy cuts in...

"...Yes, he knocked me down with the end of his rod! Pay me my money down!!"

The teacher's arms sway violently. The blubber jingles and jangles from side to side to the music.

"Scratch scratch me back...scratch scratch me back...it really is a fact...the less I itch...the more I scratch!!!"

Tommy is out of control. With each song, the absurdity of the situation increases as the chaos unfolds.

Tommy, now screaming above the class:

"And it was that good old electric washing machine. And I sure do miss those puddles of urine...stinking up the floor. Yes I do! I do!!!"

The rotund music teacher, clad in polyester vest and slacks, rolls up the next aisle. One can hear the faint sound of her voice singing along. She knows the songs well. She hears them several times a day...class after class after class. *Does she walk the aisles in every class?* One wonders. Doesn't she get tired? Does she have to be the conductor in every class?

Sit down!
Relax and let us sing!
You have nothing to prove!
We KNOW you're the teacher!
Sit DOWN and shut the fuck UP!!
AND PUT THAT FUCKING ARM DOWN!!!
...AND THE NEST ON THE BRANCH, AND THE BRANCH ON THE BOUGH, AND THE BOUGH IN THE TREE, AND THE TREE IN THE BOG AND THE BOG DOWN IN THE VALLEY...

Oh, the rattlin' bog was a-boggin' away when Georgie and Liza pulled up, and Georgie was a-bitchin' about a bucket.

"There's a hole in the bucket dear Liza, dear Liza...there's a hole in the bucket dear Liza...a hole!"

"And what kind of song might this be anyway? What is this? What about the Cars? I wanna hear "Candy-O!"

The teacher keeps walking and swinging her arms around, oblivious to the rest of the class.

Somebody peeks their head into the room.

"What happened to the GREEEEN books?!! What about Eleanor Rigby? What about Father Mackenzie wiping the shit from his hands as he walks from the bowl? Nobody flushed it!"

The voices stop singing and screaming.

You roll over in your sleep.

In the lunchroom, Louis asks Jimbo why the chicken crossed the road.

"Why Louis?" Jimbo asks.

"To get to the other side."

The two little shitstains break out into a raging fit of laughter that shakes the table into a wave of sound that carries and spreads from table to table like dominos. As the principal walks in to talk to the lunch aide, the noise reaches its climax, but is still not loud enough to drown out his voice.

"Ourrum rrruugarrawarf," he says above the noise.

The kids are relentless.

Now the whole room is screaming.

"Aarrrrmm!Ouuummaarrrrggrrrrrmrrrrrrruuurrrruuurrrr!!

Rrrruugaroaragrum sprarffaganarum! Aurrrgggrumm!! Arrrrg-ggrrrrrrggggrggrrr!!"

All of this proves too much for the seething janitor.

"HEY!!"

The voices stop.

You wake up.

The only thing worse than dreaming an entire school day is waking up to find that it's time to get up and go to school. With that thought, Tommy Dewhirst got out of bed, brushed his teeth, put on his clothes, ate a bowl of Count Chocula, took a crap, wiped his ass, left the house and went to school.

PART TWO

Through the Veil of
the Invisible Screen

9

Soccer and Smoke

When sixth grade finally started, I was filled with a mounting sense of both excitement and tension regarding the fact that it would be the final year at Cypress, as well as the seemingly "best of" assortment of students surrounding me. By that, I mean the class was an eclectic mix of strong identities whether they were the tough kids, nerdy kids, invisible kids, jocks, popular girls, nasty demonic girls and what have you. Everyone's reputation had been established over the years, and I found myself surrounded by Riley Stevens, Ashley Drake, Sharon Redshaw, Johnny Felix, Alan Horowitz, Jake Kennedy, Kevin Weir, as well as one of my best friends, Marc. Luckily, my only real detractor was Ashley Drake, and aside from her and the unknown outcome of having Weir as a classmate, I didn't anticipate much trouble...as if that weren't enough.

We did absolutely nothing that first day. The teacher's strike had thrown everything into disarray at the outset. In the morning, the sub took attendance and went through the motions with all the pre-liminary stuff, handing out textbooks and all of that junk. Sitting all around me were plenty of familiar faces. The sub did not assign seats, so for the time being we were allowed to sit where we wanted. Marc sat next to me, and Michael Covino sat on the other side of me. He was a funny little roly poly of a kid. You couldn't not like him. Sharon Redshaw, a girl quickly developing the body of a high school student sat in front of me. She loved Led Zeppelin and always made for good rock and roll talk. In front of her was Johnny Felix . Johnny was one of the brainier kids in class, and although he was often subject to teasing, he was very friendly and well-liked. He was in a way, the class mascot. I mean that in a good way. At the top of the row was Ashley Drake.

Good, I thought.

Let the snotrag stay there.

As long as she wasn't anywhere near me.

Next to her was Jake Kennedy. Of course Kennedy was famous for kicking the ball on the roof during lunchtime kickball games. He got along with the popular and the unpopular. Everybody wanted him on their team. Kevin Weir even admired his abilities. A tiny kid with monstrous power who commanded respect.

Jay Sacco, who had become good friends with Tommy over the years, was also in my class for the first time. Kevin Weir sat on the other side of the room surrounded by some girls. I was relieved that Kevin and the girls were preoccupied with each other, and that any immediate contact with any of them didn't seem to be on the hori-zon. I was glad that the sub let us sit where we wanted, and that the natural shape of the room found itself through us kids being left to our own devices. Before we knew it, it was lunchtime.

During lunch, everyone was comparing notes on their classes and their subs. There was a lot of talk about the strike, as well as all kinds of speculation as to how long it would be, and how unsettled things would be. It was an overall feeling of being in limbo. Still, it all seemed like an adventure, not knowing what was going to happen. Tommy was especially happy about the strike, as he was in no rush to begin another year with Mr. Hardenberger. The crowd in the lunchroom was especially loud that day, as Mr. Zielinski, the new vice principal walked in. We'd never had a vice principal at Cypress, and we didn't see why we needed one now. This guy was a midget John Wayne. He didn't walk, he swaggered. While he swaggered, he clipped his thumb over his belt buckle. He came across as a bad ass, probably hoping to intimidate the kids, marking his territory early on. In actuality, he looked like a pathetic, aging and decrepit small man trying to act tough. While he acted like John Wayne, he actually resembled a *Towering Inferno*-era William Holden, minus 14 inches in height. He stood at the front of the All Purpose Room and stared around the room from table to table, not saying anything. When he finally did speak, we got a good old fashioned New Yawk accent. Johnny Felix had raised his hand, asking to go to the water fountain, and Mr. Zielinski told him, "No brother John, you may not get up and drink wawdah."

That afternoon, the sub gathered the class in the front corner of the room. We all sat on the floor and talked, sharing random stories about the past summer. It was a very relaxed setting, and despite the anticipated negativity on several fronts, everybody seemed to gravitate towards the people they most got along with. The only problem during those first few weeks was the lack of consistency due to the fact that they couldn't find a sub to stay with us for longer than two days. We had around ten subs during the strike and because nobody was really setting the tone and implementing any sort of curriculum, we didn't have much homework or even class work for that matter. I remember we played a lot of silent ball during class hours.

When sixth grade started, one of the things that coincided was the announcement of Led Zeppelin's U.S. tour. They'd be playing Madison Square Garden in November. I wanted tickets, but being only eleven years old, there was no way I even knew how to go about getting them. So I asked my mom. Now, mind you, she took a part-time job in the mid 1970s working the Ticketron in Bamberger's department store. She remembered how in 1975, restless Zeppelin fans broke down the glass doors while waiting in line for tickets to their Garden shows. She referred to bands like Zeppelin, Kiss and anything rock and roll as "animals." She considered their fans to be worse. I remember she made a phone call, perhaps a fake one, and then hung up. No tickets available. I don't think she really intended to send me to a Zeppelin concert, but just to shut me up, she made a phony call to inquire about tickets. She had recently done the same thing with Bruce Springsteen, whose River tour was coming to the Garden also. Anyway, it was a sure bet that I wasn't going to see Zeppelin. A few weeks later, all bets were off when the drummer John Bonham choked on his own puke and died. I found out the next day through Sharon Redshaw. Being a diehard Zeppelin fan, she always had the scoop on them, and we often spoke about them throughout our years at the Cypress School. She was one of the few people who were hip to rock and roll, and one of the coolest girls I knew growing up. Sharon was years ahead of her time both in coolness and in looks, and was famous around the school for her denim jacket, which was covered in patches with rock band logos.

The early days of school played out quietly and the strike went on until the third week of September. With the lack of assignments during the beginning of the year, I started getting lazy when it came to doing homework. I figured it wouldn't count until Mrs. Painter took over anyway, so I didn't bring anything home at all during the first few weeks.

But then suddenly the party was over.

The teacher's strike ended, and one day we met Mrs. Painter.

It's often difficult to tell the age of an adult when you're a kid. As you age, you begin to get a sense of what a person's 20s and 30s look like. You can tell someone in their 40s for the most part. Even 50s and 60s. After that, you're just old. But when you're a kid, every adult is old. Looking back, I suppose Mrs. Painter was in her early to mid 30s. She was the spitting image of Adrienne Barbeau, the actress of *Swamp Thing* and *Escape from New York* fame.

Within just two weeks of Mrs. Painter assuming her role as the teacher, she had already become acquainted with my new habit of not doing homework. With parent/teacher conferences coming up, she was already looking forward to letting my mom know how horrible her son was doing in school. Not that I was a trouble maker or anything like that. I wasn't. I stayed silent in class and kept to myself. The extent of my horrible studentness was telling Mrs. Painter every day that my homework was lost or that I didn't get to finish it. At least once a day, she'd get in my face with a Clint Eastwood scowl and scream through her teeth, "Boy, I can't wait to meet your mother!"

But it wasn't like I was Kevin Weir who got yelled at by Mrs. Painter at least once every hour. Weir spent his time shooting rubber bands at Marc, and scrunching down to move to the end of the row to punch Marc in the arm. Then he'd run back to his seat before Mrs. Painter could turn around. Initially, he and Marc sat next to each other and were playing punch-for-punch, but Mrs. Painter caught them in the act and Weir got moved to the top of his row. Although Marc often tried to act tough around me, we both knew that Weir could kick his ass. But there was a playful brutality among the two of them...one in which Weir would destroy Marc in a random series of punches to the chest or arms. But then Marc would come right back at him. I stayed on the opposite side of the room observing them from my desk, and quietly hoped I wouldn't ever come in contact with Weir...even though he was just a few feet away on a daily basis. Still, he didn't even acknowledge me other than a quick glance here and there.

During lunch, Weir and Marc often played a violent and bloody card game called Knuckles, which involved players getting the edge of a deck of cards pounded savagely into their knuckles. That was when Weir actually stayed in school for lunch. He was one of the students who usually went home for lunch, which meant he wasn't going home at all, but instead, running off with older kids who smoked and hung out at the arcade.

Every Halloween, Miss Tripe led a giant parade with all of the students marching behind the school in their costumes. Then we'd come to a halt and sing the same Halloween songs that she taught us in kindergarten. We sang the same songs every year. 1978 particularly sticks out in my memory for two reasons. Both of them are Kiss. First, their movie *Kiss Meets the Phantom of the Park* premiered on NBC that weekend. Second, Tommy and I both dressed as Kiss members. There was nothing too creative about our costumes though. They were just the typical standard vinyl costume with the hard plastic masks and the elastic band that always hurt the back of your ears. The typical costume in Oakwoods was a bum. At least half the kids were bums. There were *Star Wars* characters, witches, playboy bunnies, cigarette girls, cowboys, Indians, *Peanuts* characters, superheroes, more bums and Kiss. And we were psyched to be parading around the school as Kiss. We wore our colors proudly. But that was two years ago. In the autumn of 1980, we were pretty removed from Kiss and had jumped on the bum bandwagon.

As the Halloween parade would get underway, we'd march around the front parking lot of the main unit and around the outside of the All Purpose Room toward the back of the building. All of the parents would be there watching their kids, taking pictures, cheering and waving. This was first-rate entertainment and we were stars onstage. Suspense was always in the crisp and biting air, and anticipation always ran high for what would happen next.

As if nobody knew what would happen next.

As if it was going to be a big surprise.

It was always the same though.

And everyone was used to it.

And everyone knew it by heart.

And everyone was probably sick of it.

Oh, I suppose it was always new if you were in kindergarten and you and your parents were hearing it for the first time. But by the third and fourth year and beyond, it just became painful and embarrassing. By sixth grade, it was a fucking joke.

The crowd is cheering. The kids march. They come to the end. They stop. The crowd goes silent. Miss Tripe in all her largeness emerges from the crowd. She steamrolls her way to the front to face the children. We never quite see her feet moving. In fact, we never quite see her feet. She just sort of glides across the blacktop. The children wait. The crowd waits. The air is rather cold and tainted with the smell of somebody's wood burning stove in the distance. Everyone wishes the music teacher would hurry up so the kids can get back inside, and all the mothers can go the fuck home and make dinner. Miss Tripe offers her blowup doll "O" smile. She looks to the left and then to the right. She nods. Her arms go up like Leonard Bernstein about to conduct Gershwin. The blubber under her arms that we're used to being disturbed by in class, jangles securely under her coat as two hundred kids sing in unison:

> *It's Halloween tonight*
> *We'll put out every light*
> *We'll set our jack-o-lanterns there*
> *And it will give our folks a scare*
> *It's Halloween tonight*
> *It's Halloween tonight...*
> *BOO!!!!*

I don't know what possessed me to sign on to Marc's idea of playing soccer. I don't even know if it was totally Marc's idea, but with some added pressure from our parents, I convinced myself as best as I could, that it just might be fun. For some reason, I also envisioned it as something that Marc and I would do together, so at least I would have my friend alongside me. Then, as usual, reality told me differently when Marc and I ended up on different teams. He would be on the Strikers and I would be on the Rowdies. In fact, we wouldn't even see each other unless our teams were playing against one another. I found myself on a team with a bunch of kids I didn't know and didn't like. None of them went to Cypress, although I recognized a few from CCD. We only had one or two really good players. Most merely just knew how to play the game and gave an honest effort despite their shortcomings. Then there were a few like me who didn't want to be there, and it showed. Our uniforms were a bile green t-shirt with white shorts. The shirts read the name of our sponsor, Lou's Luncheonette.

As we began to practice, two things became apparent. One, that I knew next to nothing about soccer except that you couldn't touch the ball with your hands, and two, that I was afraid of the ball. I was afraid of getting hit with the ball, and I was afraid of the ball coming to me. I didn't want control of the ball for fear that I would lose it, and for fear that someone would slide into me or injure me while trying to get it away from me. My dad told me I needed to be more aggressive. Aggressive was a word that I was largely unfamiliar with, and to this day I associate it with my dad insisting from the sidelines that I "get in there and get that ball." It was a word that I instantly knew was associated with that competitive element of sports that I dreaded when it came to other people...that Darwinian struggle to survive...and I fucking hated it. Plus, nothing appealed to me about a bunch of guys converging on me, all trying to kick a ball away from my feet. It usually resulted in a violent entanglement of legs and feet, and someone getting hurt...and I wanted nothing to do with it. By nature, I was not aggressive, nor could I force myself to be.

I hated being stuck out on that field for games every Sunday morning. Just standing there in my position, stranded...watching the ball being kicked around...hoping it wouldn't come to me. I often thought of places I would much rather have been, like in my bedroom listening to the new Cars album, holding a tennis racket and pretending it was a guitar while mom pounded on the wall downstairs, yelling for me to lower the volume, or to come down and eat. Sunday mornings were always filled with the smell of mom's spaghetti sauce and the sound of Casey Kasem's *American Top 40* on the radio. It seemed to be a custom of ours to eat pasta early in the afternoon on a Sunday. My grandparents did the same, so I always placed it as an Italian thing where the big meal of the day happened around lunchtime instead of dinnertime. On Sunday mornings, I woke up not to the smell of coffee or pancakes, but to the smell of an Italian meal being cooked. I'd often be sitting at the table having my cereal for breakfast while my mother worked on her sauce. If you grew up Italian, Sundays always meant pasta, or as Italians would say *macaroni*. Italians would also refer to the sauce as *gravy*.

So, on Sundays when I was stuck on the soccer field, I had the smell of the gravy in my head, and I looked forward to going home and eating. I daydreamed about the more innocent Sunday mornings when all I had to do was get out of bed, eat breakfast and watch

The Flintstones and Wonderama while mom made the gravy. I thought about how much I would have rather been at Marc's house sitting at the table in his den making comic books. Anywhere other than that horrible soccer field where the ball would come to me… and if I possessed it for more than a second or two, I would sure as shit screw something up that inevitably left me open for ridicule by those few kids who took the game seriously. Those moments at Marc's house making comic books was a comfort zone…sitting at that table for hours with Blondie or the Cars playing and the TV on with the sound turned all the way down. We'd occasionally eat something, sometimes doing off-the-wall things like plunging to the bottom of a marshmallow Fluff jar with nothing but spoons. Oh man, we got so sick one time doing that. Peanut butter too.

———

At the outset of sixth grade, things began to change very quickly. I don't recall if it was the influence of constantly being around Kevin Weir who had older friends who did older things, or just boredom and curiosity…but Marc began to take an interest in smoking cigarettes after the first few weeks of school. He also had the influence of an older sister who was a junior in high school and smoked as well. Both of his parents smoked too. Marc began telling me stories of how he would steal cigarettes from his mom and smoke them on the side of the house. His mom smoked these cigarettes called Vantage. They were one of more distinctive cigarettes I've ever seen because they had a scalloped-out hole in the filter. I remember Marc's house was filled with ashtrays that were always overflowing with snuffed-out

Vantage filters. Marc also told me how his parents found out about his sister smoking and how she was allowed to smoke in her room. He said it in a bragging tone, as if he himself would one day be allowed to smoke.

At home, my brother Franklin and I always had an imaginary parallel world where we were adults. Inspired by some Encyclopedia Brown books I read, I started my own detective agency in the house, and Franklin was my partner. He used to set up a paper car dashboard that he created with some construction paper and crayons. He'd lay it out in front of him and use a vinyl record as a steering wheel, pretending he was driving. We'd both drive to our imaginary office which was in his room, and we'd sit down at our desks and work on our cases.

In our adult world, we smoked cigarettes. I think Franklin was a smoker long before I even had a curiosity. He always had candy cigarettes, plastic cigars and pipes. Not exactly the ideal toy for a seven-year old. I remember we went to the dentist once for checkups, and before we left, we were offered various little trinkets and toys to choose from...out of which, Franklin picked a plastic cigar. I picked out a pipe. In retrospect, a dentist's office seems an unlikely place where one would learn to smoke. And even if Dr. Puma's secretary didn't teach us to smoke, she certainly offered us the opportunity to pretend we were. Around this time, Marc started rolling fake cigarettes out of office paper. He'd put a piece of tape around it to hold it together. The cigarette was hollow and he would basically inhale air through it. I started doing the same as my curiosity grew. We'd sit at our table in his living room, constructing our comics and smoking air cigarettes. Marc started to brag about how his mom had allowed him to use profanity in his comics as his stories began to resemble rated-R movies. He also discovered a picnic basket at the top of a shelf in his basement filled with Hustler and Penthouse magazines that his dad had hidden away. We spent a great deal of time sneaking into that basket, pouring through the pages of whatever book we managed to get a hold of without someone coming downstairs and catching us. Marc was growing up a lot quicker than I would have on my own, and he was taking me along with him.

10

A Change of Seasons

One Saturday afternoon in late November, Marc came up with the idea that we should steal cigarettes from the A&P. It wasn't something I would have done on my own. But as the reality of indulging an innocent curiosity seemed an actual possibility on a day that we would otherwise have spent sitting around making comic books and being tempted by thoughts of doing things we shouldn't be, the act of getting the stuff in our hands and taking it was our only obstacle...that and not getting caught. Not that there was anything wrong with sitting there making comics. It was much safer. I wasn't one to look for trouble. In fact I preferred to stay out of it. I couldn't relate to the dangerous sense of risk-taking people did all the time just to entertain themselves. This was not something I ever had to think about, much less worry about. This was the type of thing I imagined was something that maybe Kevin Weir and his older friends did, and being part of that world was not even a reality for me, and was often scary to imagine. In my narrow world, there was still a very clear and defined line between right and wrong, and good and bad. Suddenly I was presented with a new reality, imposed on me by Marc Rinaldi that was going to make me a criminal.

We walked to the A&P early in the afternoon that Saturday. When we got there and entered, I thought about how it was such a familiar place, having been there several times a week with my mom almost all my life. It was a harmless place where we bought food and toilet paper and stuff like that. It felt different though when Marc and I walked in. In the back of my mind was our reason for being there, and my nerves were not taking well to being introduced to the feeling of being up-to-no-good. I tried not to wear my thoughts on my sleeve, but Marc sensed that I wasn't happy about being there. I felt a huge sense of relief when we realized that the cigarettes were much too close to the checkout lines, and Marc knew we would have a difficult time getting away with taking anything. I figured that would be the end of it and that we would turn around and go home.

Wishful thinking.

Marc scanned the entire front of the store until his eyes stopped on the circular display of chewing tobacco all the way against the wall in the corner. He told me to remain where I was and keep a lookout. Suddenly without missing a beat, he was gone...walking casually across the store like a thief who knew exactly what he was doing. I knew I really wasn't playing much of an important role in our activity, but I guess Marc wanted to make me feel as if I were. He didn't waste any time when he got to the display, looking around once, grabbing a can of something and pocketing it while wandering away. I sauntered out of the store several steps ahead of him, anxious to be done with the situation. From there we picked up the pace and strode along through the parking lot and out onto Cypress Estates Road where we trudged onward toward Sycamore. The walk was silent but comforting, knowing the worst was over and we hadn't gotten caught. Home free.

As we turned onto Sycamore, Marc reached into his pocket for the first time since hiding the stolen merchandise.

"Oh man," he gasped, stopping in the middle of the street looking at a can of Copenhagen snuff in his right hand.

"I got the wrong stuff."

"What's wrong with it?" I asked, ignorant of what he was holding.

"This is snuff," he said in a tone suggesting that I should have known what it was and that I was stupid for asking.

I looked at him blankly.

"This is the stuff that you snort. We don't want that. We want the stuff you chew."

"We do? I'm fine not doing anything," I told him. "Why don't we just go back and make comic books?"

"Oh come on Geno, don't be a wuss."

Wuss was a word Marc used pretty frequently, often directing it at me. What he said next was unexpected, and hit me so hard that I pretended not to hear it, not even sure if he had really said it.

"We have to go back."

As those words slithered out of his mouth, I began walking up Sycamore without missing a beat, completely ignoring him. To which I anticipated Marc's response by his footsteps running up behind me and his hand grabbing the collar of my jacket, forcing me to stop.

"Geno, come on...we have to go back."

"Yeah, yeah," I said, reluctantly turning around to walk back down the street.

And walk we did. We walked and walked and walked because once we got back to the A&P, Marc decided it was too risky to go inside again for fear that maybe somebody noticed us. And so, we'd have to do even more walking...unexpected walking.

"Let's go to the 7 Eleven!" he barked like a man on a clear mission, his hands jammed in his coat pockets as he moved on, determined.

"Wait!" I choked out while tripping over myself to follow him.

He moved quickly as I sped up my pace, trying to catch up with him. He was headed toward the grass field where the giant electrical towers stood like an imposing army of tall, hideous structures cutting through Oakwoods. Beyond the field was the highway...a busy and dangerous three-lane highway where cars raced along at 55 miles per hour. And guess where we were headed.

Needless to say, I was scared shitless as we marched through the grass. This was completely unheard of in my version of reality. I could already envision my parents' reaction if they found out where I was. I had already been called a wuss and didn't want to make it worse, so as frightened as I was, I kept this one to myself. The ominous towers were terrifying as we moved closer to them, until suddenly we were passing them. What concerned me more than the thought of trying to cross the highway and getting mowed down by a car was the thought of getting electrocuted. Throughout my life I had always seen those towers, mostly from the backseat of a car.

I knew they had something to do with electricity and that the area was dangerous. The signs everywhere even read DANGER. But I had always assumed that even the grass island itself was electrical and would fry anyone who stepped on it. So as we scurried past the towers and underneath the high-tension power lines, I could feel myself suddenly have to shit. We could be fried at any second, I thought to myself. But there was an end in sight, and when we got there, I wasn't relieved in the least bit.

Big deal...we escaped electrocution.

Now we had to dodge on-coming traffic.

Very little did I think about traffic patterns in my eleven-year old mind, if at all. But apparently, Marc knew about them. He knew that the cars would all eventually pass once the traffic light 100 yards away changed to red, giving us ample time to cross to the grass median in the middle of the highway. The grass median in the middle of the highway wasn't any easier. Now we were standing on a slab of concrete and grass no more than four feet wide as we watched the traffic fly by in the opposite direction, feeling the rush of wind produced by each passing vehicle just a yard or two away from our fragile delicate bodies. But even that came to an end, as the final few cars passed and began to slow for their upcoming red light. And then we crossed, making it safely to the other side of the highway where the 7-Eleven awaited our thievery.

Inside, it seemed hot and stuffy and not at all comfortable, which is what it was supposed to be, given the chilly autumn weather outside. But being so worked up from adventuring through Oakwoods, along with the nervous uncertainty of it all, I had built up a sweat. I knew what we were there for, but I didn't have any interest in partaking in lifting some smokes, so I went over to the magazine racks and picked up a *Rolling Stone*. Michael Douglass and Jill Clayburgh were pictured on the cover, but I paid no attention. I saw Bruce Springsteen's name on the side of the cover and found the article which was about the Boss touring in support of his new album *The River*. While skimming toward the article, I came across another story about some person named Godard. The article and the name always stuck with me, and I later found out that Godard was actually the French New Wave director Jean Luc Godard. Being the aspiring film buff that I was, Godard was someone I probably should have known about, but wouldn't be turned on to his work until my early 20s. Besides, most eleven-year old American kids who are raised on mainstream movies, film buffs or not, are not aware of too many foreign films, let alone directors.

Marc walked around the store looking at various items while I looked at the *Rolling Stone*. My attention turned out the window behind the magazines, where traffic rushed by in two different directions. Beyond the highway, I could see the outskirts of our development. It looked a lot closer than the distance encompassed by our walk. From my eye to the horizon, I could have walked there in ten steps. But distance is funny that way, and often deceiving. We had been on an adventure even if the trek only took a few minutes. But what constituted adventure for me was probably just another part of a usual day for any number of kids whose parents weren't so overprotective. In other words, leaving the development and crossing the highway on foot was one small step for Marc Rinaldi, but one giant leap for Eugene Devine.

"Milanos!"

Marc's voice startled me. I jumped and turned around. He was in the aisle behind me holding up a bag of Pepperidge Farm Milano cookies.

"Sweet! I'm getting them!"

Suddenly he sounded more like a nerdy eleven-year old than a tobacco thief.

"I love Milanos!" the nerd said again.

He walked around the aisle and past me...nudging me in the back with his elbow. I followed behind.

"I can't pass up these Milanos," he said, stopping at the counter.

He reached into his pocket for money as the girl at the register rang him up. As she gathered his change, he smoothly reached for a pack of Marlboros out of the display case sitting on the counter right next to the register, all the while never taking his eyes off her. He pocketed the cigarettes just before she looked up and handed him his change. And suddenly, we were out the door. He made it look so effortless.

"I love Milanos! I can't wait to rip these open."

Marc seemed more excited about his cookies than he did about the smokes, and it didn't even phase him that he forgot the chewing tobacco. I thought about telling him, but all I really wanted to do at that point was go home and sit on the toilet. Besides, he had gotten his hands on a pack of cigarettes, which after all was his initial plan.

"I'm so glad I got these Milanos!" he roared as we made our way toward the inevitable crossing of the highway.

All I could think of at that moment was that if he had said Milanos one more time, I was going to punch him in the face. My inner hostility was surfacing more and more during that time period, as Marc always seemed to have something planned that involved breaking some law or parental rule that could conceivably get us into trouble. Not that we always acted on every idea he had. But when we kicked around things to do, his ideas rarely involved sitting around making comic books anymore, although sometimes I'd still win the toss-up of what we would do that day...and when it was up to me, we'd stay put. When we got to the grass median, I was so lost in thought that I hadn't even realized that we'd already crossed the highway. The traffic flow hadn't completely passed yet, but there was a break in vehicles that allowed Marc to unexpectedly turn toward me.

"I'll race you home. If you beat me, you can have one of my Milanos!"

And then he took off.

The next cars were less than a hundred yards away as he began to run. I surveyed the distance from the median to the other side of the highway, and then the distance of the on-coming cars. I decided that Marc needed to have his ass kicked a little...not by a fight, but in the race he challenged me to. Marc weighed more than I did, and I knew I was faster and could whip him.

So I bolted after him.

He had already reached the other side of the highway by the time I left the median, but stopped running as I was halfway across the blacktop. He looked baffled as he appeared to be searching for something. I felt something crush under my foot as I turned to my right to see the cars coming at me, but didn't pay much attention to what it was. I reached the other side when Marc realized that he had dropped his cookies in the middle of the highway.

"My Milanos!"

I spun around to see his package of cookies and came to the realization that I had stepped on it while running. Marc ran out onto the highway again to retrieve his cookies, and I damn near shit myself as I saw the wall of cars headed toward him. He picked up his cookies and looked at them in a state of total disappointment. He stood in place in the middle of the highway just looking down at them. Then he started walking back.

Walking back.

Walking.

Cars coming at him at 55 miles per hour...and he was casually walking to the curb without any hurry nor concern.

A symphony of horns wailed in unison as the brakes of several cars screeched in resenting disapproval of Marc's complete indifference.

"Hurry up, you stupid fuckin' asshole!" I yelled from the grass. "Fuck your Milanos!"

———

After Thanksgiving weekend, we went back to school and before we knew it, it was the first week of December. Before we began anything else that Monday morning, Mrs. Painter hit us with an unexpected seating change. It had been a nerve-racking few days, and the adventure wandering around Oakwoods with Marc reminded me that I just may not have been cut out for living as riskily as some kids did. I mean, one day spent lifting chewing tobacco and cigarettes while crossing highways was enough to put me on the verge of rethinking who I wanted to hang out with. How some people lived like this was beyond me.

And then it got worse.

That Monday's seating change saw Mrs. Painter moving me to the last desk in the second row. Placed right next to me in the first row was none other than Kevin Weir. We both occupied the last seats in the first two rows by the door. I avoided him during the first few months, and went largely unnoticed by him. But Weir couldn't just sit there and simply be. Wherever he was at any given moment, it was the center of chaos.

I had to get his respect, and fast...especially before something happened.

It was too intimidating sitting next to him not knowing if he was going to pick on me and if so, when. I didn't look at him. I looked down at the floor. I could see his dirty boots from the corner of my eyes. I could smell cigarette smoke on his clothes. At some point, I glanced skittishly at him. It was probably the closest I'd ever been to him. His freckled skin was unusually worn and wrinkled for a sixth grader, and he just looked older. He was clad in black from head to toe. His wild wavy hair curled down over his right eye, concealing it... adding a shred of mystery to an already tough appearance. I wanted his Harley Davidson shirt. And the chain wallet. I wanted that too. Everything about him was tough. I could still envision seeing him kick the crap out of John Bennett two years before. Bennett never came back to school, though they said Weir didn't have anything to do with that. Not sure what happened to him. He was the type of kid who moved a lot. He spent a whole childhood being a new student. He messed with Weir one day and that was it. I also remembered what he did to Rodney Sharp in the gym. Then there were the daily ritual kickball games on the playground. Weir was another one who always booted the ball onto the school roof. I wasn't that good at kickball. I played a few times during lunch, but for the most part, didn't go near the games. Weir had seen me mess up a few times. I was aware of this. It wasn't a good situation. Sitting there, I thought of a recent movie called *My Bodyguard,* and felt as though I were the main character, Clifford Peache being face to face with the intimidating Ricky Linderman for the first time. As Mrs. Painter went back to her desk on the other side of the room, I was consumed with paranoia.

I expected it, but when it happened, it really came out of nowhere. And even though I expected it, I wasn't really sure what I was expecting.

But I was expecting something.

So when it happened, I didn't see it coming.

At least not that.

POW!

Kevin Weir's fist slammed straight into the back of my left arm, causing severe fucking trauma to my tricep muscle.

Needless to say, it hurt.

Fuck.

This was it.

It was happening.

Just what I'd always feared.

Kevin Weir hit me.

Mrs. Painter was now facing the blackboard.

POW!

Again, he slammed his fist into the back of my arm in the same exact spot. I didn't say anything. I just sat there clutching my arm in pain. Weir sat gazing straight ahead as if nothing had happened. As Mrs. Painter transitioned into a science lesson, Weir waited. I knew it was coming again. I didn't know what to do. There was no way I was going to tell on him. That would've made it far worse than I'd even want to imagine. Mrs. Painter turned away. This time I was ready. Weir raised his right fist and swung. I leaned away and he missed. But then he came back. His fist, high in the air, searched for a spot on my body to land on as I squirmed around in my seat to get away from it. It was almost like a cobra to a snake charmer. Finally, POW! He struck my left leg.

Fuck!

FUUUUUUUUCK!!!

This wasn't happening!

How could this be happening?

I had to do something. I didn't know what, but I had to do something. His arm went up again, fist clenched. I slid around in my seat trying to get away as he followed my movements with his fist. Mrs. Painter, sensing that something was going on, spun around to catch Kevin in action. The look on her face suggested that she fully expected grief but somehow was surprised that it was happening so soon after a seating change.

She smiled.

The class turned around and looked at us.

"Mr. Weir! Two minutes in a new seat and you're acting up already? Perhaps you'd like to stand in front of the class and show everyone how tough you are. Would you like to demonstrate?"

Weir, now embarrassed, looked down at the floor.

"No, ma'am."

He used the word "ma'am" like he was in *Leave it to Beaver* or something. He may as well have put an apple on her desk. The teacher went back to whatever she was doing. I don't remember. Obviously, I wasn't paying attention. Attention was not something I was good at. I did very little of it. Way back to first grade, I never had the right answer when I was called on. And all my teachers always told me I was smart, intelligent and capable of doing Grade-A work, when I did work. The ability was there. The motivation wasn't. Apparently, I could've been one of the smartest kids in the school based on the some of the stuff I would surprisingly turn in from time to time. But that was sporadic. Usually, my teachers would catch me daydreaming instead. That was perfect bait for Ashley Drake, who loved those moments when I would look like a complete idiot in front of the class. That same simple utterance of "Duh," from Ashley would always initiate the usual collective roar of laughter from everyone else. As Mrs. Painter continued speaking, my ears went blurry as all sound faded out and I retreated deep into my own thoughts. Highlights of the Cypress years played over in my head like a film reel showing me flashbacks of my life...the embarrassing wrong answers...the mean and nasty girls who would yell at me and kick me if I blew the game in gym class...wimping out on the kickball field... being laughed at in the early years for being a Kiss fan...having my desk dumped on top of me in front of the class...the Bicentennial flag terrorism...all of it. It all came up like agita. I sat there with one of my best friends on the other side of the room. I also sat there with the girl I had a crush on, just a few rows away. Just at the front of my row was the girl who couldn't stand me for whatever reason. I had one of the toughest and most popular kids in the school sitting right next to me…a kid that I had feared. And he had begun to punch me. And I wasn't sure how to deal with it. Not because I was still afraid or that I was too embarrassed to say anything…but because I'd had enough. I'd had enough of worrying about what others were going to say, and I'd had enough of being defined by people whose opinions really shouldn't have meant shit to me…and most of all, I'd had enough of others setting the tone of how something was going to go.

And that was it.

That's when all of the rules went out the window.

That's when the formal classroom dynamic of a teacher/student structure implemented by rules and measured by conduct didn't matter anymore to me. The lines of "do's and don'ts" were blurred… and in an instant, the line between what I had been and what I would become was crossed. I rose to my feet, clenched my right hand into a nice tight fist, and wailed it as hard as I could into Kevin Weir's chest. Before I had a chance to think about what the consequences would be, he reached over like nothing, and slammed his fist into my left ass cheek, just as I sat back down. The speed in which his retaliation came made it seem as if he was waiting for me to do something. It began to occur to me then and there, that maybe he didn't see me as a weakling after all, and possibly thought I could handle such ferocity. Maybe he didn't have any preconceived ideas about me the way others did…or maybe he just wasn't paying attention to the others. How did he know I wasn't a psychopath who could totally fucking unleash on him without warning? Mrs. Painter missed the whole thing as she wrote on the board. We had turned a few heads though in the back of the room.

Holy shit, I thought.

I'd just hit Kevin Weir.

And I was still alive.

Maybe he wasn't so tough after all.

Maybe I was just as tough but didn't know it.

But I knew he was tough, and I knew I really wasn't.

I knew that.

But if I could just make him think I was.

Something big had happened though. I had absorbed four of his punches. They hurt like hell, but I was still alive. I had also worked up the nerve to hit him back. I wasn't sure where that would get me, and I was already second guessing my move...but it was already too late. I had hit Kevin Weir.

The next few days remarkably passed without incident, and Weir strangely avoided me, not saying a word. The only reaction I got out of him was when Mrs. Painter went on a verbal tirade regarding me never having my homework done. When the screaming was over, he kind of smiled at me as if to say "Yeah, I know how it is."

Or maybe if I thought about it a little longer, that smile could have been saying "Yeah, you wait. I may not be saying anything now, but I'll get you. When you least expect it, I'll get you."

That crossed my mind for a day or two.

11

A Strange Turn of Events Still in Motion

On the playground during the lunch hour of Friday, December 5, I was standing against the brick wall of the sixth grade unit building. I had my fists jammed in the pockets of my opened coat...a dark blue denim with wool lining inside. I was freezing, but an open jacket looked much cooler than a closed one. Image is important when you're young. Maybe Fonzie was still inside me after all. Who knows? Anyway, I was standing there watching everyone play kickball when Ashley Drake who had been studying me from about twenty feet away came walking over. Immediately, I thought she was coming to start trouble since she never had anything nice to say to me. She was looking at my shirt, which contained an iron-on of the rock group the Cars.

"Hi Eugene," she said in a bored manner.

I said nothing back.

She smiled.

Something she never did in front of me.

Still, she was probably getting ready to spit out some nasty re-mark about the Cars...or maybe how stupid I looked or something. Stupid was a word she used very often...and I was ready for it. It was coming...stupid band, stupid shirt, stupid iron-on...

"You like the Cars?"

There was a careful cautiousness in her voice as she asked me this, as if she knew I expected her to say something rotten, but was determined to let me know that she had no intention of being rotten. Instantly, I thought of striking before she had a chance to strike me.

Do I like the Cars? What the hell kind of question is that?

Was it a trick question or something?

What did she mean?

Was I just being paranoid?

Was I imagining the worst because I expected the worst?

Hold on, I thought.

It wasn't in my nature to be nasty. Whatever she was going to do, she was going to do it anyway, and I wasn't quite in the mood for playing games. I had enough on my table just standing there in the cold, pretending to be warm. I decided I would be civil. With my fists still jammed in my pockets, I reached deep down, and somehow, if only for a brief moment, conjured up the Fonz.

"I love the Cars," I said, cool yet defensive.

Musically, I wasn't afraid of anything, and I was ready to stand my ground. I was ready for her to tell me they sucked. My guard was up. You could tell me that I sucked in kickball. You could tell me how stupid I was in Math. You could even make jokes about my Tough Skins flood pants. But if you ever told me that my band sucked, I'd rip you a new asshole. Ashley smiled again. Her eyes curled up with shy embarrassment.

"So do I. They're my favorite group."

Okay...that, I wasn't prepared for.

That was almost a low blow.

There I was...ready for once to stand up to her. We were alone with nobody around to be her audience. It was just her and me. I was ready for her bullshit, and suddenly there she was, initiating a civil moment just when I had really gotten sick of her. Although I have never hit a girl nor would I ever, I almost felt obliged to at least push her down on the ground or something. I figured I owed at least that much to myself. But, that wasn't me. In the fraction of a second before I reacted, I thought carefully for a fraction of that fraction. I decided that I would see where this was going.

"Mine too," I said, letting my guard down a little.

She looked away...focusing her eyes downward, her hands in her pockets, swaying from left to right, twisting back and forth as she stared down at the blacktop.

"Well, I'll see ya in class," she said abruptly...and then slowly wandered off...walking away at the pace of a turtle as if she were waiting for me to say something else. And then my usual over-thinking began.

What did she mean by that?

I wondered.

She'll see me in class?

Of course I would see her in class...like every other day that I had unfortunately spent... seeing her in class.

And why the hell couldn't it have been Riley Stevens who said "I'll see ya in class?" Why couldn't she have come up to me on the playground instead?

Why?!

———

At two that afternoon, Mrs. Painter let us go outside for a kickball game. It was one of those rare things that happened occasionally. Friday afternoon with an an hour left. Hell with it!

Let them play ball!

Every once in a while there was that unexpected kickball game that wasn't dependant on gym class or free time during lunch. It came out of legitimate class time. That's what was so great about it. We'd play kickball for an hour, and then we'd go home. And it was Friday! It didn't get much better than that. It was the only time I didn't mind playing, simply because it got us out of class.

———

I was the tying run. I needed to score. Jake Kennedy kicked the ball clear over everyone's head, and over the blacktop and on to the next lot. Kids in the outfield began scurrying after it. I ran towards second base as fast as I could. I rounded second and headed for third. The ball was still in the outfield. I had a chance to make it home. Kennedy was behind me on his way to second. Halfway between second and third, Kevin Weir stepped in front of me and charged into my body like the asshole that I was afraid he would become...ramming his shoulder right into me, and knocking me several feet into the air. If this were a movie, the scene would be done for dramatic effect in slow motion:

The ball flying overhead into the distant lot...kids running wildly after the ball as it bounces to the point where they have to run even further...a close-up of my face as I realize how far the ball is, and I know I have a chance to make it home...my teammates at home plate jumping up and down, waving me in...Kennedy approaching as he tags along, one base behind me...a close-up of third base...a close-up of my eyes looking at third base...a close-up of an arm waving me toward third base...some poor schmuck in the outfield walking towards the lost ball because he knows he has no chance anymore...a close-up of his demoralized face...the fight has gone out of the poor schmuck. It is a priceless moment worthy of any *Rocky* or *Karate Kid* ending. Suddenly...remember, we're still in slow motion here...Weir comes out of nowhere and slams his entire body into my unsuspecting weak little frame. A close-up of the sky. The sky fills the screen, and from bottom left comes me, tumbling like a football on kickoff. I soar overhead and then disappear into the bottom right corner of the screen. Some psychedelic special effects could reveal that the trail I left in flight actually forms a rainbow. Then when it's too late, we find at the wrong moment that the rainbow is made of glass, and upon the impact of me hitting the blacktop, its seven colors smash and crash to the ground.

I woke up flat on my back. About a minute had passed, though I had no sense of time. The mind in connection with the human body seems to shut down as if to block the reality of what is actually taking place when some sort of trauma has occurred. I would imagine that the severity of trauma might determine why some people go into shock and others get up and dust themselves off. No shock here though. Felt like a little bump on my head. Or maybe a big bump. What if I had cracked my head open?

Nah.

My blurred vision slowly came into focus. The first thing I saw was Riley Steven's face. She was crouched down above me. It was kind of like Jimmy Stewart waking up to see Grace Kelly in *Rear Window*...that angelic view as if I had died and gone to heaven. The rest of the class was either behind her or all around me looking down. It was a bizarre and surreal moment. I don't remember much of what was said except for Riley asking me if I was alright. I remember trying to get up, and then going back down because I was too weak. I lifted my head up, and Mrs. Painter shrieked at the sight of the blood-soaked rock underneath me.

"Oh my God, he's bleeding!" she cried.

I reached behind my head and pulled my bloody fingers back in front of my face.

Shit!

I was bleeding alright.

I had pretty much landed on the back of my head...cracking it on a sharp rock that was sticking out of the ground. I tried to get up again. This time I sat for a minute, and then Marc and Mrs. Painter helped me to my feet. I was dizzy and confused. I don't even remember if I was mad at Weir, or if I said anything to him...or if he had even apologized, let alone got into any trouble for pushing me.

"We have to get him to the nurse," Mrs. Painter said nervously.

"I'll take him," Riley said, almost immediately.

I sat there bleeding. And as I sat there bleeding, my stomach jumped in nervous excitement. Riley Stevens had volunteered to walk me to the nurse.

"Okay Riley. Somebody else go with her!"

Without any hesitation, the devil stepped up.

"I'll go!"

FUCK!

WHY?!

And just like that...Ashley Drake was about to cut in to what could have been...

What could have been...

...could have been...

Could have been what, Eugene? You're bleeding. Just shut up. Ashley wasn't the best of friends with Riley, but they talked occasionally and were polite to each other. As it was, Riley was naturally pleasant and everybody loved her, so it was hard for Ashley to be her usual bitchy self around her. At that moment, I was so out-of-it that I didn't even really consider the reality of what was happening. I didn't even have time or room for my shyness. Both girls put their arm around me and began guiding me slowly across the playground toward the main unit building. On one side of me was the girl I had a crush on for three full school years. On the other side of me was the anti-Christ.

The three of us walked off the playground. This would usually be the part in professional sports where the audience cheered as an injured player was taken off the field. But there was no applause. Just the bitter chill of a late autumn afternoon. Behind us, I could hear Mrs. Painter directing the class to go back to the room to collect their belongings and get ready for dismissal. We walked into the main unit and started down the long hall towards the nurse's office. The hallway was filled with the sound of Friday afternoon. The strings coming out of Mr. Motolla's band room were vomiting up atonal dissonance that would make Arnold Schoenberg sound like Brahms. In the distance I could hear the power floor scrubber. The power floor scrubber's job was to scrub the floor. In the farther distance, was the crashing sound of lunch tables being folded and wheeled back into their rightful place against the All Purpose Room wall. Within a few steps, the sounds of tuneless out-of-key violins bled into "Hungry Heart," as Bruce Springsteen's current hit song blared out of the transistor radio sitting on the table in the teacher's room.

"Bbrrruuuce Sssprringsteen," I slurred out loud in recognition wandering carelessly into the teacher's room, pulling both girls in with me.

"My brother has this record," Ashley replied as she tugged at my arm and yanked me out of the doorway, pointing lazily toward the nurse's office and redirecting me along.

The walk was an eternity, and I was becoming dizzier and dizzier. I couldn't even enjoy the situation. Perhaps my dizziness took the edge off what would have otherwise been an uncomfortably nervous scenario. Yet, I was still somehow fully aware that Riley was right there. It almost overshadowed the gruesome state of affairs. I 'm walking with my head bleeding. I could feel it trickling through my hair. I'm light-headed and obviously not doing to good on the whole...and all I could think about was the fact that I had Riley to myself. Well, almost...if not for Ashley being there. But even though I liked Riley, I was terrified of her finding out. Anyway, it was probably the first time anyone in that school, let alone a girl, was nice to me like that. She was never ever cruel to me like Ashley had been, but she had never really talked to me much before that day either... which made it all the more peculiar that she had volunteered as quickly as she did to walk with me. It was almost the act of an angel to accompany me as I bled to death.

Mrs. Painter caught up with us. We got to the nurse's office. They sat me down and looked at my head. The nurse then called my dad at home to come and pick me up. Then I heard a loud familiar voice in the hallway just outside the door.

"Oughmmmmm rrrrrghrrrrrrrmmreerrrrmrrhh. Rrrmmmrgh. Arrrum. Grroumm."

Mr. Tutundjian walked in and the nurse explained to him what had happened. He came over to me and took my head into his hands, examining it.

This was one strange moment.

Mr. Tutundjian, the principal of our school, was holding my head.

"Ohhhmmmmrrmmmm. Grrruummmmmrrrghhhh. Mmrrrrom," he said to the nurse.

"Yes I know," she replied.

"Foughhhgrrrghhhrrrrrr ouummmmgrrrhh," he growled.

"Yes, his father is on his way right now."

"Mrrrruuum...crakergagruff!!!" he belched, and then sat down next to me. Just then, I realized that Riley and Ashley were gone. They must have left when Mrs. Painter got there. Somewhere, I had lost track of them. Luckily, the bleeding had slowed, and what Mr. Tutundjian was saying to the nurse basically translated to his stressing how profusely the scalp will bleed after it has taken the right kind of blow. In retrospect, I probably should have gotten some stitches, given the amount of blood I lost initially. Once it stopped trickling however, my mom slapped a Band-Aid over my head.

That night, I was supposed to go up to Oakwoods Junior High to receive my trophy from the soccer league. Even though I quit the team two games before the season ended, the coach called me on the phone to tell me that I still deserved my trophy, and that I should be there with the rest of the team. After all, it was a team effort to lose every game but one, and I was indeed part of that team effort. The only problem was that I had this stupid looking Band-Aid sticking out of my hair. I wanted to take it out, but my mom wouldn't let me, and yelled at me for wanting to do so. It wasn't even covering the wound. It was just sticking to my hair. This was one heck of an embarrassing situation in the making.

For the next few hours, I played out the upcoming scene in my head. How was I going to go before my team, and not just my team, but the entire league with this stupid looking Band-Aid sticking out of my hair? It wasn't as if I had broken my arm and had to walk around in a cast or something. People might say "well yes, he has a cast. He must have broken his arm." Or even handicapped people... people who God forbid find themselves in wheelchairs. There is an automatic feeling of sympathy for these people. And rightly so!

Here is a person who can't walk!

And they're confined to this chair!

We don't even question this.

Their situation warrants no questioning.

How dare we question something like that?!

And what about someone who breaks their leg? They walk on crutches. They can explain that!

"Yes, I'd like to thank everyone involved in the Clara Barton Soccer League who made this award possible. Unfortunately my leg injury kept me out the last few games, but I'm here tonight on these crutches to be with my team."

Crutches and a broken leg have dignity. They are explainable.

But me?

How was I supposed to explain this?

Okay, I fell! I got cut! We've seen bald men with bandages on their heads. Yes, they've somehow cut themselves. We often wonder what people do to themselves. We see people with amputations and say "My God, what happened to this person, and what kind of horribly fucked up twist of fate did this person's life take?" Then there's that bald man, who...I don't know...maybe one day, had to go dump the pressure in the boiler. The boiler was rated for maybe 140 and he forgets. Now he has to run to the boiler room in a frantic race against time before the gauge reaches 200 and the whole building explodes. Well, he may reach it in time, release the pressure and then collapse in exhausted relief, slouched over a pipe or something.

He'd say "Tsshheww! That was close. I've just save hundreds, perhaps thousands of lives. And I wish I had hair on my head because of the unforeseen twist that my life is about to take now. Maybe my hair will protect me."

But then, in deep thoughtful reflection, he may say, "But what did I do to protect my hair? I just let it fall out."

The man gets up, and without warning, hits his head on a rusty valve. Well, mind you, he's just written his story, hasn't he! And he should thank the good Lord that he's bald. A bald bandaged head doesn't look that bad. It speaks volumes of the treacherous abrasive world that awaits bald men. The measure of a man should be how well he holds up in a callous world with no hair. Perhaps men who have a full head of hair and then shave themselves bald when they're young, are in a way preparing for themselves a kind of mental boot camp, if only to practice for reality. These people spend their youths and young adulthood shaving their heads. But then, it is said that the solution only becomes the next problem. Once reality sets in, and the hair is gone because it *fell* out, some men may say, "Well, now I'm *really* bald, and why didn't I keep my hair when I had a choice?"

Yes we all have regrets. Some are bigger than others. Yet someone may tell this man, "Well, look on the bright side. It could always be worse."

In my own humble opinion, I find no solace in the thought that things can always be worse. In fact, that thought scares the hell out of me. So yes...my situation was a disaster in the making...me, myself, my full head of hair and the Band-Aid sticking out of my hair.

I ripped the fucking Band-Aid off. Once I got to the school for the soccer awards and saw Riley standing outside the auditorium, there was no way the Band-Aid was going to go the distance. Apparently, she was in the girls' league, and it hadn't really occurred to me that I would see her. She was standing at the entrance, so I couldn't avoid her. She asked me how my head was and how I was feeling, and we talked for a a second before I went in to find my team. Good thing I tore that ridiculous bandage off my head. I don't know what my mom was thinking.

It had been a crazy day. I actually had an encounter with Ashley Drake during lunch hour that wasn't hostile. Then I cracked my head open...as if that wasn't enough. Then my two encounters with Riley. What did they mean? At the age of eleven, I guess we don't think about coincidences or fate or the idea of things happening for a reason. We're more concerned with getting out of situations without shitting our pants. We don't really think about missed opportunities until after the fact.

Terrified of her finding out?

Oh bullshit.

I went to bed thinking about her as I did many nights that year, trying to imagine a situation where I was able to tell her how I felt. Imagining, or should I say daydreaming that she felt the same way. These daydreams would help me fall asleep at night.

———

Monday came. December 8. It was the first day back since my accident on the playground. Naturally, I received a lot of attention. I was practically famous. That morning, the strange turn of events was still in motion. Sometime before lunch, Riley and I got called down to the nurse's office. Apparently, we had both been absent on the day physicals were done. When we got to the main unit, several students were leaving. One of them was Weir. He walked towards me smiling. As I passed him, he reached around and tapped my shoulder.

"You have to pee in a cup, man."

Riley went into the office.

I stayed in the hall with Weir.

We both stopped walking.

"Whattaya mean?"I asked.

"They want a sample of your piss," he said.

My piss?

What the hell would they want with my piss?

Weir turned around and began to leave. His chain wallet jangled against his leg as his work boots clod-hopped down the hall. I began walking toward the nurse's office.

"Hey man!"

I turned around and saw Weir stopped at the door at the end of the hall facing me. What the hell did he want?

"What?" I asked, almost impatiently.

I think he noticed the tone of my voice.

"How's your head? Are you alright?"

I stared back at him.

"Yeah, I'm okay."

Somehow I knew it was a breakthrough moment no matter what the outcome...and at that point, I didn't even care.

"That's good," he muttered, not sounding proud of himself. His voice was sincere.

"I'm sorry I pushed ya, man."

The hallway was ringing out with the sound of the ever-present radio in the teacher's room.

"I gotta go" I said to him and turned around and began walking away.

"Eugene," he called back.

I turned around to look at him again.

"Seriously, man. I'm sorry."

 I nodded.

"I know," I said. "It's okay."

I turned back around and headed once and for all to the nurse. Miss Keller, the art teacher, was standing in the doorway of the teacher's room holding a cigarette calling out to Mr. Motolla across the hall that John Lennon's new song was on the radio. It was strange seeing a teacher smoking a cigarette. Looking back at Miss Keller, I always thought she was different from most of the teachers in the sense that she was younger and more free thinking in ideas, speech...even her clothes. She was the overly-sensitive touchy-feely type. I couldn't quite put my finger on it. I didn't really know about hippies at that young age, but that's exactly what she was. What a time to be alive! And what Miss Keller's announcement to Mr. Motolla amounted to was two humongous Beatles fans rejoicing over John Lennon's big return to music after being holed up in the Dakota apartment building through most of the Seventies. I walked into the nurse's office. It was déjà vu...the second time in as many school days that I was there.

Inside, I went to the desk. The nurse took my name down and some other information. She asked me how my head was. Then she gave me a paper Dixie cup and told me to pee in it once Riley got out of the bathroom. Riley Stevens, the most popular girl in the school was walking out of the bathroom. And she was holding a cup of her own pee. She walked out and I walked in. She looked at me with a shy embarrassed smile…a look I had never seen on her face before. It was the same kind of smile I got from Ashley on the playground just a few days earlier. I shut the door and did my thing. It took a while. Even though there were no beastly monkey men watching me like at Shea Stadium, I still had trouble producing the goods since I knew that it was expected of me. I was just glad that I didn't have to take a crap in the cup. That could have been a problem. I stood at the bowl, aiming for the cup as the bashful pee slowly began to come out of hiding. It trickled into the cup. I was afraid that it would come out full force and overflow the cup so I held back, letting out only enough to fill it a quarter of the way. Then I placed the cup on the floor, and finished peeing into the toilet. I aimed for the back of the bowl, trying to avoid hitting the water, so it wouldn't be loud enough for Riley to hear. She was just outside the door, and I was painfully aware of it. Years later in life, I would come to realize why women turn on the faucet when they pee. I finished. I walked out with my cup. Riley shot me a polite smile, but I nervously looked away as fast as our eyes met. She was sitting in a chair holding her cup of pee. It was the same color as mine. Then I thought to myself for a moment. What is it that determines beautiful people from ugly people on the outside if we're all the same on the inside? I mean you could have mixed up our pee samples to where you couldn't tell whose was whose. I sat down next to her. We waited for the nurse to get off the phone. It was awkward for both of us, but there we were… Eugene Devine and Riley Stevens…one of the most ridiculed boys in the school…sitting alone with the most popular girl in the school. And suddenly we were both on the same level. It was the first time Riley and I ever bonded in any way, shape or form.

It was beautiful.

We just sat there together holding our pee.

That night, I watched the first quarter of Monday Night Football and then went to bed. Outside it had begun to rain. It was unseasonably warm for December, but none the less, an ugly night. Across the Hudson in New York City however, the climate was about to change forever, and fate was about to change the shape of an unsuspecting world. It was about to change it into something unprecedented, shockingly unimaginable and completely unacceptable. When I go back to that month, and think that songs like "Starting Over" and "Woman" were supposed to mark a new beginning, it is still chilling to know they became haunting reminders of what could have been. The songs would spill continuously from radios through the entire upcoming winter. That night, on West Seventy-Second Street, a man and a woman got out of a limousine and five gunshots were fired.

The next day was gray and overcast. A windy drizzle. The worst kind of weather. All of the blue had fallen from the sky, and people were crying.

Everywhere.

First, I saw them crying on TV, and the ones who weren't crying just looked sad. In school, teachers were crying. Then some of the kids began crying because they saw the teachers crying. When you're a little kid, I don't think anything frightens you more than seeing grownups cry. The mental images are indelible, and they will not go away. To this day, when I hear songs that were on the charts that fall and winter, every little memory rushes back to the day the world seemed to be crying. 1980 was coming to an end...an inadvertent hangover of the 1970s...and whatever lasting remnants in spirit that remained of the 1960s had just been exterminated. The American hostages were still in Iran. President Carter would be leaving soon, and a mean scary man would be taking his place. The decade was officially over. Ronald Reagan's 1980s were about to begin, and an era had just tragically ended.

John Lennon was dead.

12

A Hard Rain

During the week of John Lennon's murder, Mrs. Painter brought in a record of "Give Peace a Chance" and played it for the class. Many kids didn't really know who he was, so she had to explain his importance as well as the significance of his death. The following Sunday saw a worldwide vigil with ten minutes of silence held for Lennon. I was at my grandparent's house for some family event where all my relatives were there for some reason. The details of such a family gathering are sketchy, but the big picture is forever etched in my memory. I wouldn't actually be personally affected by his death until about eight years later, when I would pour myself into his music and come to understand who he was and what he represented. However, the mental pictures of standing with my entire family in that living room in front of the TV in total silence, watching images of people in Central Park holding candles and crying, will stay with me forever.

The Locker Notes

During the last week and a half before the Christmas break, things began to change. I'm not sure what came over me, but suddenly I was no longer afraid of Kevin Weir. I sat in class while Mrs. Painter was doing a lesson, thinking about the punches we traded a few weeks before, and how he had pushed me on the playground. I thought about the eerie silence on his part afterward and about the underlying paranoia on my part that he wasn't done with me...especially given the occasional smiles I would get from him. I think he knew that I wasn't much of a challenge for him, and he got a kick out of the fact that I still turned around and fought back that day. It was there though, that I gained his respect. Deep down, I almost knew that he wasn't really about to kick my ass, nor was he ever. In his own demented way, he was playing. That's all he was doing...just playing.

So I decided to play too.

While my confidence was up, I decided that I would mess with him. I watched Mrs. Painter as she spoke to the class. I waited for her to turn away. When she did, I reached over and rammed my fist into Weir's arm. Then I sat up straight in my seat as if nothing had happened. A wide-eyed look of disbelief flashed across his face, as I gathered the nerve to turn around and look him in the eye.

Then he said in a whispering laugh, "You motherfucker. So, you wanna go punch-for-punch, huh?"

As quick as he completed his sentence, his fist bolted through my arm like a bullet. This time, it was much harder and hurt far more. His punch practically went to the bone. My arm vibrated as if it had been electrocuted. We traded a few more punches until Mrs. Painter caught us in the act.

"Mr. Weir and Mr. Devine! Out in the hall!"

She followed us into the hall with the entire class watching.

And just like that, I had become a bad kid.

A troublemaker.

A delinquent in the company of Kevin Weir. I didn't even know it yet, but I had also just made a new friend.

———

During lunch hour, Mr. Zielinski began walking into the All Purpose Room to disrupt our lunch by going on a verbal tirade against the entire school. He must have been a drill sergeant at one time in his life. If he caught you talking while he was talking or if you were doing something you shouldn't have been doing such as God forbid, eating, he had his own personal little punishment system. This was measured by how many minutes you'd have to stand against the wall before you could leave. For example, if Dave Mason was caught talking, he'd say, "Brother David, you owe me five." Some people received ten or fifteen minutes on the wall. Some severe sentences would run "fifteen minutes all week." Whereas it was common to stay after school, this pretty much amounted to staying after lunch. In the modern world, they call it lunch detention.

In the classroom, Kevin Weir and I became quick pals. During that last week before the holidays, Mrs. Painter kept an extra eye out for us, so it was hard to talk in class. We became like girls and resorted to note passing. Sometimes we'd think up some crazy shit for each other and leave surprise messages folded up very tiny inside the toilet paper role in the bathroom. One time, I simply wrote that he was an asshole and left it inside the toilet paper role. He wrote back, "eat shit," or something like that. We went back and forth on that one for what ended up being about two months. The bathroom itself was another story. Between Kevin, me and a few people across the hall in Hardenberger's class, the bathroom was slowly demolished. It started when I simply wrote "Rolling Stones" on the wall. Someone wrote "sucks" underneath it. I know it wasn't Kevin because he loved the Stones. Then someone else wrote "you suck." Then before we knew it, we had a thing going. Then someone else wrote what chick he thought was hot, and what he wanted to do with her. Then the language became abusive and offensive. Until one morning three days before the break, Mr. Hardenberger came into our room.

"Mrs. Painter," he barked like a little bitch.

Mrs. Painter looked up from her desk.

"Yes Mr. Hardenberger."

Hardenberger put a hand up against the wall and another hand on his hip, and shifted his weight to one side.

"You should see the profanity that's written on the boy's room wall."

That was it. We were dead.

Mrs. Painter knew who it was just by looking at our handwriting. Although we never actually admitted to anything and we never got in any trouble, there was a silent acknowledgment between Kevin, me, and the teacher. It was a very knowing glance that she gave us to make us understand that she knew...and we knew that she knew... and she knew that we knew that she knew.

———

We were relentless. It didn't stop. Boys all over the unit building began to catch on to the bathroom theatrics. The next morning we came in and there was a turd sitting on the bathroom doorknob. Someone had literally hung shit on the door. Later in the day, I got this sick idea that I didn't want the toilet to flush anymore. I went in there and concocted a lethal mixture of Crazy Glue and a roll of strapping tape that I found in the art room. With that, I went to work on the handle. When I was done, the toilet handle couldn't be pressed down. Shit piled up for the next two days before Mr. Wagner came to peel off the tape and chip away the glue. Let me stress that the bathroom only had two relief outlets...one urinal, and one toilet separated by a metal wall. Between the two classes, approximately 25 boys shared this room. That was the severity of the situation. The biggest bathroom scandal of the year came next.

On the morning of the last day before the holidays, all the boys in the unit got called down to the All Purpose Room. The vice principal wanted to see us about the bathroom. Talk had suggested that something big had happened. I had not been in the bathroom the previous day, nor did I notice anything different before, so I wasn't sure what to expect. Apparently, someone had painted a Nazi swastika on the wall. Now at the age of eleven, I had never heard of a swastika. I had no idea what it was. So when Mr. Zielinski asked who put the swastika on the wall, given his tough guy New York accent, I thought he was saying "S.W.A.T. sticker," although it sounded like "swat sticka."

I had no idea what the hell a S.W.A.T. sticker was!

The only thing I knew about S.W.A.T. was that it had been a TV show a few years earlier. And as far as I knew, I hadn't seen any stickers on the wall. In this case, I was completely innocent, and so was Kevin. Fingers of course, pointed to us, but nothing was proven and nobody else ever came forth. The only consequence of this was for the entire sixth grade, boys and girls, to sign a log sheet before entering the bathroom for the rest of the school year. Kevin and I never received any sort of punishment for anything we did or didn't do that year. In the classroom, however, Mrs. Painter decided to separate us. That day, she rearranged some students, placing Weir on the other side of the room right next to her desk. I got moved to the first seat in the first row, right in front of Ashley Drake. I could hear her sighing heavily in disgust that I was placed in front of her. Immediately, she kicked me underneath the desk.

"Now we have to sign that stupid book because of stupid you," she said pouting. She kicked me again.

I didn't react.

"You're stupid," she said, just loud enough for me to hear.

I didn't say anything back.

Then she tapped me on the shoulder.

I ignored her.

Mrs. Painter had gone into the hall to talk with Mr. Hardenberger. During these moments, little sub-worlds of conversation would form throughout the vast universe of the classroom.

"Hey Eugene," Ashley said...her voice now with the same cautious tone she had used on the playground a few weeks before. Again, I ignored her. She then rammed her fist into my back. At that instant, I spun around so fast that she nearly jumped out of her seat. She put her hands up in front of her face as if she expected me to hit her. She smiled and let out a nervous shriek.

"I'm sorry, I'm sorry," she gasped in a mix of hyperventilation and laughter.

I looked her dead in the face for a few seconds as she melted in her seat. I turned back around. I was satisfied. I scared the human side out of her. My back hurt. I wasn't happy. Ashley then tapped my shoulder with her pen.

"Eugene."

I disregarded her.

"Eugene," she said again sounding desperate.

She tapped me again.

"Turn around. I have to ask you something."

Nothing.

"Come on," she pleaded, "I have to ask you something."

Reluctantly, I turned around. I stared at her with a cold straight face. She must have figured out by then that I wasn't taking any more shit. She was smiling.

"Did you do it?"

"No," I said sternly.

"I know you didn't do it," she said with the hint of a suspicious twinkle in her eyes.

Holy crap!!

Wow!!

How about that?

What, does she have a fucking crystal ball under her desk?

She knows I didn't put the S.W.A.T. sticker on the wall!

Wow!

Well then, who did?

Could you help me out here? 'Cause people are pointing to me.

"How do you know I didn't do it?" I asked.

"I just know."

"What if I did do it?"

"You wouldn't do something like that."

She was right.

I had no idea what a swastika was...or a S.W.A.T. sticker. It was a very sensitive situation and it was a big deal. I can honestly say that we were never taught about the holocaust or even World War 2 up to that point in time. We barely even had social studies aside from talking about the early explorers and some geography lessons. Only beginning in sixth grade did we really start extending our understanding that there were other places outside of America that we would actually learn about as opposed to just hearing about. At this stage we had just begun to talk about Mesopotamia and things like ziggurats. I knew there had been world wars, and I knew that they had happened a long time ago. It's hard to fathom, that given my meticulous ability to remember dates and history, that there was a time in my life before I had an innate sense of timeline. I'd heard the name Hitler before and I probably might have even associated it with one of the wars. I'd even heard the word Nazi used in a Wonder Woman episode from years earlier, but at such a young age, I didn't have a clue what it meant or pertained to. Obviously, some kids knew what it was and many people were disgusted. Everybody seemed to know about the drawing in the bathroom. I'm not sure how much of the blame was placed on Kevin and me. I think our class at least believed us that we didn't do it.

But who did?

It was never discovered.

With Ashley, the nature of the beast was changing. She had begun to drop the veil of callous ruthlessness...a mask that I had thought to be real up until recent weeks. The bathroom antics would stop for a while after the holidays, and the final year of elementary school would take on a smooth progression into the New Year.

But things were strange.

All of the adversity of the beginning of the school year would subside, and two unlikely friendships would form...first, with Kevin Weir...and then more surprisingly, with Ashley Drake.

———

During the Christmas season, strange occurrences of vandalism started taking place in our neighborhood. A series of mysterious fires also broke out in the woods out behind our development. They were nothing the fire department couldn't contain, but after the third one within a week and a half period, word was that it was a bunch of local kids. Weir seemed to know about it and denied that it was local kids when I brought up the subject. He insisted that it was a gang from a nearby town setting the fires. He also seemed to know that the older kids were involved in some sort of gang war and stressed that it was "bad news." He never said anything else about it again, and once the fires stopped, it was an issue that eventually evaporated into Oakwoods folklore. Aside from the fires though, kids were destroying people's Christmas decorations outside their homes in what amounted to Mischief Night, Christmas-style. One night, I heard a group of kids outside my house. Before I went to check it out, I shut my bedroom light so nobody outside could see me at the window. As I slightly pulled up the shade, I heard our Christmas lights being smashed onto the sidewalk amidst footsteps walking faster and faster until they were running. I caught a glimpse of Weir's friend, Joey Franco when he turned around and literally looked up toward my window, as if he knew I was there. His face under the street light was unmistakable, and it didn't help him that our front porch light was still on.

"Devine, go to bed!" he taunted, and then ran up the street, disappearing into a shadowy cluster of five or six other bodies moving as a wall.

One of the more spookily bizarre incidents of childhood happened the day after Christmas while walking on Broad Street in Elizabeth. Every year without fail, December 26 meant the annual trip to Steinbachs to exchange clothes that didn't fit that we had received as gifts. That year was particularly rough because we were dealing with below zero temperatures and we had to walk many blocks from the car. It was me, my mom and Franklin on that Friday morning as we marched courageously toward the old ugly brown Steinbach's building to try on clothes. It was a yearly experience that we dreaded. As we approached the building, we crossed the street and I got separated from my mom and Franklin for a second or two as we walked into an oncoming wave of people crossing in the opposite direction. From the second that I began crossing, I spotted an ominous dark figure standing in the middle of the street. It was a woman dressed in a black cloak from head to toe, standing motionless. Her hair was long and black...her face pale as a corpse...her eyes, dark and swollen...and her lips, black. Although she looked dead, I could tell she wasn't that old...maybe late 30s or early 40s. As I walked past her, I saw her looking straight down at me...making eye contact. Nobody else crossing the street seemed to notice her. She stayed frozen in place and only turned her head to follow me as I moved past. I walked looking behind me, tripping over the curb as I reached it. The woman stood in place with her head turned toward me. I still had my eyes on her when she opened her mouth and let out what sounded like an exaggerated burp. Then...

"You!" she croaked in an inhuman voice, still looking me directly in the eyes as if she were trying to mentally suck my soul right out of my body.

I turned around looking for my mom and Franklin. They were already at the store entrance waiting for me.

"Eugene," my mom called out. "Let's go!"

I turned back around to where the woman was standing, but she was gone. I glanced down the street to see if she had started walking but I couldn't find her in the crowd. She was nowhere in sight and I had only turned my head for a second or two. She had completely vanished. When we got inside the store, I mentioned her to my mom and Franklin and they swore they didn't see any such woman in the street.

———

After the holidays, we returned to school. 1981 had begun. My mom sent me to school in a new sweater she had given me for Christmas. It wasn't like any sweater I had before, and although I wore sweaters, they were all pullovers. This one was different, and I wasn't happy about having to wear it. It was long and cream-colored, with big lacquer-covered wooden buttons, and a huge collar that sort of wrapped around your neck as if it were a rolled up towel. It looked almost like a shorter version of a robe. It even came with its own belt, giving it the pompous ass seal of approval. It looked like something Sherlock Holmes would wear. It should have come with its own pipe. Maybe, I could sit in a rocking chair with a crossword puzzle and a magnifying glass while I smoke my pipe and wear my sweater, I thought.

I had gotten many gifts for Christmas. The biggest was this big green box called Mr. Quarterback. It had a yellow hand protruding from it that you placed a football on. Then you wind up the timer and run like hell. The idea was that Mr. Quarterback was supposed to pass the football, and that was just fine with me. I hated the competition of sports, and I hated playing sports once other people got involved. I liked sports on my own terms, and with Mr. Quarterback, I would play football...on my own terms, and with nobody tackling me, yelling at me, or taking it too seriously. The only problem was that Mr. Quarterback was big and weighty. It came with these metal spikes that were supposed to keep it lodged in the ground. But once the timer went off and the arm flung the ball, Mr. Quarterback's power proved too great for its own weight, and the entire thing would shoot out of the ground and soar through the air right behind the football. I enjoyed playing with it at first, but once the inconvenience of securing it into the ground after every pass set in, I remained in denial for the rest of the Christmas break before I accepted that maybe Mr. Quarterback wasn't such a practical toy. What I really wanted was to have the same imaginary games that Ritchie Burke and I did for baseball. That was all I needed to kill hours when I was alone.

But then I debated with myself as I stood in the backyard looking down at Mr. Quarterback, who was clearly not cooperating. Did I really need to commit hours upon hours of imagination to a fake NFL that existed only in my head? I was going deeper and deeper into my mind and deeper and deeper into myself. Much of what I lived, existed only in my mind...the fake Kiss concerts with Tommy and Ritchie, the fake baseball games with Ritchie and Derrick, the acted-out fake movies with Marc, the comic books. Years later, I'd think of this when I'd see the Ingmar Bergman movie *Autumn Sonata*, when one of the characters said something to the effect of "I could always live in my art, but never in my life."

I always had a natural guilt complex, so after a few hours in the classroom that first day back, I started to feel bad about the sweater my mom had given me to wear. Once I got to school, I took it off and stashed it in the closet. As I sat at my desk doing an assignment, I thought about my mom. I thought about her giving me the sweater, and how when I opened it, all I could think of was selfishly wanting some game or record album or something. I thought about how she meant well, and how terrible I felt feeling anything about that sweater other than completely thankful. I thought about how much I loved my mom, and how I somehow wasn't able to vocally express things like love, and wished that I could. And then I started thinking about how she would always tell me "you only have one mother." It was usually the guilt mechanism she often resorted to as the final bomb that would end the conversation when it wasn't going her way.

And then I felt horrible about myself.

Mrs. Painter got up from her desk and went across the hall to ask Mr. Hardenberger to watch the class for a few minutes while she went to the bathroom. He must not have paid too much attention or was too busy because he never once poked his head into our room while she was out. After she left the room, I got up from my desk feeling guilty, and walked to the closet to get my sweater. I boldly put it on and went back to sit down. I didn't even have my chair pushed all the way in before Weir erupted in a fit of laughter, pointing at my sweater. He got up from his seat and walked to the front of the row where Ashley and I sat in the first two seats. He kept one hand over his mouth while pointing at my sweater, looking at Ashley trying to get her to laugh.

"Awwww," she said as if looking at a lost puppy. "Look how cute Eugene is in his sweater."

He busted out with whatever laughter he had been holding in.

"Devine, you're so gay! Hahahahahahahaha…ahahahahaa!!!"

"Oh stop it Kevin!" Ashley cut in, smacking him over the head with a three-ring binder. Suddenly, there were little chuckles from all corners of the room, but none really to rival Weir's. The few that were chuckling were probably doing so because Kevin got hit. But he only laughed harder, not even acknowledging that Ashley hit him.

"That sweater, man! Oh my god! You should be sitting in a rocking chair smokin' a pipe with that sweater, man! How gay!"

I'm not sure if I grew more upset because he was making a mockery out of my sweater in front of the class, or because I fully expected it. Regardless, I blew a gasket. I stood up, ripped the sweater off, and threw it to the floor, lashing out at him.

"Here, take the fuckin' thing! Burn it for all I care!"

And then the entire class went silent.

Weir stopped laughing.

I saw the sweater lying on the floor about six feet from my desk in the empty part of the room where reading groups gathered. When it hit the floor, it was as if I had hit my mom or done something to hurt her…as if she had felt it.

I hated myself.

My eyes welled up with tears and I could feel myself on the verge of losing it right in front of the class. So I looked down with my elbows on the desk and my palms over my eyes, somehow not bursting out into full crying.

"Eugene?" Ashley said, tapping me on the shoulder.

"Hey man," Weir began while Ashley cut him off.

"Leave him alone, stupid! You're stupid, Kevin!"

He placed his hand on my shoulder. I violently shrugged him off while keeping my face buried in my hands. He crouched down next to me. He didn't see me crying, but he must have sensed I was.

"Eugene, I was only kidding, man. Come on."

Weir got up and picked up my sweater and brought it over to me. I took my hands away from my eyes. He dusted the sweater off and put it on my desk.

"It's a nice sweater man, you're lucky to have it."

He felt like a piece of shit.

Maybe not as much as I did.

But he felt like shit.

"I was just messin' with ya, man. You shouldn't be ashamed to wear it. Was it a gift? I like it actually."

I didn't answer.

I could sense him kissing my ass while discovering that this was yet another sensitive soft side of him that conflicted with the asshole in him. But the asshole was just a façade, as I was slowly coming to find out that year.

"Eugene," Ashley said from behind me. "Did you get that sweater for Christmas?"

I turned around to face her.

"Yeah."

Weir took the sweater and held it up to me.

"Come on, man. It's a nice sweater. You should put it back on. I'm an asshole, man. I didn't mean to laugh. Come on man, put it on."

He opened the sweater around me so I could slip my arms into it, helping me get it back on.

"There. Look. That's a nice sweater, man."

The monster that I thought Kevin Weir was for the past six years had dissipated into the reality that he was just another kid, and one with a heart sometimes, even if those moments came after he had been mean. I knew by now that yes, he was a troublemaker. But he wasn't a bad kid. Somewhere, his soft side always surfaced.

Mrs. Painter walked back into the room clueless to what had been taking place. She had been out for a while. She must have taken a long nasty crap or something.

———

Ashley brought out our playful sides. It was a side that was hidden behind that "I'm too cool for this shit" attitude that boys can have. Besides the obvious gradual gravitation she had toward me that year for whatever reason, our friendship was sealed over penguins. She was obsessed with penguins. She always had them on her shirts as far back as I could remember. She also had penguin patches on her jeans, penguin folders, book covers, Color Forms, Shrinky-Dinks, etc...

One day, she asked me to draw her a picture of a penguin, and when I refused, she proceeded to jab me in the shoulder with her pen. It was an Ashley Drake thing to jab people with her pen or pencil. I guess it was her way of telling you she liked you. How I didn't die of ink or lead poisoning the second half of that year is beyond me. She must have broken dozens of pencil points on me. Knowing I couldn't defeat her persistence on the desired penguin picture, I complied. Kevin also joined in, and we had penguin-drawing contests. Of course, it was the girl who imposed the contest on the two guys who were suddenly competing. She was constantly beating the crap out of him too, and he wasn't about to fight her either. In a way, we both loved the attention. Ashley's biggest contribution to my elementary school life besides years of grief, was when she turned Kevin and I on to Saturday morning cartoons.

But not really.

I occasionally got up to watch the Saturday morning cartoons with Franklin who was much more into them than I was. But in an epic lunchtime conversation about them, Ashley sort of re-sparked my interest in them. Kevin seemed to be into them much more than I was, and was able to relate more to what Ashley was talking about. It was the kind of conversation that went "Hey did you see that one when Shaggy and Scooby Doo..." So, prompted by Ashley, Kevin and I began waking up early on Saturdays to watch cartoons. On Monday mornings, we would shamelessly talk about what we watched on Saturday. There was an innocent silliness that she was able to bring out of both of us. Kevin deep down really wasn't a bad kid. I don't think there was a bad bone in his body. Maybe he needed an audience sometimes, but he wasn't a bad guy. I kind of wonder today what kind of life he had at home. Eventually, he became very protective of me, as he knew my newly-found delinquency was just a front for a kid who was really scared. Ashley had also been a kid badly in need of attention. I think after a while, we were all able to drop the veil that we wore outside the classroom. In reality, she was just an eleven-year old girl. Without knowing it, she reminded us time and again that we were kids...maybe not little kids anymore, but still kids. Kevin didn't have to be a tough guy around us, and I no longer had to impress him, nor defend myself from her.

What had been taking place on a much larger scale since September was more change than I had probably seen during my entire stay at Cypress. All of that fear and trepidation had begun to subside to a certain degree, although I was never completely at ease. There was still that unexplainable feeling that something terrible could happen at any given moment, and that probably had something to do with being friends with Kevin Weir. When I think of autumn and everything after, those months really become a dividing line...a kind of summation for the first part of my life that seems to end where the next part begins. There was no overlap...just a very defined radical shift, perpetuated by the need to be cool and the needs of two other kids whose stars aligned with mine on their own inadvertent quest for change in their own lives.

13

The Dumpster

Sixth grade obviously did not come without its consequences. Yes, counting kindergarten we had waited seven years for this, and we had climbed the ladder, and were now kings and queens. And we were in the much-revered position of sixth graders. But with status also came the dreaded sixth grade chorus. As the end of every school year approached, so did the sixth grade concert, where every kid and teacher went into the All Purpose Room to watch and listen to the sixth grade class sing Broadway show tunes. The time inevitably came for try-outs, and everyone was required to participate. Just what I had always feared, and it was finally coming to pass. Kevin, Marc and I decided early on that we weren't going to take part. Chorus just wasn't cool. The audition was for each student to sing an a cappella version of the "Star Spangled Banner" in front of Miss Tripe. Of course the three of us purposefully sang out of key and botched it up. We ended up being the only three kids out of the entire sixth grade who didn't make it. So on Monday afternoons at two o'clock when the rest of the class went to chorus practice, the three of us sat in the classroom with Mrs. Painter and got a head start on our homework.

The hour alone with the teacher was interesting. She got to know us all a little better than the troublemaking punks that she thought we were. Kevin had acted up so much that year that his desk was now literally up against Mrs. Painter's. She wanted to keep an eye on him as well as make an example out of him. The period was supposed to be quiet. It usually wasn't. At first, Mrs. Painter used the same stern disciplinary tone that she used in class, but eventually let her guard down a bit. As Kevin would continue to crack jokes, she would lighten up a little and smile. She knew he was funny and actually began to take a liking to him. When a full class was in session however, she showed no appreciation for his antics. I remember the day I myself broke the ice with her. Marc came in one Monday wearing a jersey with The Doors on it. On the backside was a picture of Jim Morrison and the caption: *Jim Morrison: An American Poet*. Mrs. Painter

was out in the hall talking to Mr. Hardenberger when suddenly Kevin turned around and looked at Marc with his usual mischievous smile.

"I bet you can't name five Doors songs you fat piece of shit."

Marc got up and ran over to Kevin. Very quickly, he delivered a thunderous blow to Kevin's shoulder blade and then ran back to his seat. While walking back into the room, Mrs. Painter caught him in the act.

"Mr. Rinaldi, got a problem?"

She was furious.

She walked to the front and turned around to face us.

"I suggest you take your aggression out on Mr. Weir after class."

"Oh, thanks a lot!" Weir said sarcastically.

"Shut up!" she shot back, "I wasn't talking to you!"

"Yeah, but you just told him to beat me up after class."

"Mr. Weir, I said shut up!"

She was pissed. She looked in the back at Marc.

"And Mr. Rinaldi, I suggest you get busy. Or an American poet is going to be a dead poet!"

She sat down.

Then there was morgue silence.

But I had personal issue with what Mrs. Painter had just told Marc. Jim Morrison had died in 1971. With total self-confidence, I stood up. I had to correct her.

"He's been dead for ten years."

"Shut up you!" she snapped, almost cutting me off, her voice breaking into a trace of laughter.

She chuckled to herself and then broke out into a hysterical laughing fit. At that point, we all started cracking up. I don't think it was my comment as much as the absurdity of the whole thing that made her laugh. I think she realized that she was up against a wall of absurdity. It was pointless to fight us as we fed off each other. She knew we weren't bad kids. She knew we did our work, at least in the classroom. And so she was okay with us having fun in the process. From that moment on, she mellowed out until the year ended. She let us be ourselves without any real threat of consequence. That doesn't mean she let us beat the shit out of each other, but a mutual respect developed between Mrs. Painter and us, and we began to look forward to that weekly hour alone with her.

———

Cable television came to Oakwoods in late February 1981. I raced home from school on the day it was installed. I was amazed at the control box, with its three tiers of thirteen channels each. Holy crap, I thought. There were channels that I never imagined. I thought it would simply be HBO. There was ESPN, a channel dedicated to sports. Ingenious! There was a Philadelphia station and an Atlanta station. There was even a weather channel! I got a kick out of that one...a channel that only shows the weather...imagine that! I watched it for hours, just because I could. I remember turning on HBO for the first time, and seeing the rainbow color spectrum that served as a logo along with the accompanying beep that signified when the channel wasn't in service. This of course, was before HBO was a 24-hour channel, and it didn't really go into operation until around 4 or 5 PM. When it finally came on the air, the first thing I saw was a preview of the John Carpenter film, *The Fog*. Carpenter had done *Halloween* a few years earlier and was probably responsible for bringing the slasher film into mainstream America. Gratuitous stabbings were nothing new in cinema, but let's face it...the majority of American suburbia was not watching *Suspiria*. Following *Halloween* though, the next few years saw a fad in slasher movies that made up a large percentage of the much larger trend in horror movies that included but was certainly not limited to *The Shining, The Changeling, Friday the 13th, He Knows You're Alone, Prom Night, Motel Hell, Deadly*

Blessing, The Boogey Man, My Bloody Valentine, Happy Birthday to Me, The Hearse, Halloween 2, and the Silent Scream. It seemed like for every *Ordinary People*, there were ten horror films. They were all on cable during that first year in Oakwoods. On that first night, however, the first thing I watched was a Sean Connery movie called *Meteor*. I couldn't get over the fact that there weren't any commercials either. Nor could I believe what I was hearing. The curse words weren't cut out like on regular TV. It was a momentous occasion in my house, when I turned on *Apocalypse Now*, and heard the word *fuck* coming out of the TV speakers.

A few weeks later on a Friday night, Tommy and I slept over Marc's house for what was planned as an all night cable TV marathon. Part of the cable package included the WHT channel that Marc's family had for years before cable even came to New Jersey. The original plan was to watch an X-rated movie called *Emanuelle* that went on after midnight on WHT. That, however, was thwarted as we snuck downstairs to find that Mr. Rinaldi was still watching TV, or else had fallen asleep in the recliner. Since we could only see the back of the chair, we couldn't tell. Back upstairs, we wrote love letters to Riley, and as the result of a dare, Marc volunteered me to sneak them into Riley's bag on Monday. By the end of the night, Tommy and Marc both wussed out and tore them up. I folded mine up, intending to dispose of it, but not immediately doing so for some reason. Later that weekend, when I found myself at home still with the letter, I hid it inside my stereo. It was one of those old wooden Motorola console stereos that stand on legs and open up like a coffin. Inside, was an 18-inch slot to store albums, so I tossed the letter to the bottom so as not to deal with it.

That same night at Marc's, we came across Federico Fellini's *Amarcord* on one of the Public Broadcasting stations. For a long time after that, I never knew the name of what we watched, and would rack my brain trying to describe it to people. Mind you, this was decades before IMDb and Google. Years later, as I'd get more serious about cinema and absorb foreign and independent film, I'd come to realize that *Amarcord* was the film we saw that night. What initially attracted us to it as we channel surfed, was that it just looked funny, and we couldn't understand what they were saying because it was in Italian. So, we just watched it, not really paying attention to what was going on or bothering to read the subtitles on the screen. We began to place our own words in the characters' mouths, inventing our own dialogue on top of it. Then came the scene with the fat woman. We joked about how she looked like Miss Tripe. Then the fat woman began stuffing a boy's face into her naked breasts, forcing him to lick them. Suddenly the thought of Miss Tripe wasn't funny anymore. It was traumatizing. What if that *was* her? And hypothetically, what if the boy was me, being forced into her boobs and suffocated like that? I could never look at Miss Tripe the same way again. I didn't want to go to music class anymore.

———

One day, Kevin talked me and Ashley into leaving with him for lunch. He had always been one of the few to leave school during lunch period under the guise of "going home," while he really went for pizza at Luigi's, and then next door to the arcade to play video games. For me, it was an experience similar to walking the highway with Marc, and I wasn't happy about it, but I tried to act like I didn't care, so as not to come across as an uptight killjoy. I was tired of the monotony of the lunch room anyway, so leaving was a welcome change. Even though there usually wasn't anything to buy during the school day, my mom never sent me out of the house without some money in my pocket. It had been over two years since the Kiss card incident, so some time had passed to where I was allowed to have money again. I had a five dollar bill on me, so I was able to buy a few slices of pizza and a Coke, and pay for Ashley's as well since she didn't have any money on her. I wasn't worried about having to account for it. I figured I would just tell my mom the truth if she noticed that I spent my money. Why I left school grounds was another story that I would have to invent a lie for, but I wasn't prepared to deal with that kind of stress yet, so I tried not to think too much about getting caught... at least not through lunch.

While we ate at Luigi's, Kevin was telling us about how the Chinese restaurant a few doors down in the stripmall, was busted for serving cat as their meat. Nobody could prove what they were cooking, but apparently there was a dumpster full of cat heads in the alley behind the Kon-Tiki. Oakwoods was subject to many urban legends, one of which consisted of a haunted tree with arms on the other side of the Forbidden Zone out behind the Sleepy Hollow apartment complex...which was one of the contributing factors that kept me out of there. The most recent thing we'd hear about around the neighborhood was the cat heads in the dumpster behind Kon-Tiki.

"Eww, that's digusting, but I don't believe it," Ashley kept saying.

"It's true," Kevin insisted.

I was indifferent to the entire conversation and just sat there listening, although Kevin kept asking if I believed him or heard the story. After a few minutes, he got up from the booth and started walking out of Luigi's, motioning to us.

"Come on, let's go take a look!"

I wasn't finished with my pizza.

Really?

Is this what we're doing now?

Looking for cat heads in a dumpster?

Ashley and I got up and followed behind him.

"Oh my God Kevin, you're ridiculous. You're trying to ruin my love of Chinese food," she said.

"I know," I chimed in. "I love it too, and I don't think we're gonna find any cats in the dumpster."

"Neither of you will ever eat Chinese again," he mocked.

"Yeah right," I said.

"You won't. You'll both get grossed out and not want anything."

"Never," Ashley retorted.

"You'll be sitting there looking at the menu and decide everything on it is made of cat!"

"Bullshit," I charged.

Kevin was relentless in his sudden mission to gross us out.

"What are you gonna do? Order just rice? Maybe the one scoop of ice cream they give you for desert?"

I smiled and conceded by laughing. Not at Kevin really, but at the thought of the one scoop of ice cream they gave you for desert at Kon-Tiki. That much was true.

"But I love that one scoop of ice cream," Ashley said, giggling.

As we approached the end of the stripmall we turned the corner to see Riley Stevens and Sharon Redshaw walking in the same direction, but about twenty steps ahead of us.

"Hey!" Kevin called out to them, as we stopped at the dumpster.

"What's up dudes?" Sharon said, nodding back and waving at us.

Then she turned around and headed back toward us. Riley kept walking along the back of the stripmall.

I turned back and watched her.

Paying no attention to Sharon, Ashley was now focused on ice cream.

"Now you got me thinking about ice cream, Kevin!" she scolded.

I took my eyes off Riley long enough to turn around to respond to Ashley.

"Ice cream is my favorite," I said.

"Oh my God, Eugene, mine too!"

"Chocolate's the best."

"No way, strawberry!"

"Strawberry sucks. Eww, nasty!"

"Chocolate looks like poop!"

"Chocolate!"

"Strawberry!"

"Chocolate!"

"Strawberry!"

Christ, really?

We left school grounds in the middle of the day, and were probably going to get in trouble if we got back late...and there we were, standing at a dumpster in an alley behind a Chinese restaurant...nitpicking about ice cream.

"Are you guys gonna smoke a doobie back here?" Sharon inquired.

Kevin smiled.

"I wish. You got any?"

"Nah, man, I'm dry," Sharon shot back as she started walking again, catching me looking at Riley.

"Whattaya like Riley or something, man?"

I turned back around almost embarrassed. Sharon was a straight-up kind of chick. She was cool and called things the way she saw them. She was one of those stoners who could smoke lots of pot and still be a straight-A student. I didn't know much about her at all, but I suspected she was very much like Kevin in that she probably hung out with kids a lot older, and got away with things I wouldn't even dream of attempting...things like hanging out in the woods, smoking, riding in cars, leaving Oakwoods and going God knows where at all hours of the night...leaving her own block.

That was one that really began to bother me. The more I thought about some of the things kids were doing while I was barely allowed off my own street, the more it pissed me off. But then again, what exactly *were* they doing?

I wasn't quite sure.

It was all one big elusive mystery...this giant wall of luring fantasy sequence that always got the better of my imagination when I went deep into thought about what everyone else got to do, versus what I couldn't do. It never really did occur to me that maybe these kids weren't allowed to do half the things they were doing, and it's just that they were sneaking around with their parents not knowing.

Who knows?

But there I was, hanging out with Kevin Weir.

And what were we doing?

Walking the back alley of a stripmall to see if we could find dead cats in a dumpster.

Big fucking deal!

I would rather have been talking rock music with Tommy at the lunch table. I mean there was definitely a sense of adventure in wandering outside the box and off the script of daily routine, but I seriously didn't care about the contents of a fucking dumpster. Plus, it was freezing outside, and I wanted to be inside.

"Sharon, I'm leaving…I'll meet you back at school!" Riley shouted from the opposite end of the alley.

Sharon turned to Kevin who was hanging on the dumpster as if it were a pull-up bar, trying to see inside of it.

"Oh come on man, screw this dumpster. If there's no weed, I might as well get back to school. Riley wait up!"

And suddenly Sharon was running through the alley to catch up. As she got near the end of the stripmall behind the A&P, she began to slide.

"Wooooah shit…watch out guys it's icy!"

"That's black ice, watch yourself!" cried a coarse gravelly voice from the loading dock of the A&P. A grey-bearded middle aged man wearing brown overalls and a ski hat emerged.

"And what the hell are you kids doing out of school? Where are your parents?"

Sharon turned back at the man.

"And who the hell are you, ya poor bastard?"

Kevin started laughing hysterically as he climbed to the top of the dumpster, overhearing Sharon's wiseass response.

"Ha! Poor bastard!" he wailed as he jumped in, landing on a pile of God knows what.

Ashley was stunned that he jumped in.

"Oh my God Kevin, are you crazy?"

"Go on, go back to school...get an education! Don't end up in a dumpster like me!"

From a very close distance, I heard the rumbling sound of an engine, but before I could process the sound, a Ford Econoline box truck with a Breyers logo turned the corner and chugged away as the driver threw it in park.

"Seriously, I'll meet you guys back," Kevin called out from inside the dumpster.

I turned around and saw that Sharon was already gone. Kevin was no longer visible, and it was just me and Ashley. As we approached the back of the A&P, we glanced up at the workers inside. They looked cold and miserable. In fact, they were.

"Look how cold and miserable they look," I said as we tried to walk around some ice.

"I know," Ashley smiled sadistically, "I'd hate to be that poor bastard."

The poor bastard sat cold and miserable on the loading dock as the delivery truck began slowly pulling up. The frigid winter chill sent the rest of the poor bastards to the other side of the dock where they gathered round a space heater, occasionally sneaking into the store for warmth. It was a day where nothing much was happening, and the loading dock was empty. The poor bastard watched as the truck began backing in, its tires cracking against a lengthy sheet of ice. The truck came awfully close to hitting us as we made our way out from behind the building, carefully watching our steps as we walked along the ice, which was now spread too vast to avoid. As the truck passed, I noticed the back door was opened and some crates were ready to fall out.

"Look out," I said pointing to the ground.

"Watch, WATCH!" I screeched as Ashley's foot went into a pile of dog shit.

"Oh my God, Eugene, dog poop!"

Somehow, I got the impression that it was the poor bastard's job to remove all of the dog shit from the premises before the workday started. It was an inconvenience and a drag to have to walk on the property of a food store and find such unsanitary conditions such as dog shit near the loading dock. Not that I even took into account that we were in a way, trespassing. But that didn't matter...my friend stepped in shit.

But then something caught my eye.

"Look!" I pointed to the ground.

Ashley looked down.

It was a spoon...a white plastic spoon, perhaps dropped by some lazy bastard, or even the poor bastard himself while he and his co-workers had takeout Chinese food and didn't dispose of the cutlery in the proper fashion. It was resting in a narrow groove of visible pavement between slabs of ice. It was caked with dirt. Now it would be caked with shit.

"Yay, a spoon," Ashley said while bending over to pick it up. "Now I can scrape the poop off my boot."

As we stopped, I realized we would be blocked in as the passing truck began to slow down. It was going to stop, and we probably wouldn't be able to pass. At a sudden instant, the brakes began to screech as the truck slid to a complete stop with some crates reading "Ice Cream: Keep Frozen" falling out of the back and onto the icy ground. The crates hit the pavement with the sound of a wooden thud.

Ashley looked up, concerned.

She stopped scraping her boot and stared straight ahead at the crates, still holding the shit-caked spoon.

"Duuuude," I whispered.

"Yay," Ashley grinned as she immediately took off on the frozen ground, her boots stampeding the ice as she ran toward the back of the truck. I took off behind her, my shoes also trampling the crackling surface, as we were both unaware of the fact that we were running on ice.

"Ice cream!" she wailed at the top of her lungs, her mouth smiling ear to ear. The sound of two sets of running feet trampling the ice filled the alley.

"Ice creeeeeeam!" she railed again with glee. "And I just happen to have a spoooon in my hand!"

14

The Visitors

Late in January of 1981, Ronald Reagan was sworn in as president. On Inauguration Day, just hours after he took the Oath of Office, the American hostages came home from Iran. The public really thought nothing of it at the time, but it was said that Reagan had struck a secret deal with Iran to delay the release of the hostages until after he took office, which many who still regard him as a hero, remain in denial about. In class, we watched the events unfold live on TV. When you're a kid, you're very impressionable. When the hostages came home, it was a great day for America, and you weren't really thinking about how the rest of the world viewed us. Politics had not entered your awareness. The return of the hostages coinciding with the inauguration, to a group of sixth graders made Reagan seem like a hero. And that's exactly how they intended it. I can't really account for all the adults who fell for it.

Around nine weeks later, President Reagan was shot. That day, word had just gotten out to us during the last half hour of school. I found out by overhearing the secretary in the main office as I was delivering an envelope that Mrs. Painter asked me to bring down. The ladies in the office seemed distracted and upset, and everyone seemed to be holding their noses or burying their faces in their shirts. I could hear the deafening roar of some kind of vacuum coming from the All Purpose Room. As I became aware of the issue at hand, it hit me that the entire unit building smelled relentlessly of shit. I gave the secretary the envelope and she told me to get back to my class as quickly as I could.

"Why did they have to do this now?" I could hear someone angrily ask in the principal's office.

As I walked out of the main office, I became distracted by the blending sounds of a sanitation truck and a monstrous vacuum coming from outside the school. I had to step over a large hose that ran from outside, into the building and into the All Purpose Room.

"Where's Leon?" I heard Mr. Zielinski cry as he walked out of the office.

Nobody answered him.

He walked past me and into the All Purpose Room. One of the office ladies was walking out holding her nose.

"Where's Leon?" he asked again.

"Who?"

Mr. Zielinski was livid.

"Leon! The plumber!"

Leon the plumber wasn't having a good day. He had an uncooperative partner who had been getting on his nerves for some time.

First, he arrived late to the Cypress School where they were cleaning a grease trap. The man's name was Moses. Moses looked already dead, so his life couldn't have been much worse. He wore shit-caked boots, yellow hip waders, a raincoat of the same color, and a black pullover ski cap with a large ball at the top. Facially, he was a real-life version of the old man who opened the door in the Fat Albert Halloween Special and took the kids' candy. But the tardy Moses didn't even give Leon the chance to be angry. Moses himself was angry. It seemed that every time they went to do this particular grease trap job at the Cypress School, there was always a catch. There was always a second job besides the grease trap. But this job was usually done during the summer while school was out of session. It was a job that nobody in their right mind would ever impose on a school building while school was in session, especially with kids around. But nobody could avoid the foul odor that began to permeate the air that week, so Leon the Plumber had to return on an emergency call. Once Moses heard that he had to go to Cypress, he knew there would be that catch. The grease trap, as bad as it was, was a day off. Let's throw a cliché in there for good measure. The grease trap compared to the second job that went along with it...was a piece of cake. Even with the deathly stench that caused one to gag and vomit, it wasn't as bad as the catch...and the catch was the hole in the floor. The hole in the floor was located in an otherwise uninhabited room behind the All Purpose Room. It was behind that one door that never opened and every kid in the school always wondered where the hell that door led.

The hole in the floor was simply unfathomably cruel. It was a rather tiny hole...one of 8X8 inch proportions, with a six inch pipe that trailed along the ceiling, down the wall and into the hole. If you pulled away the large metal plate on the floor, the eight inch hole became a five foot hole. It took a while for the staff of the main unit to figure out what had been taking place…but apparently, the pipe ran all the way from the Board of Education office upstairs above the All Purpose Room. It was an angry, ruthless pipe that ran directly from the restroom of the personnel office, and every time one of the women had a bowel movement, it was flushed and delivered safely into the hole in the floor below. And then came the mysterious stench that only last week had been discovered during routine inspection. The unfinished business of cleaning the remnants of shit pilings underground were left to Moses who had seen this occur in the industrial world far too much for his liking, and was furious that he had to go climbing down into the shit again.

"Why do I gotta go down in the shit again?!" he screamed hoarse-throated and gravelly.

"Always me! I'm always the one that's gotta climb down in the shit!"

Of course Leon saw to it that Moses climbed down into the shit with the hose, sucked the shit through the high-powered truck-vac parked outside and did his job properly. At the end of the day, Mr. Zielinski complained to Leon when Moses tracked shit through the main office after forgetting to take his waders off.

"Did you forget to scrape the shit off your shoes?" Leon began.

He had a go at Moses, and it escalated after weeks and weeks of pent up rage. Leon lost his head and fired Moses right in front of me.

"Hey!" Mr. Zielinski barked, pointing at me.

"Hey!" he said again. "You can't be in here. You gotta get out!"

He grabbed me by the hand and in the process, sidetracked Mrs. Santorini, the teacher's aide as she walked out of the office.

"Mrs. Santorini, please escort this young man out of the building and back to his class."

"Sure, Mr. Zielinski," she said in her Don Corleone voice, clearly annoyed.

As we began down the hallway, Mr. Tutundjian walked out of his office, and he too, wasn't happy. He began yelling at Mr. Zielinski.

"Arrgruurrugum!"

He spoke short and to the point.

"Mmrogorum, argagrabapaw! A senanoof naaww! Grrroughm!"

"Okay," Mr. Zielinski replied respectfully, "no problem."

Mrs. Santorini continued down the hall.

"I've never had to be taken back to class," I told her as we moved toward the door.

"I know honey, he's being ridiculous. He's acting like this is some big emergency, this smell. I've smelled worse before, haven't you?"

"Not really," I said, "it's pretty bad."

"Think so? You should smell my bathroom after my son-a-Carmen gets done with it. Nobody does a smellier number two than my son-a-Carmen. My son-a-Carmen is a growing boy, but he's also a stinky boy. God bless him, my son-a-Carmen."

———

In the spring, the puffballs came. One night, the sky was bright blue and it didn't get dark out. The midday sun burned around the clock as the puffballs blew aimlessly through the mild air. They danced playfully, not touching the ground but continuously blowing through invisible patterns, endlessly crossing and circling a canvas of sky blue. The fallen pink and white of blooming magnolias covered the ground. Birds unheard all winter suddenly emerged in morning song...singing... calling...celebrating the arrival of Persephone's return to Earth.

Demeter was dancing when I sat up in my bed.

Was it morning?

Night?

I looked around what I thought was my room, but nothing looked familiar.

The walls are blank.

I threw the covers off.

I was sweating. My clothes were soaked and stuck to my body. I put my feet on the floor and stood up. I was dizzy. I saw the hallway outside my bedroom door. It looked familiar. I had to get to it. I thought that I might be able to, but I had to walk through fire to get there. Everything was black. Black and orange. And red. There was red. I had to walk through red. There were little devils shouting things from the living room, but their voices echoed loudly as if they were shouting from the center of my own brain. As I walked out of the room, I was suddenly running up Sycamore Drive, leaping over sidewalk cracks. I was taking massive leaps in the air and floating about in slow motion. As I slowly landed, barely touching the ground, I'd leap up again, flying through the air for several more yards until I'd land again. I did this all the way up Sycamore, yet I wasn't getting anywhere. I just kept running, leaping, and flying through the air in a treadmill-like standstill. In sleep, I could always fly. In the wrath and fury of a fever dream though, it was as if I were in a Bosch painting. I stood at the top of the stairs in the hallway. From the bottom of the stairs, the voices became more familiar, and suddenly my mom was asking me what the matter was.

Hours after I had woken up, I began to drink some tea that mom had made for me. I sat up in my bed and placed the cup on the night table. The room was filled with mid-Monday morning brightness, and I wouldn't be going to school. In fact I had a doctor appointment coming up within the hour. I looked around the room. Some traces of Kiss were still there, but Deborah Harry and some Mets and Yankees pennants had recently been added to my walls. I enjoyed the friendly serenity of my room. I couldn't help but notice the way the sun came through the window at that hour in the morning. Since I was usually in school during the day, I wasn't used to seeing my room at that hour. Weekends when I was home, it was different. Weekends were always different. Saturday and Sunday just had that Saturday and Sunday look about them. I went over to the window and looked out. It was sunny and warm outside, but the puffballs were gone. In fact, they had never been there. I sprung around to scratch my back. It itched like crazy. I had been itching all the day before, and it was becoming annoying. Suddenly my stomach itched. The Tylenol that mom had given me reduced my fever, but it was clear after the visit with the doctor, that I wouldn't be going to school any time soon. I had the Chicken Pox.

———

Deep into spring, talk began to loom large over the approaching end to the school year, and the larger reality that we would be graduating and going to "middle school" in the fall. I put middle school in quotes here because, as I mention early in the story, what was long known as junior high literally became known as middle school the year we started there. Oakwoods Junior High was now being referred to as Oakwoods Middle School. And another of the little sixth grade perks was the annual bus trip to the school to get a preview and a tour. It was a little ridiculous that we all had to get on a bus as if we were going on a long-distance class trip, only to travel three blocks up Oakwood Avenue. When we got there, our class and Mr. Hardenberger's class merged together into one giant mass of sixth graders.

We walked in with our teachers, and Mr. Rogers, the principal greeted us. We were told to wait outside the main office while Mr. Rogers took care of some business. The business just happened to be Derrick Adler who was sitting in a chair with the vice principal, Mr. Flagg interrogating him. Mr. Rogers was obviously distracted by the presence of the visitors. He motioned uncomfortably to us while looking at Mr. Flagg.

"I'm going to take them around the building, okay?"

Mr. Flagg nodded.

"I've got this," he said, referring to Derrick.

Mr. Rogers closed the door behind him and smiled. Adler smiled at me through the window. Mr. Rogers caught us exchanging glances.

"Mr. Adler was doing a little smoking in the bathroom this morning," he said, looking at us. Mrs. Painter gave Kevin and me the hardest glance we'd seen since the bathroom incidents earlier in the year. She looked at us as if we had something to do with Derrick and had been caught smoking ourselves. She didn't say anything, but there was a full-length lecture and reprimand in her eyes.

During the tour of the hallways, Mr. Rogers explained to us how there were three main halls...one for seventh grade, one for eighth grade and the old ninth grade wing. I had heard about the mythic ninth grade wing. Legend had it of a hippie teacher with long hair who taught rock and roll classes after school. We stopped at one classroom and Mr. Rogers opened the door to let us peak in. He explained to the teacher and the students that we were sixth graders who would be going there in the fall. Many of the kids looked big and mean, and already, there seemed to be an underlying joke of how we were the scared little sixth graders.

What could possibly be so great about this?

It took all those years to become kings of the school, and in just a few short months, we would be the little kids again.

I couldn't help noticing the desks though. They were attached to the seat and *looked* like school desks...at least the kind that I used to see the Sweathogs sitting in. How great it was going to be not to have those stupid desks in which you keep the entire contents of your life... the kind of desk that if things got too cluttered, your teacher would dump on the floor and make you clean it up.

No more of that.

No more cubbies.

We'd have lockers.

We'd have homerooms.

And since homerooms went alphabetically, Tommy and I would finally be in the same class.

In the cafeteria, we all sat down at lunch tables while the administrators spoke to us, telling us about the school...trying to welcome us as best as they could.

Outside the window, a garbage truck was pulling up to a dumpster. I was bored. I watched it, tuning out Mr. Rogers as he spoke. I thought about Derrick Adler sitting in the office. The thought scared me a little. How bad could that be? How much trouble do you get into for smoking in school? Or for smoking period? I couldn't conceive of what would happen to me if I were in his shoes. The whole thing freaked me out. I wasn't sure if I was ready for middle school. I looked at Kevin who sat next to me. He seemed to be enjoying the trip as if it were one big joke. Many of his older friends went to the middle school. And he seemed completely at ease. These were the thoughts that were running through my mind just before the bomb exploded.

———

Some of us jumped out of our seats while some of us just flinched. A scream could even be heard from down the hall...a female voice... then an outburst of collective gasps in the distance and an overall feeling of disruption and unease in the building. Something had blown up.

But wait...that couldn't have been a bomb! Could it?

That was the immediate thought as everyone remarked that the blast that shook the entire wing of the building sounded like a bomb.

Or maybe it was a gunshot.

School shootings were not yet a weekly thing back in 1981 and neither were lockdowns, so the protocol for this type of disturbance was more a case of teachers and students alike wandering around in confusion and all asking each other "what was that noise?"

We all left our seats and looked toward the outside hallway. Mr. Rogers stopped speaking and ran out of the cafeteria and down the hall. Mr. King, the guidance counselor told us all to stay put. Concerned, he peaked out the door, while we talked among ourselves.

"Oh man," Kevin said with a smile, "I told you it's the end of the world. We're all gonna die now!"

Ashley jumped out of her seat, reached across the table and punched him in the chest. Mrs. Painter didn't notice. She was too concerned about what the noise outside had been. Down the hall, Mr. Rogers could be heard telling someone to get to the nurse and a boy's shouting could be heard. It grew louder as he approached and Kevin recognized the voice. He knew the kid. It was a friend.

"What the hell?" Kevin curiously mumbled while running to the door.

"Mr. Weir, take a seat!" Mrs. Painter said from the doorway raising her arm, trying to block him from walking past. He stood next to her, looking out the door, paying no attention. He smiled at his friend who was walking with his hand out. It was dripping with blood. The skin had been burnt off and three fingers were stuck together.

"What the hell did you do, you stupid shit?" Kevin asked. The kid looked stunned and wasn't smiling.

"Fuckin' M-80 went off in my hand," he mumbled.

Mr. Rogers was behind him.

"A firecracker doesn't just *go off* in an English class. I'm telling you, you're making a great impression here in front of the sixth grade."

"Fuck the sixth grade!" the kid shot back at the principal. "And fuck you. I'm tellin' ya it went off!"

Kevin turned around smiling. He looked at Mrs. Painter and then turned to the rest of us at the table.

"What a stupid shit," he said grinning from ear to ear.

Mrs. Painter could only shake her head.

***

One day while working on a science project with Ashley and Kevin, I began to thumb through a *National Geographic*. I turned a random page and jumped out of my seat, flinging the magazine across the room where it hit Sharon Redshaw in her rapidly-growing chest and then landed on her desk.

"Oh my God, Eugene," Ashley cried while laughing nervously.

The rest of the class grew silent, partly in shock and partly waiting for the fallout.

"What the hell, man?" Sharon screamed from across the room.

"Yeah, Jesus Christ man! What's up with you?" Kevin chuckled in amusement.

Mrs. Painter looked up from her desk, removing her glasses. She stared at me, as did the rest of the class.

"Uhhh, Mr. Devine, do you wanna please explain yourself?"

15

Sandinista!

With a little more than one month of school left, Marc announced he'd be having a birthday party at his house, and invited just about everyone we knew in the sixth grade. Growing up in Oakwoods, the usual thing for our parents to do for our birthdays would be to invite the entire class to a pizza party at Luigi's. It was either Luigi's, or McDonalds. That was okay when you were younger. This was going to be different though. People were talking about this one for weeks in advance. Just about everyone in Mrs. Painter's and Mr. Hardenberger's class were whispering about it. Word was quickly spreading that this was going to be a major happening.

That school year brought many new kids from the neighborhood into the Cypress School with the closing of the old Fruit Tree School. Many of them had bad reputations that surpassed what the average eleven or twelve-year old usually did. Of course Kevin knew all of them, and his connection with Marc initiated us as part of them, and them as part of us. Two schools of sixth grade delinquents had joined to form one giant band of outsiders. Most remained unnoticed throughout the school year because they were all in Mr. Hardenberger's class, and Marc and I didn't have much contact with them except for on the playground during lunch hour when they happened to be around and not sneaking off to the arcade. One of the kids was Joey Franco, the local criminal who tolerated me only because of my connection with Kevin. Otherwise, he saw through me, and that my heart really wasn't in what they were all about. I never liked him, and Kevin knew it...especially after I revealed to him that he was one of the douchebags who smashed my dad's Christmas lights. Another kid who hung around Kevin was a mysterious shaggy-haired, tie dye-wearing figure who suddenly appeared one day named Frank Zappa. He must have gone to another school because he wasn't in any of the Cypress classes. Either that, or he didn't go to school at all. He seemed to know everyone in Oakwoods, and like Kevin, he had lots of older friends. He was the same age as us, but seemed to be an Oakwoods celebrity. Maybe he was too famous to go to school. Rumor had it that he was bringing drugs to the party. Rumors also flew of a toga party straight out of the movie *Animal House*. Kids walked around chanting "Toga! Toga! Toga!" On that note, it cannot be overstated how the advent of cable TV changed the way pop culture influenced kids. Where R-rated films were once taken seriously, as was the entire Motion Picture Association's rating system, kids were having access to films they would otherwise have never seen in a theater. We suddenly had access to *Animal House, Cheech and Chong's Up in Smoke, American Gigolo, 10, The Blue Lagoon* and *Stir Crazy*, all in the comfort of our living rooms. Most parents would never have taken their kids to see any of these films, which contained nudity, sex, drug use, profanity, nudity, sex, male prostitution, nudity and sex. All of these films by twenty-first century standards seem rather tame...but on the inevitable journey towards an "anything goes/access to whatever you want" Internet culture, the early 1980s were barely halfway there. It was a time when some things were still considered shocking. Given the desensitizing effect that the Internet would later have on kids, resulting in humans with the indifferent feeling of having seen it all, some might find it difficult to imagine...but back then, we hadn't yet seen it all.

To top off the anticipation of the party, was the fact that Riley Stevens and her best friend Nicole Somethingorother had both confirmed that they were coming. Nicole was in Mr. Hardenberger's class and had a huge crush on Kevin. Not that that mattered to any of the other guys who had crushes on her and who thought they had a chance with her.

And Riley?

Half the school had a crush on her. But the question always remained...who did Riley like? She was such a celebrity and so unattainable that I think even she knew enough to keep up the mystique and work it as if she was above liking *anyone*. And a few dozen guys all making idiots out of themselves thinking they were going to be the one to get with either of these two girls was far past the point of ridiculousness. Still, the idea of promised games such as Seven Minutes in Heaven and Spin-the-Bottle made the possibilities of this party seem endless.

We began seeing Tommy more often since he was in the same unit building as us, and there were a lot of mutual friends and acquaintances between our class and Mr. Hardenberger's class. He too was looking forward to the party, mainly because of Riley. It was a little funny how the party was supposed to be for Marc's birthday, but all of the attention leading up to it was centered around Riley and Nicole, and the fact that they were both going. Both Tommy and Jay Sacco who had become buddies on the outside of school had worshiped Riley for years. Jay was in class with Marc, Weir, and myself, which merged the few subgroups of friends that Tommy and I had branched out into. Everything was coming together.

On the Saturday of Marc's party, a unique and rare set of circumstances created the perfect storm for an entire 24 hours of total freedom away from my house. First, my parents were up bright and early to leave for a wedding out in Pennsylvania and I was up with them to pack a bag to stay at Marc's house for the entire day and night. The birthday party would be at night, followed by a sleepover. I wouldn't be going home until the next day. Franklin had already left the night before to go stay with our grandparents. During the ten-second ride down Sycamore, my mom told me to behave and be careful. After I said goodbye to my parents and headed toward Marc's front stairs, Elena Rinaldi appeared at the door, smiled and waved as my dad beeped the horn and drove off. I walked up the stairs noticing Elena's cutoff shirt behind the screen, but was stunned when she opened the door for me.

"Come on in, kiddo," she said, revealing naked legs and butt cheeks falling out of a skimpy pair of tight pink Dolfin gym shorts that disappeared into her crotch. She was already one year out of high school and I hadn't seen her much since she started college. It was the last weekend of May though, and her semester had ended weeks ago.

"Marc is out in the backyard," she said, closing the door. As my eyes popped out of my head, I pretended not to notice the full display in front of me.

Out back, Marc was shooting a BB gun into a foam target. I walked outside and down the back stairs to see an open guitar case with a Gibson Les Paul copy sitting on the picnic table. Marc shot the gun and looked at me noticing the guitar.

"See that bad boy?" he asked.

"Yup."

"Like it?"

"It's cool...is it yours?"

"That's my birthday present from my uncle. You gotta get drums or something Geno...we gotta start a band."

I too was thinking about playing guitar, but now that Marc had made the first step between the two of us, I didn't want to be thought of as a copycat, so it was then that I started entertaining the idea of playing drums instead.

"I'm growing my hair long," he said, aiming his automatic 45 at the target. "You're gonna have to grow yours too. Is your mom gonna let you? My mom already said I don't have to get anymore haircuts."

I didn't respond. He shot his gun.

"Your mom isn't gonna let you," he charged. "She's always making you get those dorky haircuts at the mall."

The back door opened, and Elena with a telephone pressed between her ear and her shoulder, poked her head outside.

"Marc, cut the shit with that freakin' gun already!"

Elena wasn't happy, not just with Marc using the gun, but we could hear her arguing with someone over the phone inside.

"Where's your mom, by the way?" I asked curiously, not having seen either of his parents as I walked through the house.

"The parents are out shopping around. They left right before you got here. My sis is hanging around the house today."

Speak of the devil, Elena's voice called out from the kitchen window.

"Marc, come in here a second."

Marc set the gun down on the table next to the guitar and headed for the door.

"We got all day, Geno," he called back while walking up the stairs. "We gotta think of something to do. Maybe we can go see that new movie *Death Hunt*."

The movie he spoke of was the latest Charles Bronson film.

"It's rated R," I replied. "Is your sister gonna get us in?"

He didn't have time to respond, as he had already gone inside. The door banged shut behind him. I wondered what we could possibly do all day, and started hoping he didn't get any bright ideas that consisted of breaking any laws or going too far from home. It had been half a year since we stopped doing comic books the way we were regularly doing them in that end-of-innocence summer of 1980. We were weeks away from the summer of 1981 and a lot had changed. Still, at the moment I was really hoping we could just sit inside and watch movies or something...maybe draw comics.

"Eugene," Elena called from the window. "Come on in, we have a plan."

A plan?

Suddenly I wasn't feeling as worried. If Elena was involved it couldn't be that bad. I walked into the house where they were both standing there in front of me.

"Geno, we're goin' to New York City!" Marc exclaimed anxiously.

"Huh? What?"

Elena held out her hand to stop Marc from talking. She seemed in a rush and found it better to explain the situation herself.

"Eugene, we're going to see the Clash. Do you want to see the Clash?"

The front door opened and Elena's friend Debbie walked in. Debbie was 19, tall and blonde. She wore tight black jeans, pink Converse, a pink cutoff t-shirt and blue and pink feather roach clips in her feathered hair. I was confused.

"The Clash? The band?"

"Yeah, Geno...the band...duh!" Marc chided, rolling his eyes.

Elena took over.

"Eugene, listen. We don't have much time. See, Debbie and I have tickets to see the Clash today, and our friends can't make it. My parents put me in charge over here today without knowing I have these tickets."

"They're not supposed to know," Debbie cut in, entering the kitchen.

I was still confused.

"But don't we have the party tonight?" I asked.

"Yes, that's tonight," Elena said. "The concert is at one o'clock today. We'll be back in time."

Now I was even more confused.

"A concert at one in the afternoon?"

"Yes, it's an all-ages show and we can get you in, but we really have to get going because it's getting late and we have to make a train."

"Sis," Marc cut in. "Mom and Dad don't know we're going to New York to a concert?"

"No, I'm leaving them a note that I'm taking you guys swimming at Debbie's for the day, and that we'll go to McDonalds for lunch and be back in time for the party."

"Good thinking!"

That's when I started wondering a little too much about the situation.

"Um...do you know your way around New York?" I asked Elena.

She turned around and took my face in her hands, bending down slightly to where our eyes were even.

"Don't worry, kiddo...I go to the city all the time. I need to go get dressed now and then we can go."

She turned back around to head upstairs to her room, leaving the three of us in the kitchen. My eyes followed her out of the room, noticing her shorts were completely lodged up the crack of her butt, and her entire right cheek was exposed. Before she got to the stairs, she turned back around. I turned away nervously, hoping she didn't notice me watching while pretending to look at the newspaper on the table. Some woman in China named Soong Ching-ling had died.

"Everything will be fine, kiddo."

<hr>

In the city, it was anything but fine. The train ride was fine and even the walk through Penn Station could be considered fine. But once we got up the stairs that regurgitated us out onto Seventh Avenue, it quickly became clear to me that we were on our own in the middle of nowhere. And I already had to pee.

Elena and Debbie argued over which direction to go in.

"I thought you knew where we were going, sis...what's up?" Marc immediately cut in, surveying the situation and the traffic moving south.

"We have to go to Forty-Fifth Street," Debbie announced to anyone who was listening.

"Well," Marc interjected, pointing north..."if this is Thirty-Second and that's Thirty-Third, we must need to walk *that* way!"

Walking up Seventh, I discovered that I already had a sentimental feeling for the past, as memories of the New York City of early childhood all rushed through me...courtesy of the wonderful assortment of midtown metropolitan stenches...that glorious combination of hot dogs, hot pretzels, sewage, garbage and piss that remained indelibly with me since my first visits there in the mid-1970s. I became obsessed for a short while with skyscrapers when the *King Kong* remake came out at the end of '76. Knowing we had the Empire State Building and newly-constructed World Trade Center practically in our backyard, I pestered my parents to take me there during the summer of '77. There were quite a few other trips into the city...several to museums with my Aunt Teresa, basketball and hockey games at the Garden with my dad, and even baseball games in the outer boroughs...and somehow those scents of the New York City streets had stayed with me. And so, at 12, I was already feeling old, missing a more innocent time and longing for something I wasn't sure of... something I couldn't quite put my finger on.

We soldiered on through ten blocks before Marc wanted to stop and get a hot dog just as we were approaching Forty-Second Street.

"Marc, are you kidding me?" Elena complained, watching him walk back toward a vendor we had just passed. We had no choice but to walk back, following him.

"Come on sis, I didn't have breakfast."

"We're okay," Debbie cut in. "We still have another hour any-way...we made good time."

Elena glanced over at me.

"Eugene, do you want one too? Are you hungry?"

"No thanks," I said, politely declining.

While we waited for Marc to get his hotdog, a song called "Shaddap You Face" blasted out of a boom box sitting on the ground.

Debbie started cackling like a little girl...breaking the cool persona she seemed to be enveloped in from the moment she entered the Rinaldi home.

"Oh my God...this song," she chuckled. "Have you heard this?"

"Yeah, it's cute," Elena smiled, counting out change to pay for Marc's hot dog. In the distance we could hear nondescript chanting going on, but couldn't make out what it was. The sights and sounds of the city all blended in with each other...especially as you approached Midtown, and it all amounted to one enormous and often overwhelming experience of kaleidoscopic sensory overload.

"Geno, check it out!"

As I started walking again with Debbie, I looked back to see Marc pointing out a woman in a tight leopard-print miniskirt and skimpy top to match, pacing back and forth approximately twenty feet from us.

"That chick is a hooker!" he said authoritatively as if he were giving us a tour of Times Square. Elena, embarrassed, put her finger to her lips and lashed out.

"Sssshh…you little asshole…what's wrong with you?"

Marc could only laugh. He and Elena caught up, and he walked beside me.

"Did you see that hooker?"

At the next light, I glanced out at the sea of yellow Checker cabs all stopped to let the cross-town traffic move west along Forty-Third Street. The chanting we heard was growing louder.

"We shoulda took a cab!" Marc shouted. "I wanna ride in one of those bad boys!"

As the light changed and we started to cross the street, it seemed all at once that a wall of car horns began competing with each other a block or two away, as the wailing sounds now merged with the chanting, which was slowly revealed as a bunch of teenagers screaming "Hell no, we won't go…hell no, we won't go…" over and over again.

"What the heck is going on over there?" Elena wondered as we got closer to a massive crowd moving in on Times Square with mounted police officers on horseback hovering overhead.

"That's it! That's Bonds!" Debbie exclaimed, pointing across the avenue at a block-long yellow marquis with big red letters that said BOND. "We're here! I don't know what's going on with this crowd, but we're here."

We crossed Seventh along Forty-Fourth walking against a growing crowd of visibly angry kids that also spilled onto the merging Broadway intersection. A trail of bodies up Broadway in front of Bond International Casino extended to Forty-Fifth Street and wrapped around the building as police with bullhorns sounding increasingly impatient told the crowd to disperse. I had seen the sign in historical pictures and had known Bond to be a company that sold clothes. I wondered quietly to myself why the Clash was playing at a clothing store.

"I paid ten dollars for this fuckin' ticket!" screamed one kid, passing us.

"Fuckin' pigs!" screamed another.

"It's not the cops, it's the fire department," said a third.

Then a fourth...

"It's the fucking city!"

"What's going on?" Elena inquired to anyone who cared to answer.

"Concert is cancelled," someone shot back.

Then several other voices arose from the gathering mass of humanity.

"What's going on?" a woman called out.

"Concert is cancelled."

"No, it's not, it's postponed!"

"Fire department shut it down...they oversold the shows and there were too many people inside the other night."

"They were hit with a vacate order...they can't open the doors. Clash ain't playing."

"Hell no, we won't go!" they still screamed in unison from around the corner on Forty-Fifth.

Amidst the various overlapping explanations overheard from within the wall of people moving toward us was a sudden change in the nerve center...wherever the nerve center was. It could have been at the end of the line, or it could have been in the middle of the line...but at some point, the line was no longer a line, as the crowd surged forward with a violent thrust of overpowering force...unlike anything I've ever been hit with, both physically and figuratively... knocking me to the ground and sweeping me along to be trampled underfoot. I wailed out as loud as I could, as several bodies actually stepped on me or tripped over me before I found a pocket of space to roll over, falling off the curb and into the street where a police officer quickly helped me up. As fast as I got my bearings, I was pushed back into another wave of kids storming Broadway in all directions. By the time I realized how much ground I had lost and how far past my friends that I had gotten, they were nowhere to be found.

The traffic moving south on Broadway was stopped dead, so I threaded my way through a bunch of cars across to a median in the middle of Times Square. I needed to get out of the crowd and view the sidewalk from a distance so I could hopefully locate Marc, Elena and Debbie. Trying to avoid the oncoming sense of disquiet, I sat down on a raised planter containing dirt and some freshly planted trees that sat on the end of the concrete island. There were assorted people standing around and a few people sitting next to me watching the melee take place across the street. It then hit me that I was suddenly alone in the middle of New York City, and all I could think about was that I had to pee really bad. In situations of potential panic, I'd come to find out throughout the course of my life that I had a high threshold for chaotic situations. The crazier things got around me, and the more unglued people became, the more calm I was. For the moment, my priority was to find someplace to pee. I looked at my surroundings which were filled with places to pee, but they were all business establishments that would require some sort of patronage. Across the street were restaurants, bars and two movie theaters. There was even a school of some sort called the Sobelsohn School, but that appeared to be on the second floor. I thought about the two movie theaters and crossed the street to the Loews State where I was immediately met with hostility and a woman motioning to me from behind a locked door that I needed to leave...as if I were part of the mob outside trying to destroy her movie theater. Nothing of the sort was going on. I scurried past posters for *The Fan, Happy Birthday to Me* and a giant ad for a soon-to-be-released new Cheech and Chong film called *Nice Dreams*...and I decided to try the other theater, which was right where I lost Marc, Elena and Debbie...or where they lost me. I pushed my way through the crowded sidewalk and entered the Criterion Center where *Death Hunt* was playing...the movie Marc wanted to see. They were also showing *Outland, This is Elvis, Excalibur, Nighthawks* and *The Final Conflict*...all films that I'd see on cable within the next year. I was able to walk straight in and through the concession area where I eventually found the restrooms. The halls were filled with random scattered kids of various ages in their teens walking around. I went into the men's room and was met with three guys going out the door. It was empty, but at that point, I didn't care who was in there...I had to unleash a torrent that had remained suppressed and painfully avoided since I left the house hours earlier... and that's exactly what I was going to do.

In the restroom, I tried to forget for a few seconds that I was in a public place and focus on something particular...which in this case, was a plan to find my friends. As I peed, I planned my next move. I was going to go back outside, and if I didn't find them, I was going to ask one of the cops for help. Outside the door was the sound of collective disturbance, as the stragglers wandering the halls were being addressed by an upper-echelon staff member of the theater telling everyone they needed to leave. Whatever was going on in the streets outside had found its way into the theater as a bunch of disgruntled kids suddenly had to pee. I myself wasn't bothered in the least bit because I had no emotional attachment to the concert since I only learned about it less than two hours earlier. Plus, I didn't know that much about the Clash other than a minor hit that had been on the radio about a year earlier called "Train in Vain." What I didn't know at the time was that the Clash was just on the cusp of becoming the biggest band in the world. I also didn't know that they were the only band that mattered. They were critics' darlings in a time when rock criticism also mattered, and when a week's worth of shows in New York City were put on sale, more people than could ever be imagined tried to buy tickets. Bond International Casino, according to the New York City Fire Department, only allowed a capacity of around 1500 people, and each night was oversold by twice that amount. The fire department showed up two nights earlier after word quickly spread that there were some 3000 people stuffed into the club. It was too late to shut down and the show went on without incident. Now, two days later, they were able to shut it down...and consequently, we walked straight into a riot. As I zipped my fly, the door burst open and a group of older teens spread themselves around...laughing, cursing and making it clear that they were in charge...at least until management got the cops inside to bust it up. But I wasn't about to wait around for that to happen. I exited without washing my hands and kept my head down in the process. Walking out the door, I was grabbed by a guy in a suit who looked like Rocky's boss, Tony Gazzo.

"Where's your ticket? Are you watching a movie right now?"

"No, I had to use the bathr..."

"You had to use the bathroom...well you can't be in here, you gotta go!"

"I'm going...I couldn't find my friends and had to go to the bathroom."

"Yeah well you don't just walk in without paying...this is a movie theater, not a public toilet...come on, let's go or I'll get the police."

"I need the police too...I can't find my fr..."

"Oh, are you gonna get the police too? Spare me the tears kid... just go."

"I *am* going...I just had to use the bathroom!"

"So does everybody else! You think you're special?"

It didn't sit very well in my gut that there was an inordinate surplus of older, more threatening kids around the theater for such an ungodly early hour, and Tony Gazzo was singling *me* out. It was yet another one of those moments when my tolerance for this kind of shit was past its limit. I got to the theater exit, turned back around and gave it right back to him.

"Yeah, motherfucker...*I AM* special!!"

The glass door behind me opened out and I was grabbed by the arm again. Startled, I spun around to pleasantly find that it was Elena.

"Oh my God, thank God! Come on, Eugene…let's get out of here!"

We took the train back to Oakwoods and got to Marc's late in the afternoon, just in time to catch the last half hour of *ABC's Wide World of Sports* and the women's national motocross championship. Elena brought us to McDonalds on the way back because we were all starved and couldn't wait for the pizza that we'd be eating for Marc's party. We told Mr. and Mrs. Rinaldi that we went to Debbie's and then to the mall and Elena did all the talking for us. Nobody ever found out that we were in New York City. But as the evening and Marc's party approached, I began to feel far more anxiety than I had even come close to while in the city. That growing feeling of ever-present danger that seemed to increase by the week was palpable. I felt like I was in a runaway car with the pedal stuck to the floor.

When the party finally went down, it didn't nearly live up to all the hype. Most of the invitees didn't make it, and to the heartbreak of many guys, Riley was one of them…although Nicole Somethingorother showed up with another friend of hers named Jen. Ashley didn't show up either, although Kevin invited her. I wasn't bothered too much by Riley's no-show because on top of being shy, I didn't like competition and refused to deal with it on any level…not with sports, and certainly not with girls. For me, it was more of a "why bother" situation…so I found it best not to take part in being just another guy chasing someone as elusive as Riley. Sometimes I wondered...among the sea of girls at Cypress, if there were any I could have been overlooking due to my focus on Riley.

Yeah right.

I knew them all.

And if Riley was a waste of time, the rest weren't even worth a thought. And the night didn't go without its embarrassment on the girl front when Nicole landed on me during Spin-the-Bottle, and got up and kissed Kevin instead.

The most popular person that night was unquestionably Frank Zappa. He sat in Mr. Rinaldi's recliner most of the night like a king... his long shoulder-length dirty blonde hair hung over a Grateful Dead t-shirt. He wasn't big or tough looking. In fact, he was the same size and build as me, but there was an intimidating aura surrounding him, and something very familiar as thought I knew him from somewhere. Weir, Franco and some of their cronies sat around him, almost at his feet. It was obvious that Frank Zappa was well-liked. It almost seemed like they were protecting him...as if you had to go through them to get to him. If there was an elementary school underworld that nobody knew about, Frank Zappa was probably the Godfather. He had a strong presence in the room, and for a long while before the party really got underway, a lot of the icebreaking seemed to revolve around him and the fact that he brought the drugs, and that everyone in the room was about to take them for the first time in their lives. I felt completely uncomfortable around Frank Zappa as he put his hand out to shake mine.

"Eugene, how ya doin'?"

I was stunned that he knew my name.

I sat down on the floor next to him.

"Good, man. What's up?" I said trying to sound tough.

He extended a pack of Marlboros to me.

"Ya want a cigarette?"

Suddenly, my heart stopped. In an instant of trying to be cool and dismissive at the same time, I died right there in front of him and said the stupidest thing that ever came out of my mouth.

"No thanks, man. I only smoke pot."

Without missing a step, Frank Zappa pulled out three funny little twisted cigarettes unlike anything that I'd seen in real life except for what Officer Anderson had shown us at the school assembly.

"You wanna go outside?" he asked.

I stood up.

"Uhh...maybe later, man...it's kinda early."

Fuck!

What did I just do?!

What did I just say?!

Who did I think I was talking to?!

I stumbled away, shaking. I went through the kitchen where Marc's parents sat smiling at me, as if they'd heard the entire conversation. I went past them and up the stairs and into the bathroom to check my underwear. As I entered the bathroom, it dawned on me that Frank Zappa was the same kid I once saw walking up the street with the older crowd...the kid who was looking at me and smiling. The one who kind of creeped me out.

———

In the bathroom, I could hear everyone going out the back door and into the yard. I went into panic mode. I leaned against the counter thinking about what I was going to do. I couldn't *not* go out there. So I had to come up with something. I started planning. I played out the entire scene of the joint being passed around and what I was going to do when it came to me. I wondered if I could somehow play it off as if I was smoking it, but not inhale. I was terrified. Every bad warning about drugs that the teachers, parents and Officer Anderson had drilled into our heads from day one came to me at once. There was the *Scared Straight* movie we watched the year before, and all of the ABC After-School Specials starring Scott Baio smoking pot and then falling out of a boat. I thought of a 16-year old Helen Hunt jumping out of a window. I saw all my friends losing control and doing something crazy. I envisioned them jumping out of windows or maybe even off the roof. I actually believed the fiction and propaganda. Marc's parents were down in the kitchen. *If something happens they'll know*, I thought. *And his mother talks to my mother!*

I walked out of the bathroom and downstairs past Marc's parents. I went into the living room and looked out the window. Beneath me, I could see the silhouettes of everyone standing there as a lighter flickered on and off. Mr. Rinaldi called out to me from the kitchen. I froze for a moment and then went in to see what he wanted.

"Why don't you go outside with everyone else?" he asked smiling.

It was a knowing smile, one that seared through me like a laser.

I knew that he saw fear in my eyes.

"What are you doing? What are you afraid of?"

Somewhere in the back of my mind I got the feeling that Marc's parents knew what was going on outside. Or maybe they didn't. Maybe they thought I had some sort of social phobia or something. But just as I turned around to go outside into the yard, something miraculous happened...and it was perfect timing. Derrick Adler walked through the front door and into the house.

"Hey Derrick, everyone is out back" Mr. Rinaldi said greeting him.

"Hey Mr. R, I just wanna show Eugene something. Hey Eugene, come here."

At first I thought *oh shit, now what?*

"What?" I asked hesitantly.

Derrick only offered a devilish smile, as if he was up to something that the Rinaldi's couldn't know about.

"Come out front with me, I have something to show you."

Although I was suspicious of him, I'd never been so glad to see him. Maybe if I went out front with him, everyone would at least know that I was doing something rather than just sitting inside alone looking scared. It's not like the entire party had to be in one particular spot at the same time. Parties were supposed to be like trees. They branched out...some people in one room, and some in another. In this case, most of the people were out back, and now I'd be out front with Derrick Adler. Plus with Derrick's reputable credibility, I couldn't miss. He was already in his second year of middle school, and the only reason that Kevin Weir had been the toughest kid in Cypress, was because Derrick was no longer there.

"Come on, Eugene! I got something to show you!" he insisted.

Still, I wondered if it was a trap. It had been years since he and Marc had ganged up on me, but I still wondered. Yet, my inner reasoning told me that he wasn't really part of the Kevin Weir / Frank Zappa crowd and actually existed above it. Nor was he into the drug scene. His recent brief experimentation with cigarettes ended with a suspension from school, so he was probably trying to stay out of trouble, as well as probably looking for someone to socialize with while everyone else was out back. I doubted that he would do something to put me on the spot in front of everyone out there. He just may be my ticket out of having to pretend to smoke pot in front of everyone. So, reluctantly, I walked through the kitchen with him and out the front door of the Rinaldi home.

When we got outside, Derrick was looking at me with a huge smile plastered on his face.

"What?" I asked.

What I got from him next, was pure Derrick Adler.

"The Merker's are testing Granny Morbid in the basement. Go by the window and look."

I looked straight into his face...something I almost never did, as eye-contact had always been intimidating for me. But on this occasion, I channeled Jack Nicholson in *The Shining* and looked him straight in the eye.

"Are you out of your fucking mind?" I barked, looking up at him, as I sat down on the Rinaldi's front steps.

There he goes, I thought...*Adler and his obsession with the Merker's.* He grabbed my hand and pulled me up.

"Come on Eugene, you gotta go see Granny Morbid. It's all true what I been saying all these years about the Merker's doing experiments on her."

"Yeah, right."

"Go see for yourself. I looked into the basement window and saw Malbert chasing her around with a needle. Then Big John the Bouncer came out and tied her up to a chair."

"You're crazy!"

I got up and sauntered away, putting my hands in the pockets of my jeans, trying to look casual.

I went two houses up toward the Merker house, stopping by a bush. Derrick caught up and stood there with me...staring at the house. Looking back, I can imagine how peculiar and up-to-no-good we must have looked to any adult looking out their windows that night...two kids just standing on the sidewalk staring at a house without a care in the world. Then he insisted again that I go up to the basement window.

"Come on man, it's funny. Go look."

I glanced up at him. He was taller than me. He now had a serious look on his face, but still with a hint of mischievous smile. What was it with him and the Merker's? I remembered the incident from a few years earlier when Big John the Bouncer exposed himself out the window while I was outside with Derrick's sister Stephanie. Suddenly, it was too much. I fell to the ground in an exaggerated fit of childish laughter. It wasn't so much that the situation was funny, as much as a feeling of euphoria to be out of my house at such a late hour. It was the exhilaration of knowing it was Saturday night with no school the next day, and that I didn't have the pressure of having to go home because

I would be sleeping at Marc's. I felt free, probably for the first time ever...or maybe not free, but possibly what it felt like to kids like Kevin Weir and Frank Zappa who didn't have a curfew or weren't confined to their bedrooms late at night when others were walking around outside having a good time. I felt like one of the big kids who they hung out with...the ones I would always hear walking up the street at night as I was laying in bed. I felt like I could do anything I wanted. I laughed uncontrollably as Derrick, now cackling himself, tried to pull me up.

"Go, Eugene...go see Granny Morbid!"

I dusted myself off while working up the nerve to somehow get across the Merker lawn unnoticed in the hopes of catching a glimpse of the mythic experiments. Instead, I scaled the walls of the house next door. This was the house in between the Rinaldi's and the Merker's.

It was an eerie dark marked by a sinister silence.

I moved closely against the side of the house and came even with the Merker's basement window. Derrick kept watch from behind a bush. He gave me a hand signal that it was okay, motioning me to move toward the window. I crouched down and hobbled over to it. The light in the basement was on. Most of the window itself was dark, covered by a curtain or something, but I could see through various cracks that there was a light on inside. Other than that, it was hard to see anything. In the distance, I could hear laughter coming from Marc's yard. I wondered if they noticed I was missing. It sounded like they were having fun without me. Maybe I should have been back there with them after all. There that night, I found myself standing on a line. I was torn between good and bad...and not just what I had purposely become in the classroom. That was more about not taking shit anymore, and not believing people were better than me. I needed to become cool again.

What did that mean though?

Did it mean staying quiet and invisible while continuing to accept people's bullshit? Did it mean overcoming the obstacles of peer pressure by caving in and going along with the crowd? Did it mean standing up to the crowd? Initially, cool was about standing *out* in a crowd. Then came a time when standing out was no longer acceptable, and often became a problem. Now suddenly it was about fitting *in* with the crowd. At the same time, I knew I was cool... and that attitude of knowing it was still just beneath the surface. I just needed to conjure it back up. Somewhere just beneath the surface was a star.

As I sneaked around between the two houses, I envisioned a camera following me with the world watching in amusement. In the back of my mind, I was always imagining that I was on camera in some movie or something. Decades before reality TV, I always pictured myself on some screen with everyone who didn't like me watching. That meant the girls of the Cypress school...some of whom who had been mean to me...and they would be able to see a different side other than the timid quiet kid in class. Somewhere just beneath the surface was some devastatingly charismatic character who was dying to leap out, if only I could work up the nerve to *let* him out. Somewhere within those thoughts of the invisible camera was this idea that girls like Ashley and Riley were watching...and the even crazier delusion that Riley would somehow miraculously fall in love with me through the veil of the invisible screen. I crouched in the grass. The ground was cold. The day had reached a sweltering 85, but there was now a slight chill in the late spring air. I looked out toward the street. Derrick was no longer there. I could no longer hear the kids two houses away. I was alone. I immediately became distracted by Derrick's disappearance, and was therefore frightened by the hand that reached out of the darkness and grabbed my arm. I jumped up as a man came out of the bushes. It was Barker Merker himself. He had come out to murder me. I had already died earlier in the evening of natural causes in the presence of Frank Zappa. But there was Barker about to commit the grizzly. I fought him off, struggling to break out of his clutches.

"What the hell do you think you're doing, huh?!" he sputtered.

His breath smelled like a dirty ashtray. I broke loose and ran.

"Go on, get outta here!" he yelled from the side walkway. I could hear Derrick laughing from Marc's front lawn. I stopped running as I got back to the house, collapsing on the grass. At that point, I was feeling a combination of terrified and overall disgusted by people in general, and didn't even care if Barker Merker had followed me back to Marc's house. Not only did he not follow me, but he completely vanished almost as quickly as he appeared. Derrick flopped down next to me.

"Yeah, Eugene!" he belched while playfully punching me.

I gave him one good shot to the chest and he backed off, still cackling. Somewhere in that moment for whatever reason, the dark clouds hovering over me had burst into nothingness. I exhaled all of the tension that the night had held, and lay in the grass looking up at the stars in the sky. I later used the distraction as my excuse for not being out in the yard with everyone else, and as it turned out, nobody even noticed or thought anything of it anyway. I was in the clear...at least for the time being.

16

The Music Never Stopped

One day, Mrs. Painter was absent. It just happened to be a Monday, and Miss Larch was our substitute. She had no idea what she would be up against come two o'clock when the class went to chorus, and me, Marc, and Kevin stayed behind with her. It would be the last chorus rehearsal before the year-end concert. Ashley started busting me about being exempt from chorus shortly before the class was to leave.

"You guys are lucky. You don't have to go to chorus."

I only smiled.

"I wanna stay too. I don't wanna go to stupid chorus. You guys are stupid."

I let out an evil laugh.

She punched me in the back.

I turned around and grabbed her penguin folder, tossing it on the floor. All of her papers fell out.

Miss Larch wandered over.

"Now that wasn't very nice. Why did you do that?" she asked as Ashley crouched to the ground to pick up the papers.

"Answer me!" the sub said growing furious.

Ashley cut in.

"It's okay, he was only playing."

Miss Larch walked away and directed the class to line up and wait for Mr. Hardenberger to walk everyone over to chorus. Ashley stayed behind as the class lined up. She then jammed her pen into my back. As much as it hurt, I didn't so much as flinch or react. She mellowed a bit.

"Hey Eugene."

I didn't answer her.

She tapped my shoulder.

"Eugene."

No answer.

Miss Larch called out to her. "Ashley, aren't you going to chorus?"

"Yes, I'm going." Then she turned back toward me.

"Eugene," she said, sounding desperate.

"Go to chorus," I said without turning around.

The class began to walk out with Mr. Hardenberger's group.

She got up real close behind me and whispered something I didn't expect to come out of her mouth.

"Do you think Riley is pretty?"

I didn't react.

"Let's go Miss Drake!" Mr. Hardenberger belched from the doorway.

She didn't move though.

Not wanting to hear Hardenberger's obnoxious voice anymore, I turned to see if he was gone, and he was. Then I turned back around facing front.

"Eugene," she said again.

Nothing.

"Do you like Riley?"

Silence.

"Eugene!"

"Go to chorus," I said, not even turning around to look at her.

She took the hint. She got up and headed for the door.

The room was quiet. I could see the sixth grade classes through the window, walking across the blacktop. But from behind me, I could still feel her presence. I turned around and she was standing in back of the room, stopped at the door.

"Seriously Eugene. Do you think she's pretty?"

Now the room was painfully silent. I glanced over at Marc and Kevin who were looking at me as if they were waiting for me to answer. Then I turned back to her, but before I could respond, Mrs. Santorini poked her head into the room with her chesty, phlegm-filled voice.

"Ashley Drake, are you coming to chorus?"

"Yes, I'll be right there."

"No honey, you have to come with me right now. You're gonna be late. My son-a-Carmen is always late for things. You should ask him what happens when you're late. He's a gooda boy, my son-a-Carmen.. but he has to learn to be on time."

"Okay, okay, I'm going," Ashley screeched, throwing up her arms in disgust as she walked out of the room.

I sat there watching her through the window as she walked with Mrs. Santorini the entire length of the playground toward the main unit building, trailing after the rest of the sixth grade class. In a way, I felt bad for her that she had to walk the entire way to chorus while listening to Mrs. Santorini talk about her son-a-Carmen. For a minute or two, I sat lost in thought. Her questions were completely unexpected. She never mentioned Riley again after that, and at the time, I never thought anything of it as to what provoked a question like that, seemingly out of nowhere. But was it really out of nowhere?

The hour alone with the sub started quietly. Just as Miss Larch remarked on how good we were being, Kevin got up, walked over to Marc and bombarded him with an all-out assault of punches. All Marc could do was crouch in his seat and hold his arms over his head in an attempted but failed defense effort as Kevin machine-gunned and drum rolled punches into his body.

"Stop it," she cried without flinching or moving from her desk.

She was still, like a mannequin. There was no attempt to control Kevin outside of her monotone words. She had subbed for Mrs. Painter in the past, and knew to pick her battles with him.

"I have to use the bathroom," Kevin said after the beating.

He was still standing over Marc. He looked at Miss Larch. She just stared at him.

"Can I go use the facilities?"

The rumbling guffaw that came from the pit of my stomach was the result of hours anticipating the insanity that was about to happen, and now that Kevin had started, I erupted in hysterics.

"What's so funny?" Miss Larch asked.

 I didn't answer.

Damn, I thought. She was afraid of Kevin, but she really had it in for me.

"Please," Kevin continued, "I need to go have a bowel movement."

Miss Larch continued to stare at him.

"Ohhhhhhh,plllleeeeeeeze substitute, I have to go use the facilities. It's an emergency."

I was beginning to sweat from trying to contain myself.

"Go ahead," she conceded. "But hurry back."

"Oh thank you, substitute...thank you!"

He bolted out into the hall and then into the bathroom. We heard him slam the door behind him. Miss Larch, concerned, glanced over at Marc.

"Mrs. Painter will get a nice note about Kevin's behavior. Are you alright?"

Marc just quietly nodded, looking on the verge of crying.

A minute or so went by. The room fell silent again. The sixth grade unit was a fun and cozy quiet. We were the only four people in the building. Suddenly, in the vast stillness, we heard Kevin flush the toilet. Another minute went by and we heard it flush again. Miss Larch looked up from her book. She gazed curiously at the open doorway leading to the hall. Then she looked back down. Marc sat pouting from the beating he had just taken. I was chuckling to myself and trying to get his attention, but he wouldn't look at me. I didn't do anything to him, but he was probably embarrassed because I'd just watched him get his ass beat. The bowl flushed again. As soon as the water ran its course, it flushed a fourth time, and then a fifth...then a sixth. After that, there was a rapid unbroken succession of flushes. Miss Larch looked up at me and slammed her book down.

"Will you go see what he's doing in there?"

With pleasure, I obliged. Outside the bathroom, I could hear Kevin still flushing nonstop. I knocked on the door. If he answered, I couldn't hear. I knocked again.

"Come in," he said, sounding purposely dorky.

I knew he was up to something. I slowly and cautiously opened the door, afraid of what I might find behind it. I expected at first to see his legs protruding from behind the partitioning wall with his pants down around his ankles. But Kevin was not sitting on the bowl. Instead, he was standing on it. His left hand was holding on to the metal partition. His other hand wasn't visible. For support, one of his feet was resting on the flush handle, and whether he was slipping or moving around unknowingly, his foot kept flushing it.

"Come on in," he said.

I stopped in my tracks looking up.

"What the hell are you doing?" I asked.

"Hold up," he said while fidgeting around behind the wall.

What ever he was doing, I wasn't having any of it.

"I'm outta here," I said, shaking my head and stepping outside the door.

"What're you doin' man? Get back in here!" he shouted from inside. He didn't seem to have any concern for the carrying volume of the constant flushing. He was almost oblivious to it. Next, I heard his heavy boots stepping down off the bowl and onto the floor. He opened the door and looked at me with the same shit-eating grin that I had come to know so well.

"It's all yours," he said.

But I didn't need to go in there.

"She just sent me out to see what you were doing."

"Go," he said, pushing me into the bathroom.

"I don't need to."

"Go to the bathroom man."

"I don't have to go."

"Yes you do."

Our talking had to have been heard by Marc and the sub. There's no way that our voices didn't carry into the classroom. I stood inside the bathroom looking at Kevin who was now on the outside. He began to pull the door closed, leaving me in the bathroom and insisting I stay there.

"Look inside the wall, man," he said standing outside the door.

The door was now closed.

"What?" I asked growing slightly pissed off.

"Look in the wall," his muffled voice seeped into the door.

The wall?

Look in the wall?

What does he mean by look in the fuckin' wall?

I stood there wondering for a few seconds. Then I grabbed the door and opened it violently.

"What do you mean look in the wall?"

"Just look in the wall, man!" he screamed in a whisper, pulling the door closed again.

Now I was just plain disgusted.

I looked up at the metal partition wall from the urinal side. Then I went around to the toilet bowl side. I stared at it, trying to figure out what he was talking about.

What the hell was he talking about?

What was I supposed to see?

Maybe he left me some secret message.

He opened the door and peeked in.

"Did you look in the wall?"

"Fuck off!"

"Look in the wall!"

He pulled the door closed again.

I looked *at* the wall. But how was I supposed to look *in* the wall?

I stepped onto the toilet seat where his boot prints were caked. I had my left foot on the seat and my right foot positioned on the Royal Sloan piping, trying to avoid the handle. I reached up to grab the top of the partitioning wall, when I heard the sub coming. Kevin knocked on the door. It was a quick nervous knock.

"Hey man," he whispered frantically. "Don't look in the wall!"

Miss Larch came out of the classroom. I heard her raise her voice at Kevin outside the door.

"What is going *on* out here?"

I began to step down off the toilet. But as I took my hand off the metal partition, I noticed to my horror that the bolts had been taken out, separating it from the tiled wall that it was attached to. As quickly as I realized this, it began to fall. I tried to catch it, but as I reached up for it, I only had one foot remaining on the bowl. The wall fell away into a reverberating and ear piercing crash against the perimeter of the room, leaving me to slip...losing one foot in the toilet bowl. My heart was now racing in fear and shock. Weir had obviously flipped his fucking lid this time. My shoe was soaked, and so was the bottom of my pants as my left foot sat at the bottom of the bowl.

The door opened.

The bewildered substitute stood there with my two friends, looking at me as I just stood in place like an idiot with my foot in the toilet. Miss Larch peaked in with her neck stretched into the room but her body still outside the door. She saw the partition wall leaning against the tiled wall.

"What happened?" she asked nervously.

"Yeah, what happened?" Kevin had the audacity to echo.

How did one explain something like this?

The only consolation was that Mrs. Painter wasn't there to see it, nor was anyone else. The sub didn't concern me. I'd have time to think of something. Until then, I decided to tell her the truth. With my foot in the bowl, I pointed up at the metal partition.

"The wall...it fell down."

———

The Locker Notes

The sixth grade concert took place on a Friday afternoon during the final hour before dismissal. Since everyone was in the chorus, our entire class had to leave the classroom a half hour early, except of course for me, Marc, and Kevin, who walked down to the main unit building with Mrs. Painter. Inside the All Purpose Room, folding chairs were set up for every kid in the school, but there was no room for the three outcast sixth graders who were not participating in the concert, so we had to sit on the floor next to Mrs. Painter who had a chair. Mrs. Painter had been out sick all week and seemed to be in a pretty bad mood. The three of us sat crossed legged on the floor on the side of the room where the teachers sat and Mrs. Painter glanced down on us from her chair once or twice as if to see if we were situated and quiet, and then seemed to forget us as the concert got underway.

From the first notes of the show, I knew I had made the right choice in massacring my chorus tryout. There was no way I could see myself standing up there singing to the entire school. I tried imagining the view from the stage and seeing a large mass of people all looking at me, and I cringed. On that same note, I knew I would have to face the same situation if I was ever going to be a rock star, and maybe if I'd had a guitar in my hand, I might conjure up the courage to stand there and go crazy in front of everyone. But these were show tunes we were hearing, and there was just no way. One of the more uncomfortable moments was a solo spot for Alicia Allen who had to take the lead in "Oom-Pah-Pah" from the musical, Oliver. I sat there embarrassed for her and everyone around her who had to take part...not wanting to look, hoping to be stricken with sudden deafness, and wishing I could be anywhere else at that moment.

Mrs. Painter even began squirming around in her seat. Marc and I looked at each other, silently acknowledging the painful moment. Kevin just sat there looking down with his elbows on his knees and his face in his hands. I tried to distract myself from the song, but could only notice the fat of Miss Tripe's arms jiggling back and forth as she stood in front of the chorus trying to act like a conductor. I glanced up to the left of me at Mrs. Painter, and had to do a double take when I noticed that she was sitting exactly like Kevin was. She was hunched over with her elbows on her knees and her face buried in her hands. I nudged Marc and motioned toward her with a subtle nod. He looked at her and gave me a sort of "what the hell?" glance. Kevin was still sitting in the same position and didn't even notice, nor did he look up when Marc tapped him.

Just then, Ashley caught my eye.

She was standing on the bottom level of the chorus all the way at the end. She was smiling but looked timid through the entire thing, focusing probably on empty space in the air, not looking at anyone or anything in particular. And then I became distracted again as Mrs. Painter stood up for a second, and I went to move over thinking she was trying to walk past but instead, she quickly sat back down. I noticed she was sweating and just plain didn't look good. Then she bent over and put her face in her hands again. Mr. Hardenberger noticed her behavior and leaned over from his seat.

"Are you alright, Mrs. Painter?" With that, Mrs. Painter, green in the face, sat up, leaned over and vomited the entire contents of her lunch into my lap.

"EEEEWWWWW!!!" one girl screamed.

"Ohhhh my lord, Mrs. Painter," cried another teacher.

Marc and Kevin jumped up instantly as an entire chunk of the audience broke away and scrambled out of the room.

I sat there stunned, almost in shock.

Then I looked down and saw it.

Then I smelled it.

And then I vomited myself.

In what was reduced to merely background noise, the chorus kept singing and the music never stopped.

A few weeks later, we'd graduate, leaving the Cypress School forever.

In the end, there was a sixth grade party in the All Purpose Room. And once again, this vindicated the All Purpose Room as a room for all purposes. Tables were set up around a dance floor that once served as a torture chamber of Skin-the-Cat games, Mr. Wagner yelling "Hey!!," Mr. Zielinski's long drawn out "Brother David" speeches and Mr. Tutundjian's incoherent moaning. We ate food that our mothers had collectively cooked, and walked around freely, leaving at times to walk amongst the unit buildings to let all of our previous teachers sign our yearbooks. Then we passed them around to each other in the dance. This way we could get them signed from kids in the other sixth grade classes. In the case of Riley Stevens, there was a line to get her signature. She stood like a celebrity signing yearbook after yearbook all taken from one long pathetic line of fanboys. I left the building long enough to revisit old classrooms and collect signatures from Mrs. Jacobson, Miss Keller, the dreaded Mrs. Aarons, and a few of my other teachers not mentioned in this book. Mrs. Greco and Miss Collins had since retired. I did not want Mrs. Aaron's signature, but for some reason, I went to her classroom because I thought that we were required to visit our old teachers, and had no idea that it was optional. On the way back, I caught Mr. Wagner walking across the playground and gave him my book to sign as well. Upon returning to the party, I was greeted by an assault of playful but devastating punches from Kevin Weir, to which I responded by grabbing him by the sleeves of his t-shirt, and proudly slamming him against the wall. I had come a long way since the beginning of the school year, and was quite pleased with myself.

Ashley approached me a few minutes later while I was taking a break sitting next to Miss Tripe's Univox record player, which was spinning a vinyl copy of The Rolling Stones latest album *Emotional Rescue*. She sat down in a chair next to me, opened her yearbook and smiled.

"Wanna sign mine?"

It was that same shy smile I had come to know ever since that awkward moment on the playground. In an instant, I wondered how in the world such a pain in my ass that had made my life miserable right up to that year could suddenly appear so innocent and angelic. It wasn't as if I liked her or anything. Well, not in that way I guess.

Or maybe I did and was just in denial?

I mean, it was Ashley Drake, and just being her friend had taken a while to digest. But that whole *evil Ashley Drake* thing had long vanished, and it was quite honestly hard to even associate her with that same hideous creature of the Cypress School's yesteryear. In a nutshell, she was no longer Ashley Drake to me.

She was just Ashley.

And there she was, delivered to me straight from the gates of hell into pure sweetness...sitting there next to me smiling, and looking into my eyes as if she wanted to say something...

...or was waiting for me to say something.

"Oh...yeah...sure," I said, taking the yearbook from her, acting surprised as if she had interrupted me deep in thought, pretending to not fully be aware of her presence, when I was in fact learning at that very moment that it just might have been her I had been overlooking all of that time in favor of Riley. I handed her my yearbook and took out a pen.

Then she started getting weird on me.

"See my face, Eugene?" she asked looking me straight in the eye.

"Huh?"

"You see my face?"

"Um...yeah?" I said with a hint of nervous laughter.

"You see me smiling?"

Of course I saw her smiling. What was she driving at?

"Um...yeah?"

"Do I look happy to you?"

I kind of thought everyone was happy.

After all, it was the last day of school.

"I'm really not. I'm smiling on the outside but crying on the inside."

I wasn't sure what to make of that.

Was she about to tell me her dog died or something?

Was she waiting for me to ask her why?

Was one of us going to say something before the moment got much more uncomfortable?

I looked deep in her face to humor her, and I was a split second away from asking her what was up, but before I could open my mouth to speak, she ripped the sky wide open and the rain came falling down.

"I'm moving, Eugene. I'm moving away."

I pretended not to hear and opened her yearbook.

I searched for a spot to write.

"Eugene, my mom told me last night that we're moving away to Georgia in August."

————

Ashley signed my yearbook and left me her phone number and address, but said that she wouldn't be at that address much longer. She said she wanted me to call her, and if I wanted to hang out for half the summer, we could. When I signed hers, I felt like I had a chance to leave her some sort of message...a few words...a confession...anything. But instead I just wrote my number. I didn't even consider that there would be a next year, or other girls, or that the end of one thing marked the beginning of another. I was young and not yet experienced in the wisdom of the evolution of life. To us, that day was only an end, and I suddenly felt sick.

But none of these troublesome things of Ashley and Riley really phased me for too long that day. At least not on the surface.

I was too cool for it all.

I got it all back.

I conjured them all up that day...Fonzie, Ace Frehley, Al Pacino... people who had become heroes for one reason or another. Despite all of my neurotic anxieties and insecurities, I was tough as steel on the exterior and didn't flinch. The only difference between Fonzie and me though, was that he always got the girl. But that didn't matter either. The music was flowing through one awesome song after another. I even found it a little funny when Rachel Santos and I brought in the same Cheap Trick album. Where she was listening to disco four years earlier and was mean to me, we both were able to share a brief rare conversation about music—one that didn't end in a confrontation. The soundtrack of the day consisted of The Rolling Stones, Led Zeppelin, the Cars, Cheap Trick, the Doors, the J. Geils Band, Joan Jett, AC/DC, Bruce Springsteen, Pink Floyd...and someone...not sure who, but someone even threw in Kiss.

In the end, rock and roll had won.

———

We walked out of the Cypress School for the last time that afternoon. It was me, Tommy, Marc, and Kevin. At the end of Cypress Estates, Frank Zappa and his cronies were waiting to meet us. As we crossed Oakwood Avenue, and walked into our development, I felt a surge of excitement that I hadn't felt before, but I wasn't sure if I liked it or not. It was a kind of looking forward to the next chapter of our lives, but with a certain sadness and fear. It seemed as if something was ending...and it was. Sure, we'd all be going on to the middle school, but it was like we maybe wouldn't get there. The only way to explain it would be like that feeling we get about history. We study and hear about things that happened before we were born. We think we may understand it, but can we really relate to something that we haven't lived through? Did these things we learn about or read about really happen? Or did the world start with us? Realistically, we know it will all go on long after we're gone, but from the vantage point of a twelve year old kid not knowing what was around the corner, the end was always near. Then, we find that age does not discriminate against that sentiment.

Aren't we all kids?

Some of us are just a little older than others? Some with a little more experience? Some a lot more weathered?

Aren't we all afraid?

On the bright side, it was a new beginning. We decided that we were going to form a rock band. One of us would learn drums. A few of us would learn the guitar. I'd put the tennis racket down, and get a real guitar. Maybe even a synthesizer. It was, after all, the 80s. We'd grow our hair long! We'd play Battle of the Bands and all of our classmates would see how cool we really were. It was going to be great! That summer, a little channel called MTV would appear on the cable lineup. It would otherwise be known as Music Television, and it would show these little song clips of bands and artists called videos. We would be able to see music as well as hear it. We'd see other things for the first time too. Within a year, a channel launched by Playboy magazine would join the cable lineup with content made up of nothing but softcore porn. Cautious parents didn't subscribe to the Playboy Channel, which meant that their kids watched it on a scrambled screen late at night when nobody else was in the room. Eventually, we'd learn to unscramble the channel by pressing three specific buttons together. This really was the end of one thing, and the beginning of another.

What is it then that causes the uncertainty?

Once upon a time, there was a kid who was so deathly afraid of snakes that he would jump in fear whenever he unexpectedly came across a picture of one in a book or a magazine. He could be casually and randomly turning pages, and then if there was a snake, he'd jump in shock, throw the book or magazine in the air, and run out of the room. If he somehow knew in advance that there was a snake in the book, he could control his fear by slowly peeling back the pages, stealing peaks, and revealing the horror in small pieces rather than all at once. He'd go to the zoo, but wouldn't go near the reptile room, and if he somehow found himself in it reluctantly, he'd go through it face down, unable to look at what was in the tanks. He'd go through it quickly, with the paralyzing sensation that something was about to creep in on him and pull him away from the world he had known...a world of something much more safe than whatever was pointing him down into the cowering little fear hole that he wished he could get out of. As he'd grow older and into an adult, one of his girlfriends would unexpectedly find out about his fear. One day he'd come across a snake, fling the magazine, and it would hit her in the head. She'd say, "What the hell is your problem, hun?" He'd play it off and tell her there was a spider crawling on him and it freaked him out, and then say "sorry" for hitting her in the head. Then one day in a moment of trust and honesty he'd say to her, "Hun, remember that time I flung that book and hit you in your head?" And then he'd proceed to tell her of his issues. There would indeed be issues. Plenty of issues. Twelve of them. They would be

National Geographic issues. Someone would give him a year subscription for Christmas, and *National Geographic* would just be loaded with snakes. How would he be able to read it? How would he ever enjoy it? Soon afterwards, she would proceed to go through all of his magazines searching for snakes, tearing out any that may have been there, making them snake-free for him to enjoy without fear of cardiac arrest. She'd even go through the TV Guide, which would always contain advertisements for Shark Week or Snake Week on the public stations. In time, the relationship would fall apart. Of course there would be all the scarring emotional baggage that goes along with a breakup, but that's another story. What is significant to this one though is that he'd be on his own again in turning the pages. There was always that wisdom that said to break down every fucking inhibition you may have and stare it in the face. And at times, he'd feel brave enough to do that. Those were the rare occasions though. Most times, he'd safely peel back the page to peek and see if it was safe to go all the way in. And in those rare moments of exhaustion... those moments when all he wanted to do was just live and take chances and go out on a limb for something...anything...he'd just dive in head first without looking. Sometimes he would make it in all the way, and sometimes he would end up flinging a magazine at someone else's head. Either way, as is the case in life, nobody knows what is on the next page.

And so, in Oakwoods, when the sun goes down, and all the residents gather under their roofs in rows of houses that all look the same, the story is written for every suburban community across America. Families sit in their living rooms watching TV. The young ones play video games and do homework. The kids with limited to no adult supervision wander the streets, scarred by their parents' separation, while other kids remain at home in the line of fire and forever in the middle of their parents' war. Some homes are structured to the point of boredom, routine and cliché, while others are broken by drugs, divorce, violence, alcoholism and neglect. And just outside, there is that protective wall. It tranquilizes, lobotomizes and hides us from the truth. It shields us from reality. In the end, we become exactly what we once rebelled against. In Oakwoods, another generation of young wary-eyed parents cautions their children through their own inherited behavior. They watch suspiciously out the window at night, as another generation of young punks walks the street towards the fence at the top of the block. And so, the full spectrum of another generation of suburbia is complete...parents, kids, good, bad, black, white, the end of the road and the end of the world. How we perceive the world is ultimately not up to us. It is injected into us.

And every generation lives at the end of the world.

As me, Tommy, Marc, and our extended group of new friends walk up Sycamore Drive in an early-summer twilight, the neighborhood now looks different. It is as if I'm seeing it from another angle. The sun is just about beyond the horizon in a pinkish, purplish blend of infinite possibility. The coming night will magnify this feeling. We walk across a field of overgrown grass to the end where there is an opening in a fence. We continue, as I watch Frank Zappa light a cigarette and offer one to Marc and Tommy. They take them and light them. Kevin looks at me, smiles, and pats me on the back.

"You alright, man?" he asks in a serious and sincere manner.

I force a smile.

"Never better," I say, looking behind me nervously, as the last remaining sights of the swaying grass disappear from view. And with that, all familiarity with my surroundings comes to an end.

We keep walking.

It feels good.

A little scary.

But good.

It is then that I realize where I am.

And it dawns on me, that I have gone into the Forbidden Zone.

Epilogue

The end of the world came on a Wednesday in early March of the following school year, our first at Oakwoods Middle School. It was a much different world. A Saturday morning cartoon called The Smurfs, a video game system called the Atari 2600, and a small plastic color-oriented puzzle called Rubic's Cube had taken the country by storm in the first months of 1982. Those who weren't talking about Smurfs, Atari, or Rubic's Cube were talking about a tiny otherwise overlooked film running on cable called *The Man Who Saw Tomorrow*. The film, narrated by Orson Welles, was based on the prophecies of Nostradamus, and speculation according to received information from the old man's predictions was that the world would end in 1997. This cat had the world ending at the hand of a third dictator. The first two were Napoleon and Hitler, both of which his prophecies stunningly foretold. The third dictator would come from the Middle East and blow up the world in 1997.

But then there was the Jupiter Effect, which didn't call for a man-made end of the world at all, but was merely a cosmic occurrence that would obliterate the planet. That's at least how we interpreted the hearsay, which could possibly have been blown out of proportion.

In short, a planetary alignment was supposed to wreak havoc on the solar system and create the ultimate bad day on Earth.

Our interpretation?

The end of the world.

So on the morning of March 10, 1982, we were already sick to death of the end of the world, but it was supposed to happen around noontime. Everyone had been talking about it since the week before. The teachers had gotten a kick out of it, but tried to reassure everyone it was a hoax based on some stupid book. Many of the students however, especially the girls, took it seriously. Kevin and I were in fifth period English when at around 11:45 he got a pass to the bathroom and I got a pass to the water fountain. Our hippie teacher Mr. C was cool, and let us both out of the room at the same time as the rest of the class listened to The Beatles "Lovely Rita." Down the hall we could hear the chorus practicing in the music room. We walked toward the door and listened. We made no effort to hide the fact that we were there, and Kevin even stepped into the doorway to make himself visible. If the world was about to end, why should we care if we weren't supposed to be there? We listened to the chorus sing the last few lines of "Edelweiss" and when they stopped, Kevin applauded.

"Thank you Kevin," Miss Verilli the music teacher said cheerfully.

"Is everyone ready for the end of the world?" Kevin asked.

"Yes Kevin," she said pleasantly while closing the door on us. "We're all set. Thank you."

We headed back down the old ninth grade wing toward Mr. C's class. The halls were unusually empty and there was a sense of barren desolation suddenly hovering in the air. Neither of us felt any urge to run around the halls any further. When we got to the door of our room, Kevin stopped me, putting out his hand.

"Hey."

"What?"

"What if the world really is about to end?"

I didn't say anything.

Then an awkward silence.

"Ya know?" he asked.

"Yeah, I know."

"I mean, seriously. What if everything just ends right now?"

"Yeah, man...I know."

I tried not to show the same concern that he was bringing to the surface. Man, I was cooler than ever. At least I was going to die cool.

———

We walked back into the classroom where the opening notes of "A Day in the Life" were beginning. We sat down in our seats. The class was silent and Mr. C was in his glory as we all soaked in the final moments of The Beatles *Sgt. Pepper's* album, in what were to be the last minutes of all existence. We all sat listening quietly and attentively to John Lennon tell us how he read the news about a lucky man who made the grade, blew his mind out in a car and didn't notice that the lights had changed. It was our last song before the Earth would crack, and fire and blood would rain down on our classroom. A fidgety nervous little girl named Sophie Shaw sat there sobbing to herself as she watched the clock.

We *all* began to watch the clock.

As it struck 11:57, Paul McCartney woke up and fell out of bed.

Just then, the bell rang.

Class was dismissed with the music still playing, and during the three minute interval between fifth and sixth period, the world ended.

Then we went to lunch.

www.ingramcontent.com/pod-product-compliance
Lightning Source LLC
Chambersburg PA
CBHW072047190726
48294CB00005B/1441